A THIN VEIL

Also by Jane Gorman

The Adam Kaminski Mystery Series
A Blind Eye
A Thin Veil
All That Glitters

A THIN VEIL

*Book 2 in the Adam Kaminski
Mystery Series*

Jane Gorman

Blue Eagle Press

This is a work of fiction. Names, characters, places and incidents are the product of the author's imagination and used fictitiously. Any resemblance to actual events or persons, living or dead, is entirely coincidental.

To Chuck.

CHAPTER ONE

SOUND EXPLODED through the morning air. Grating and angry, it ricocheted off the walls as if trying to scrape a layer off the tawny stones. The roar of the gun hit the group gathered on the mansion's drive and they dove for the ground at the force of it.

Only one person hit the ground with the dull thud of death.

Diplomatic Security Agent Sam Burke and the other agents with him were the first back on their feet. The five agents had ducked at the sound, but turned toward it rather than diving for cover. Each heard it coming from a different direction, scraping off a different wall, spinning up from the trimmed grass below or surging down from the mansion's tiled roof.

Agent Sam Burke pulled his weapon and scanned the drive leading back to the house, seeking movement in the shadows behind the hedge or around the corner of the residence. He stood still, focusing on the direction the sound had come from, his grip tight on his gun. With the shot still ringing in his ears, he relied on his eyes for any sign of movement. Two of his colleagues ran to assist those who had fallen while two more chased the sound into the shadows around the house.

Ambassador Alain Saint-Amand knelt on the path, his hands clasped over his bowed head. One of the agents placed a hand on his back as he spoke, his fingers whispering against the gray silk. "Ambassador, come with me. Quickly."

Unfurling gracefully, Saint-Amand grabbed the agent's arm, his grip puckering the thin polyester. "Run! Run!"

His cry came out as a hiss, the fear it conveyed carrying almost as loudly as the shot. The two men scuttled, still bent low, toward the heavy oak door and the safety that lay behind it.

Another agent moved to Senator Lisa Marshall. She lay curled on the ground, her arms bent underneath her, her fingers over her ears. "Senator," he shouted, as if the silence that followed was as deafening as the shot. "Can you hear me?"

She turned and nodded, her helmet of blond hair showing gaps in its defenses. Rolling onto her knees, she leaned into the agent as she stood. His arm hovered over her, offering what protection it could. She glanced back as they ran toward the safety that waited behind the oak door. Her eyes focused on the figure still lying on the path behind them. Her face crumpled, she blinked and shook her head, turning back toward the house.

The agent followed her glance, saw the inert form.

"Damn." The swear came out between clenched teeth as he shook his head. "Sam!" he called out, then gestured with his chin toward the path. He said no more, but turned his attention back to the senator and her safety, his top priority.

Sam scanned the area once more, then turned to focus on the man they had failed to protect. Jay Kapoor lay with one arm flung out, the other crossed in front of his chest. As if defending himself to the last. His charcoal suit was impeccable, his red tie still in a tight knot at his collar. Only the spot of blood blossoming on his white shirt revealed the futility of his optimism when he had dressed that morning.

Sam put his fingers on the young man's neck, his dark brown skin jumping out in contrast to Jay's greenish-yellow hue. He found a weak and slowing pulse. Jay's chest moved once, then was still. He interlaced his fingers and pressed his hands down over the wound, applying pressure as best he could. When another agent crouched next to him, Sam used the handkerchief he offered to stanch the blood. The spreading pool of red on Jay's white shirt slowed. Stopped.

Sam nodded, risking a glance over at his colleague. He could stop the bleeding out with his pressure, but the color of Jay's skin made it clear there was more internal damage. He had seen wounds like this before. After ten years on the force in DC, Sam knew chances were slim the ambulance already on its way would make it in time.

Agent Collins, the lead Diplomatic Security agent for this assignment, stepped out of the house. The two remaining agents had returned from their search, one holding a gun wrapped in a white handkerchief. The wail of approaching sirens grew louder as he stepped onto the path. "Sam?"

Sam didn't look up, just shook his head. They had failed to protect Jay. The most he could do now was keep him alive until the ambulance got to them. He coughed and found his voice. "Doing what I can, sir. And we can pray."

Agent Collins looked at the others. "What'd you find?"

"Could be the weapon used, sir. Still warm." An agent indicated the gun. "In a bush to the right of the front door. Techs can confirm, but it looked like it had been thrown there, not dropped."

A blue sedan swerved onto the drive from the street, its tires squealing as it turned to the right side of the U-shaped drive, leaving room for the ambulance that was only seconds behind. Diplomatic Security Agent Collins gave final instructions to his team, then moved to meet the FBI.

The driver of the ambulance kept to the left, the back of the bus angling toward the group clustered on the path. Two medics jumped down. Within minutes, the young man had been strapped to a gurney and carted back to the ambulance. Sirens screaming, it pulled forward around the drive and back out into the street.

Sam heard Agent Collins conferring with the FBI agents who had arrived, saw his colleagues escorting the drivers into the house with the others, knew he had to move, too. But his eyes felt glued to the patch of dark brown pavement at the curve of the drive.

Without moving his gaze away, he reached into his pocket and pulled out his phone.

DETECTIVE ADAM KAMINSKI jumped for the phone to stop the rattle of its vibration against the nightstand. Next to him in their bed, Sylvia yawned and settled further under the covers, her back towards him.

He'd been lying awake for half an hour, watching her sleep. Thinking. She'd had her back to him since he woke up. He assumed she always slept like that, curled away from him as far as the bed would let her. When he put a hand out to touch her shoulder, she pulled the blankets up even higher without opening her eyes.

His expression hardened as he put thoughts of Sylvia out of his mind and glanced at the phone. Surprised by the caller, he slid out of bed and walked into the living room. He had been expecting Sam's call, but not this early. The delegation wasn't due in Philly until ten.

"Sam, what's up?"

"It's not good news, Adam." Sam's voice was grim. "The visit's off, at least for now."

Adam caught the tension in Sam's voice and stopped moving. "What happened?"

"A shooting. Senator Marshall and Ambassador Saint-Amand are fine. The senator's aide... he wasn't so lucky."

Adam nodded as he listened. He could hear noises in the background. The all too familiar sounds of a crime scene investigation. "Did you catch the guy?"

"Not yet," Sam answered. "We have the weapon." There was a pause and a muffled sound, as if Sam had put his hand over the phone. "Listen, Adam, I gotta go," Sam's voice came back on the line. "I'll call you later when I know more."

The line went dead.

Adam looked at the phone for a second, then tossed it onto the coffee table and sat back into the futon that served as their living room sofa, running both hands through his thick chestnut hair.

This had been just another routine dignitary visit for him. He'd been preparing for a few days, sure, but five months into a six-month detail on the Philadelphia Police Department's Dignitary Protection squad, he knew none of these visits were going to offer the challenges he'd wanted.

Or the opportunities for advancement Sylvia had hoped for.

He let his head fall back against the futon, the feel of the bar through the thin mattress reminding him that their so-called temporary furniture was still cluttering their living room while he and Sylvia waited impatiently for the permanence they both wanted. Waited for the opportunity to invest in their future. And in real furniture.

Closing his eyes, Adam brought his mind back to the victims in DC. The senator, working hard to leave a positive legacy in her last few months in the job. The French ambassador, striving to preserve relations with a government that too often disagreed with his own. And the staff who, like the dead aide, were caught in the middle.

CHAPTER TWO

THE WHITE TIPS of Senator Lisa Marshall's French manicure tapped against the glass as rivulets of condensation dripped toward a pool gathering on the coaster. She tightened her grip on the glass as if to take another sip, but instead she tipped the glass and turned it rapidly in her fingers a few times before resting it once again on the polished end table that matched the others dotting Ambassador Saint-Amand's morning room.

Sam watched her as she shifted in her seat, the light from the residence's ornate windows catching and highlighting a ladder that ran along her nylons, starting mid-calf and disappearing under the knee of her red suit. She crossed her legs, hiding the run, then patted her hair back into place one more time.

The tall man fidgeting next to her put his hand out, as if to touch her knee, but she pushed him away. A sad smile crossed his lips, then vanished. Mr. Marshall returned his hands to his lap.

Ambassador Saint-Amand, on the other hand, seemed perfectly at ease. He flipped through the pages of a leather-bound folio, glancing up occasionally to look across the room toward the open doorway. With his back to the door, Sam couldn't see what the ambassador was looking at, but he wasn't willing to turn his attention from the room to find out.

Sam could hear the men outside, searching the

grounds more thoroughly than before. FBI technicians draped in white scoured the path where Jay Kapoor had fallen. One or more of the searchers passed before the tall front windows every now and then, casting shadows into the otherwise bright room. With his height advantage, Sam could see the technicians at work, like ghosts crawling over ground tainted by death.

Diplomatic Security Agent Frist stood on the far side of the room in the same pose as Sam, hands crossed in front of him, feet parted. He didn't move, but the stillness of his expression told Sam that Frist was as alert as he was, paying close attention to the activity outside the house as well as the people in the room.

A small door at the back of the room opened to admit a painfully thin woman in a demure black dress. She used both hands to hold a silver tray loaded with a crystal decanter, several glasses, and a pitcher of water and she winced as the door slammed shut behind her. Her narrow lips shifted into a frown, then she looked up and around the room, identifying her targets in order of importance.

"Merci, Elise." Saint-Amand accepted a snifter of brandy from her, swirling it gently in his hand as he returned his attention to the papers in front of him. The senator waved Elise away with a jerk of her hands and Mr. Marshall simply shook his head.

Elise then moved to the other people sitting in the room, carefully ignoring the agents. A fair man in a navy suit accepted a snifter of brandy, watching Senator Marshall over his glass as he took a tentative sip. He kept a tight grip on the glass as he lowered it, his eyes darting back and forth between the senator and the agents guarding the doors.

When Elise made it around to the two drivers sitting on smaller chairs near the back of the room, she left the brandy on her tray, topping up their glasses of water instead.

"How long must we wait here? What's going on?"

Senator Marshall stood as she spoke, but did not step forward.

"Be patient, my dear, it's okay." Her husband stood as well, putting his arm around her shoulders and keeping it there despite her effort to shrug it off. "They're doing everything they can, you know that. Let them do their work."

"Your husband is right, Senator Marshall," Frist said. "Our agents are checking the scene one more time, making sure we're safe. Agent Collins will be here soon to fill you in."

Mr. Marshall patted his wife's arm with his left hand, then seemed to almost push her back onto the yellow silk sofa. She sat stiffly, her back hard against the elegant curves of the sofa, chewing on her lower lip.

"Madame Senator," the ambassador said without rising, "if there is anything else I can offer you to make you more comfortable while you wait, please do not hesitate to ask." When Lisa Marshall did not respond, he continued, "Some coffee, perhaps, or some food. Or you might prefer to wait in one of the rooms upstairs, to be more comfortable?"

She looked up hopefully at that, but Sam intervened. "I'm sorry, I can't allow that. You're going to have to wait down here until Agent Collins has had a chance to speak to us all. I'm sure it won't be long now."

Collins proved Sam's point by choosing that moment to walk into the room. A second man followed close on his heels, a man Sam recognized immediately as the FBI Assistant Director responsible for the Bureau's Washington field office. Assistant Director Burnett had an easy two inches on Collins and walked like a man on a mission, hindered only by the smaller fellow blocking his way. Collins ignored him, just as he ignored the three men in suits who trailed behind them both. More FBI, Sam assumed, men Sam didn't recognize. One of them, a burly man with a round face and curly red hair, looked vaguely familiar but the other two looked fresh out of college. No older than Jay Kapoor had been.

"Senator Marshall, Mr. Marshall." Collins crossed the room and looked down at the seated couple. "I am very sorry to have to tell you that your aide, Jay Kapoor, is dead. He was pronounced dead on arrival at the hospital, death due to a gunshot wound."

Collins paused, then squatted down in front of Lisa Marshall. She closed her eyes and rested her head against her husband's shoulder. Tears shone against her cheeks.

"He would have died quickly, Senator," he continued in a softer tone. "He wouldn't have felt any pain."

Senator Marshall inhaled deeply as she raised her head, wiping the tears away with her hand. With her other hand she reached for her husband, who put both his hands over hers and squeezed.

"He was a good assistant. A good man. Why would anyone kill him?" she asked softly.

Saint-Amand coughed gently, and Assistant Director Burnett stepped forward to answer before Collins could respond. "It seems most likely, ma'am, that the killer was aiming for either you or the ambassador. We do have to treat this as an intended assassination gone wrong."

"But —" Sam started to speak, then cut himself off, his frown deepening into his forehead.

Collins lowered his eyebrows a fraction as he threw a glance in Sam's direction, then turned back to the senator. Sam stood still and stayed silent, turning his palms up as he looked down at them. He still had blood on his hands.

Collins stood. "The Capitol Police will increase your protection detail, Senator. We're going to keep a close eye on both of you." He turned to face the ambassador. "And you, Ambassador Saint-Amand. We'll be doubling the detail assigned to you."

The ambassador nodded silently, placing the folio carefully to his side.

"I know you'd all like to get home — or to be alone." Assistant Director Burnett spoke again, nodding to

Saint-Amand. "My men need to ask you each a few quick questions, then I can let you go."

Getting no response, Burnett turned to Collins, who asked, "Ambassador Saint-Amand, will you have any objection if Special Agent in Charge Hennessy talks with the senator first?" Collins indicated the burly man beside him as he spoke.

"Of course, of course." Saint-Amand rose, gesturing to the hallway and a smaller room visible there. "Please, use my assistant's office. You will have privacy there. Take as long as you need, I will wait here."

"Thank you. Mr. Marshall, we'll get your statement next. Mr. McFellan?" Burnett had resumed control and with his last question he turned to the fair man seated against the wall.

"Me? Yes?" McFellan's phone hit the ground with a clatter. He fumbled as he leaned over to pick it up, then tucked it into his pocket as he stood.

"We'll need to talk to you as well, so please be patient."

"I see." McFellan nodded and sank back onto his chair, his hand moving into his pocket to retrieve his phone.

Collins stepped back to allow the senator, Assistant Director Burnett, and Special Agent in Charge Hennessy to pass. Collins glanced once more at Sam, then followed the group out of the room. Sam heard the office door close as he turned back to the others who were still waiting. He headed across the room toward the two drivers, but McFellan stood again, blocking his path.

"Yes, Mr. McFellan?"

"It's just... well..." He glanced at the ambassador. "Do I really need to wait? I don't think I should be part of this. Your boss said this was about the senator or..." He drew a circle in the air with his finger, pointing toward Ambassador Saint-Amand. The Frenchman harrumphed and shifted in his seat without responding.

"It will be necessary to get your statement as well, Mr.

McFellan. I appreciate your patience."

"I don't see…" McFellan's voice trailed off as he frowned and stepped back to his seat, the fingers of his left hand still gripping his phone.

Sam watched him sit, then turned back to the drivers. "He'll need to talk to you both as well, once he's finished with the senator, the ambassador, and Mr. McFellan."

Both men nodded and one said, "Of course, but I didn't see anything."

"I know," Sam said. "Agent Hennessy will ask you a few questions, and you can get home."

"Would be nice." The other man spoke under his breath as if making a blessing or a wish. When Sam raised his eyebrow, he added, "I only get paid when I work. I can't afford to go home. I need to call in and get my next assignment."

"Well, hold off calling until Agent Hennessy is done with you. I don't know how long this will take."

The man frowned but said nothing more, and Sam returned to his post at the door. The blood on his hands had dried long before and now lay caked in the tiny crevices and wrinkles across his palm and around his fingers. He rubbed his hands together, trying to wipe off the blood, trying to shake the feeling that he owed more to Jay Kapoor.

"HEY, LI'L SIS, how's it going?" Detective Adam Kaminski intentionally kept his tone light, ignoring the mess and noise surrounding him. His temporary workstation in the Philadelphia police headquarters affectionately known as the Roundhouse was the opposite of the organized desk he and his partner Pete Lawler shared in the homicide unit. And would be sharing again once this detail in dignitary protection ended in a month.

"Adam? What's wrong?" Julia wasn't fooled by his voice.

"Nothing, I'm fine. I'm fine." Adam ran a hand across his forehead as he spoke, rubbing away the tension gathering there. "Just calling to check in, see how you're doing."

"Same as I was when I saw you at Mom and Dad's two days ago, you know?" Adam heard the question in Julia's voice, knew he'd never been able to hide things from his little sister. "What's wrong, really?"

"A kid got shot this morning."

Adam thought of Jay, only a year out of college, his whole life ahead of him. He hadn't known him well, had only spoken to him a few times on the phone in preparation for this visit. But that didn't change the distress he felt over Jay's death.

"Oh, Adam. I'm so sorry." She paused for a moment, and Adam was struck by how silent it was on her end of the phone. No conversations going on around her, no sounds of people going in and out of doors, phones ringing, sirens in the street. Nothing like the desk Adam sat at.

"I know how much that must hurt you," Julia continued. "Were you there? Want to talk about it?"

"No, no, nothing like that. It was down in DC, I wasn't there. A young man who was part of the delegation I've been preparing for. It's just..." He heard Julia take a breath to speak, so added, "I'm fine, really. I guess I wanted to make sure you're okay."

"That's sweet, but you know I'm good. I see you every week, big brother. What kind of trouble could I possibly get into with you watching out for me? So are you going to focus on solving your latest murder, or spend all your energy worrying about me?"

Adam smiled for the first time that morning. Calling Julia had been a good idea. "I'm not involved in this investigation, not this time. And you know I worry about you. That neighborhood you live in isn't the best in the city."

"I know, I know." Her voice held mock anger. "You

tell me every time you come over. But you see the potential for crime everywhere, thanks to your job. It's a great neighborhood. I love it, I love my neighbors, I love my loft. I'm not moving, Adam. Redirect, please…" She drew out the last word with a smile in her voice. "There must be something else you can focus on."

This was a conversation they'd had so many times it had become routine. But he wouldn't stop worrying about her. He knew she was stubborn, but he also still knew her as the little girl who'd adored her big brother. Even when he'd tickled her until she'd peed in her pants. Even when he beat up the boy who'd made fun of her in the eighth grade. Well, maybe especially then.

"I know you're okay, Jules, I just like to hear you say it."

"I love you, too. Now go do your job. I always love to hear from you, but I'm fine. I promise."

Adam hung up the phone and turned his eye to the worn leather-bound appointment book open on his desk.

"Hey, Kaminski, how's it going?"

Adam looked up to wave at a fellow member of the Dignitary Protection unit across the room. "Not great today, McDonnell. My VIP got shot at this morning."

"No kidding?" McDonnell worked his way over to Adam's cubicle, almost knocking over a stack of papers piled precariously on a low bookshelf along the wall. "That's not good. Any news on it yet?"

"No, nothing yet, the locals are working on it. With FBI, I think."

"Probably." McDonnell nodded, leaning against the narrow strip of solid wall that formed one side of Adam's gray, square work space. A space that hammered home the fact there was nothing dignified about working in Dignitary Protection. "With a senator involved, they would take the lead."

He looked like he was about to say more when a shout from across the room drew his attention. "Yeah,

yeah, I'm coming," he called back, then turned to Adam. "Sorry about that, Kaminski. And here you'd thought you'd gotten out of homicide for a while, huh? Let me know if there's anything I can do to help."

He tapped Adam's shoulder as he headed back out across the room.

Adam watched McDonnell weave through the mess of desks, shelves, and walls that crammed the room, patting colleagues on the shoulder as he passed, sucking in his gut occasionally to squeeze through the narrow aisles created by the line of cubicles.

He closed his eyes, just for a moment, and let himself drown a little in the raucous noise that filled the squad room. Finding solitude in the controlled chaos. He took a deep breath, opened his eyes, and brought himself back to the task at hand.

He had taken it upon himself to call the venues that were part of the planned trip. To let them know the VIPs wouldn't be coming. It wasn't his job, but it was something useful he could do from this end. Plus it gave him a chance to connect one more time with the people involved in the visit, now that the situation had altered so radically. He had one more call to make.

The phone was answered on the second ring, a young woman's voice, sharp but not unfriendly. "Barton McFellan, Advocacy Consultants."

"Detective Adam Kaminski, Philadelphia Police Department," Adam introduced himself. "I'm calling about Senator Marshall."

"Yes, we heard about the attack this morning," the woman replied. "One of our partners was there."

"I see." Adam realized belatedly that he shouldn't be surprised. A company like Barton McFellan, shelling out thousands of dollars to cover the costs of this weekend jaunt, would want to get some face time with the senator as part of the deal.

"I wanted to make sure that someone on your end was doing whatever you needed to do to cancel the trip," Adam continued. "You know, calling the hotel, things like that?"

"I'm sure someone else on the senator's staff will be taking care of that, Detective." There was a flicker of a pause, as if the woman's cool cracked briefly. But only for a second. "Since Jay won't be able to do it."

"Right, of course. Did you know him? Jay, I mean?"

The woman paused before responding. "Not personally, no. I believe our partner, Mr. McFellan, worked with him on a number of projects that involved Senator Marshall. In fact, he planned to talk with Jay at the residence this morning, that was one of the reasons he was there."

"Really?" Adam frowned. "Did they get to talk?"

"I wouldn't know, Detective, you'd have to ask Mr. McFellan." Her voice dropped again. "This really is a tragedy."

Adam nodded, though she couldn't see him. "Yes, it is. I hope they catch the guy who did this, and fast."

"Yes, Detective, we all do. If nothing else so that the senator and ambassador can sleep at night, without worrying someone is coming after them."

CHAPTER THREE

THE SUN WAS HIGHER in the sky but still low enough to cast a sharp shadow over the tiled roof of the ambassador's residence. It drew a stark line on the drive in front of Sam and Agent Collins as they walked toward their cars. A demarcation Sam was reluctant to cross. He stopped short of stepping over the line and turned to Collins.

"You sure you want to leave this with Hennessy and the Bureau?"

"Drop it, Sam." Collins gave him a look that left no room for argument. "It's the Bureau's case now, you know that."

"I know." Sam shook his head as he looked back toward the gloom of the front yard, the technicians still at work. "I just want to do more, sir, that's all."

"I get it, I do." Collins offered a small smile. "Let the FBI do their job. You know they're good at it."

"It's our job, too, isn't it? Protecting the ambassador, ensuring his security while he's a guest in our country?"

Collins shrugged. "I know there's overlap in our missions. I don't need you to lecture me on the inefficiencies of the system." He turned and kept walking, crossing the line into the light. He spoke to Sam over his shoulder. "If you've got any bright ideas, let me know, I'll pass them along."

"What about MPDC? Will the they be involved?"

Collins stopped again, gave Sam a look whose meaning was clear. "If the Bureau needs boots on the ground, they'll call the police department, like they always do."

"Good. That's what I wanted to hear."

"What are you after, Sam? What's bugging you?"

"Not sure." He looked down at his hands, now scrubbed clean. "I feel like I owe Jay more, an effort to find who did this to him." He took one more look back at the scene. "The shot was clean... why not take another?"

"What do you mean?"

"The shooter. If he missed his target, why'd he stop? Why not take another shot?"

"He only had one chance, he knew we'd be coming for him within seconds."

"It was such a clean shot." Sam shook his head. "Could it really be a miss?" Collins gave him another look, but Sam persisted. "And you know as well as I do, you need to keep it simple in an investigation. In any shooting, the dead guy is most likely the victim."

"Don't lecture me on how to conduct an investigation. When a madman shoots into a crowd, we don't look into why he shot the people he shot, we just try to catch him."

"Well, maybe we should. Maybe we're missing something."

ADAM SHIVERED as he hung up the phone, glad to be done with those calls. It felt too much like stepping into a dead man's shoes. He jumped when a hand fell on his shoulder.

"Sorry, partner, didn't mean to scare you." Pete smiled as he leaned into Adam's cubicle, his arm running along the top of the low wall. Even as he relaxed, his fingers kept rhythm along the top of the wall, tapping out some drumbeat only Pete could hear.

Adam laughed and stood, leaning against the opposite side of the cube and crossing his arms in front of him. "Good to see you, partner. What brings you over to the Roundhouse?"

"Just checking things out." Pete looked around the disorganized room and smiled again. "Wanted to make sure you weren't getting too comfortable up here. I guess I had nothing to worry about, huh?"

"Very funny." Adam bowed his head, accepting his partner's observation that this wasn't the sort of environment Adam would have chosen for himself. "It's been a good detail. Up to today, that is."

"Why, what's up?"

"A murder, of all things." Adam looked back at his partner. "I thought I had gotten away from that for a while, coming over here, but I guess not."

"Want to tell me about it?"

"Not much to tell at this point. Someone took a shot at Senator Lisa Marshall and the French Ambassador to the U.S. They were planning to come up today. They're both fine. But the senator's aide got hit. He didn't make it."

"Ah…" Pete screwed up his eyes and shook his head. "It's always the bystanders, the ones who want to be near power, who get hurt, isn't it?" Pete looked at his partner, knowing Adam's background well enough to know how personally he took it when a young person was killed. "That's why they need us. To give them a voice. To get them justice."

"I guess so. He was a nice kid, you know? Friendly, easy to work with, easy to talk to."

"I'm sorry, man. Are you going down there?"

"Me?" Adam's surprise showed on his face. "I don't think so. I mean, I haven't been asked."

"Aren't you interested, though? Could be fun working with the fancy brigade down in DC, couldn't it?" Pete smiled, and even after all these years working together Adam couldn't tell if he was being serious or sarcastic.

"You know," he said instead, "I do miss my old job. Babysitting VIPs isn't as great as it sounds."

"You don't say." Pete looked overly perplexed and now Adam knew he was joking.

"I know, I know," Adam continued. "Look, it was worth doing. I met some good people, got to know the deputy commissioner. That can't hurt, can it?"

"I see you talking, partner, but I'm hearing Sylvia's voice."

"All right, give me a break. A couple more weeks and I'm out of here and back to our old job. Doing our part to help the victims, stop the bad guys."

"And this murder in DC...?" Pete let the question hang in the air.

Adam shrugged and toyed with some papers on his desk. "FBI is taking the lead, I think, and Diplomatic Security's involved, because of the ambassador. And if they really need a cop, they can call on DC police. The best thing I can do is wrap up the details on this end, let the Bureau know of anything that doesn't sit right..." Adam's voice trailed off as he thought of what he'd learned about Jason McFellan.

"And it looks like you thought of something to tell them. Okay, do your thing the way you want to do it, Kaminski. Better for me if you don't go to DC, you know? I can't wait for you to be done with this detail and back out on the street with me. Let me tell you."

Adam smiled. "What, things not working out with Slap-Happy Harry?"

"Yeah, you can joke about it." Pete tried to look serious, but a smile crept across his features. "He earned that nickname for a reason. I'm telling you, the man's insane. I can't believe the captain thought it would make sense to partner me with such a crazy bastard. I swear, he finds risks where there aren't any, just so he can take them."

Adam laughed out loud. "I think the captain thought you could teach him a thing or two about being a detective, Pete. You know, help him out a bit?"

"As if." Pete narrowed his eyes. "I don't give a rat's ass what happens to that guy. As far as I'm concerned, he shouldn't be a cop. You either do your job, or you don't. Don't do it half-assed, for the kicks. That's all I'm sayin'."

Adam put his hands up as if to stop Pete in his tracks. "I know, I know. Sorry I brought it up. Hey, I only have a couple more weeks here, then I'm back in the Sixth District with you. You can make it that long, can't you?"

Pete bit back whatever smart-ass retort he was coming up with when Deputy Commissioner White stepped out of his office.

"Kaminski." The deputy commissioner didn't yell, yet somehow his voice carried across the busy room, stopping all conversation.

"Yes, sir." Adam winked at Pete as he turned to follow his boss into the corner office.

CHAPTER FOUR

"HAVE A SEAT, Kaminski." Deputy Commissioner White gestured to the chairs facing his desk as he closed the door behind Adam.

Dust motes dancing across the office on rays of late morning sun floated over file cabinets filled with reports, each its own story of loss, of devastation. As Deputy Commissioner for Special Investigations, White commanded a number of different units, including dignitary protection. And including homicide. This was nothing new to him.

White walked around to the other side of the desk. A shockwave of aftershave mingled with the musty odors already in the room as he moved. Adam inhaled deeply, recognizing those musty odors as hours upon hours spent poring over reports, analyses, and photographs, working day and night to catch those who would do harm to the people of Philadelphia.

Adam respected this man and everything he stood for. If he could help, he would.

"I have a request for you, Kaminski." White surprised Adam by saying, "I need you to go to DC for me."

"Of course." Adam didn't need to think about his reply. "What do you need?"

White paused as he lowered himself into his leather chair, adjusting his jacket as he sat. "I got a call this morning. From the Kapoors. Do you know them?"

Adam blinked and took a breath. "Jay's parents. No, I never met them. They must be devastated."

White frowned down at the files on his desk. "You could say that, I suppose. I never know what to say to parents who have lost a child through senseless violence."

Adam waited silently. There was nothing he could add to that sentiment. He fought back the memories that crept into his vision whenever he thought about the dead children. Three plain wooden coffins being lowered into the ground. Three fresh graves holding three victims. The children he was supposed to protect. The children he had failed.

The sound of sirens from the street below the window carried over the regular street traffic, reminding Adam that every day on this job could be another day dealing with murder. It was worth it, he knew, chasing justice for those who needed it. Justice for those who deserved it. But it was tough.

Finally, Deputy Commissioner White looked up again. "In some ways it's worse for them... if it can be worse in a situation like this."

He looked closely at Adam as he spoke, and Adam saw the light glinting off the hint of whiskers around his mouth that his razor had missed that morning. He must have shaved in a hurry.

"Their son is dead, but we're looking for someone who wanted to kill the senator. Or the French ambassador. You see the problem? From what I know about you, Kaminski, this is the sort of problem that's of interest to you."

Adam nodded. "Who's looking for the person who killed their son, you mean?"

"Exactly." The deputy commissioner picked up a pen from the surface of his desk and starting tapping it gently, quietly.

"It's the same thing, though, really, isn't it?"

"Of course. Find the man who took a shot at the

senator and you find the man who killed Jay Kapoor. They're doing the right thing. The same investigation we would run." He nodded, as if convincing himself.

Adam thought about the situation. The investigation had to focus on the likely intended victim. In this case, that was either Senator Marshall or Ambassador Saint-Amand. But Jay Kapoor was dead. He was the actual victim, if not the intended victim. And his parents needed to know that someone was paying attention to his death.

"You're right, I want to help. What can I do?" Adam asked.

"They're not just another family, you know?" White's comment didn't seem to be in response to his question, so Adam waited until White continued, "They're influential, I mean. Here in Philly. He owns a chain of jewelry stores. Not national, at least not yet, but they're a big business. And she's used that money to establish herself in Philly society."

"So they're looking for extra help?"

White blew out his lips in frustration. "It's hardly special treatment. Nothing like the senator and ambassador are getting. And their son is dead." He looked at Adam once again. "They've asked for our help. And we have to help them. Because they're influential here in Philly and can help the department. And because it's the right thing to do."

"How can I help the investigation, sir? I haven't been invited to join. I'm closing out my report here, and my role in this is done."

"I know, I made some calls. After I spoke with Mrs. Kapoor."

Adam raised his eyebrows. "So I'm going to DC?"

"Just as an observer, technically." White shrugged. "I called MPDC, a deputy commissioner there. He understood when I explained it to him. MPDC's not really involved in the investigation, you understand?"

"Sure, it's FBI and Diplomatic Security, right?"

"That's right. Metropolitan Police in DC are asked to help, sometimes, when the feds need some on-the-ground footwork, people who know the area."

"I don't know the area," Adam pointed out, but White waved his hand as if to wave away Adam's concern.

"You'll be there, assigned on a temporary detail to MPDC. That's the best I can do, it will have to be enough."

"Yes, sir." Adam stood, then turned back to White. "I'll do my best, sir. You know even with me there, this investigation is still going to focus on the senator. Not Jay."

"Understood, Kaminski. Do what you can to watch out for the boy's interest. For the family's interest. And make sure you keep them informed of all progress. They need to know we're there for them."

"Yes, sir." Adam headed back out to his desk to make a few more calls.

THE PAVEMENT under Sam's feet vibrated with a passing bus. The rattles and groans of the cumbersome vehicle as it passed the World War II Memorial and turned onto the loop around DC's famous Tidal Basin drowned out Officer Ramona Davis' next words.

"What?" Sam asked, frowning and shaking his head.

"I said, who the hell do they think they are?" Ramona repeated without raising her voice.

Sam laughed. "They think they're the FBI. Working for the good of the American people." He kept his left arm draped over the roof of Ramona's patrol vehicle, but bent lower to look at her as she leaned toward him from the driver's seat. "I don't have a problem with that. Why should you?"

"I don't know." She shrugged, glancing past Sam at a couple of joggers making their way toward the path along the water. "You were there, Diplomatic Security has the lead for the ambassador's security, it was at the ambassador's residence." She looked back at him, this time her voice rising. "Seems to me it should either be DS on the lead, or MPDC — this is our city, you know?"

Sam smiled and looked down at the serious young officer. He had known her father years before, when Sam was a rookie on the police force for the District of Columbia. Sam had since moved on to Diplomatic Security while his friend and mentor had retired to a quiet life, waiting to become a grandfather.

Ramona was the spitting image of her father in so many ways. From her broad cheekbones, wide smile, and perfect pearly white teeth to her overpowering sense of justice. Where her father's face had accumulated ridges and valleys of experience and wisdom, Ramona's was still smooth as molasses, clear and bright.

They both looked over when they heard the sirens of an approaching motorcade, a common enough occurrence in this part of the district. Blue flashes from the headlights and dashboard of the lead SUV identified it as the law enforcement detail protecting whichever dignitary followed in the black limo.

Sam's eyes followed the limo, its tiny American flags whipping angrily in the wind as the car sailed past. He couldn't see through the tinted windows, but didn't particularly care which politician or VIP was going to what meeting or party.

He turned back to Ramona. "Do you still claim this is our city?" He nodded toward the back end of the motorcade. "It's their city now, and you know it."

She shook her head and tapped her hands on her steering wheel. "No way. It's theirs when they want to drive through town without hitting traffic. It's ours when some kid is killed or some hospital's missing meds. And when any of that crime comes a little too close to those bigwigs, who do you think they blame? Hmm?"

She moved her arm in a broad sweep, indicating the

scenery around them. The top of the Washington Monument peeked from over the trees to the north, while Thomas Jefferson kept a serene eye on them from his granite pedestal across the Tidal Basin to their south. People jogged, walked, and biked past, enjoying the majesty of history as only DC could provide.

"No, this is our city. These are our citizens. And we're tasked with protecting them." She looked back at Sam. "We're the only ones who are. Who are actually thinking about them, and not the voting tendencies of some group of donors in Ohio."

"Okay, okay, I'm not going to debate this with you." Sam laughed and put his hands up in surrender. "I am on this murder investigation, even if the FBI has the lead. And I wanted to ask you a favor."

"I was wondering when you were going to get to that."

"Come on, I can't stop the daughter of an old friend for a casual chat?"

She smiled, and Sam couldn't help but smile back. "Of course you can. I wish you would more."

"I know, Ramona. I'm sorry. There's always just so much going on."

"Like this murder?" she prompted him.

"Right." Sam tapped his hand twice on the roof of her vehicle, getting his mind back to the situation at hand. "I got a call that Philly PD is sending someone down."

"What?" Ramona interrupted him, her voice incredulous. "It's not enough that we have federal agencies jostling us out of the way. Now Philly PD wants to get in on the act?"

"I don't think it's like that." Sam's voice didn't carry the conviction of his words, and she smirked and raised her eyebrows.

"I've been working with this guy for a few days on the Philly visit. He's been my local liaison with their Dignitary Protection Unit. He's a good guy. Seems like a good cop." Sam nodded, his voice more firm now.

"That's great. What's he going to do down here?"

"Well…" Sam hesitated briefly. "He's going to be assigned to work with MPDC."

"What?" Ramona's voice rose to a level even Sam wasn't expecting.

"Look." He tried to speak calmly. "The senator is from Pennsylvania. Her aide was from Philly. And looks like his family has some pull locally, at least with Philly PD. They've been making a bit of a ruckus, saying they want someone to keep a focus on their son."

"Hmph." It was nothing more than a loud exhale, but Ramona managed to let the sarcasm carry on her breath. "That won't be the FBI, then, will it?"

"No," Sam admitted, "and it won't be DS either, I'm afraid."

She frowned. "Really, Sam, even you?"

Sam shook his head. "Look, Ramona, this isn't a big deal. We're all working together. FBI's got some great agents on this. We're a strong team and we'll get this solved. But no, we won't be focusing on Jay Kapoor."

"So Philly PD will be the voice for Jay." She looked back up at Sam, but he was staring off across the Tidal Basin, his attention caught by movement on the water. "And where do I fit into this little scene?"

Sam looked back at her. "Keep an eye on Kaminski, our friend from Philly." He leaned into her car to put a hand on her shoulder. "He doesn't know DC, doesn't know how people work down here. He might need someone to hold his hand a little."

"Gee, thanks. It's babysitting, then?"

"Look, it won't be so bad. He's been good to work with. Plus I asked around a little, and I've heard good things about him."

She shrugged. "Fine, then. I'll keep an eye out for him. How do I know I'll even be assigned to work with him?"

"I'll have DS request your assistance on the case. That

way you'll be involved, you'll be the one assigned to partner with Philly PD."

"So I'll be in on the investigation, even though I'm not a detective?" Ramona smiled and shook her head. "I don't know how you do it, Sam, but you manage to annoy the hell out of me and give me exactly what I want all at the same time."

"Hey, I may've left MPDC years ago, but I still have some pull, some favors to call in. And I'm always watching out for you. You're not the lead on this, remember. This is an FBI case. You're just there to serve as a liaison with MPDC when they need one. And to keep an eye on Kaminski."

"Of course." Ramona shrugged, but Sam recognized the look in her eye. Determination. Excitement. Ambition.

Sam shook his head as he stepped back from her patrol vehicle. He hoped Kaminski knew what he was getting himself into. "Right. Now get back to work, before someone notices you're not on your assigned patrol."

"Yes, sir." Ramona gave a token salute, then pulled out into the 17th Street traffic.

CHAPTER FIVE

ONLY THE TIPS of Sylvia's sandaled toes touched the sand below the swing as she tapped at the earth to get it to move her in the right direction. No one else could make sitting on a child's swing seem elegant. Sexy.

Adam crossed the grass towards her, the Roundhouse looming behind him.

A swarm of children from a local daycare center darted among the swings and slides, slipping in the sand around the swing set. Sylvia watched them as they ran, laughing when they laughed, smiling back at them as they ducked around her. She tucked her hair behind her ear whenever the light breeze moved it in front of her face. Her skirt floated in the same breeze, but managed to stay just above the surface, never touching the sand below.

She looked cool and happy, and Adam envied her that as he felt a trickle of sweat working its way down between his shoulder blades. The daily uniform in dignitary protection was a dark suit, even in the summer months. And this was only early June — Adam hated to think what it would be like in the heat of August.

Approaching the swing set, Adam leaned around Sylvia, planting a kiss lightly on her cheek, then grabbed at the next swing over. It groaned as he squeezed his bulk into it, but it held his weight.

"You should be careful." Sylvia smiled. "I don't think this set can hold a large man like you."

"No, I suppose not." Adam laughed as he stood, then reached his hand out to her. She took it and he barely felt her weight as she pushed up off the swing with a little jump, almost floating down to the ground. "You look beautiful," he said with simple honesty.

She smiled and placed a hand against his cheek, playfully tapping a finger against the dimples that Adam found so embarrassing. "And you look hot. And stressed. Why did we have to meet this morning?"

As they stepped out of the sand, a group of children ran towards them, one little girl reaching out to pull on Sylvia's skirt.

"Hello, Sasha, how are you today?" Sylvia smiled as she bent down toward the girl.

The girl smiled shyly, one finger tucked carefully into the corner of her mouth, and stepped back into the group she was with. Sylvia laughed and looked over to the group's caretaker, keeping an eye on them from the far side of the playground. Sylvia shared a wave with the woman, then patted the little girl on the shoulder. "I'll see you again another day, okay?"

The group ran off, shouting and laughing. The little girl turned to give Sylvia a tiny wave before joining her friends.

Adam watched Sylvia with pride, in awe, as always, of her ability to make anyone, even children, feel comfortable with her. He chose a bench deep in the cool shade of a nearby tree. "Turns out I have to go to DC. Today. I don't know how long I'll be gone."

"Is this about that shooting?" Sylvia's face showed nothing but concern as she leaned forward and placed her hand over Adam's as it lay in his lap. "Will you investigate that boy's death?"

"Looks like it. At least I'll be an observer, not an investigator."

Sylvia made a sound somewhere between a laugh and a snort as she stood. "An observer? What does that mean?"

"Sylvia. It means I'm going to help out however I can. Why does it matter? Julia didn't see a problem with it, why do you?"

"Julia?" The pink spots on Sylvia's cheeks turned a darker shade of red. "You talked to Julia before you talked to me?"

"Honey, I didn't mean anything by it. I wanted to see you, in person."

"No." She crossed her arms over her chest as she turned her back to him. "Sometimes, Adam… sometimes I think she's more important to you than I am. She's your sister. I'm… I don't know what I am."

"Sylvia, honey, please." Adam put a hand out to touch her shoulder but she shrugged it off. "It doesn't mean anything. I don't have to choose between my family and you. I love you both. And Julia really needs me."

"And I don't?" Sylvia turned back to him. The breeze caught her hair again. She didn't catch it behind her ear, instead letting her hair and her skirt wave against her slender frame. The lavender scent that Adam had grown so accustomed to carried over the air to him and he felt a pang of loss so acute he had to look away. He knew what was going through her mind.

"I don't want to fight if you are leaving," Sylvia said, interrupting his thoughts. "This must be an important investigation, no?"

"The deputy commissioner himself asked me to do it."

Sylvia sat down and again took his hand. "I do love you, Adam. And this will be good for your career."

"I suppose… that's not really why I'm going…" He shook his head as he spoke to her. "It may be true, I don't know. In fact, it may not be true." When Sylvia looked confused, he continued, "I'm going to protect the interests of the boy who was killed — Jay Kapoor."

"The boy?" Sylvia's frown deepened. "Surely you want to know who attacked Senator Marshall? Or the ambassador?"

"It's all the same thing in the end, you see?" Adam explained. "We're trying to find the man who fired the shot. Right now the FBI and Diplomatic Security are treating the VIPs as the victims. Deputy Commissioner White wants to make sure we have someone there who remembers that Jay was the victim. Intended or not."

Sylvia frowned. "I see… that makes sense. And the deputy commissioner asked you to do this?"

Adam smiled as he saw what had changed her mind. Not the fate of the victim. The deputy commissioner. "Yes," he said out loud, "and the boy's family, the Kapoors. Quite influential in Philly society, apparently."

"Really?" Now Sylvia was smiling again. "Then you must go and do your best." She paused and examined him closely. "I know you, Adam Kaminski. I know you think I'm being selfish… that I don't understand. I do. Better than you do, I think."

"What do you mean, Sylvia?" Adam asked with a sigh, recognizing where this was going.

"You remember always those children, do you not?" Sylvia asked, her Polish accent coming out stronger as it did whenever she got worked up. "You think of the students when you were a teacher, the ones who were shot?"

Adam nodded mutely. He didn't want to talk about this again. Didn't want to think about the coffins, the funeral, the memories that wouldn't leave him in peace.

"And that is good, Adam. That is because you are a good man. You are also a good detective. If you want to help people — help children like that — then you must succeed in your career. These are not opposite goals, Adam. It is all the same goal."

Adam shrugged and turned to look out over the playground, the calls of the children carrying over the sound of traffic passing by the green city square.

"We have the same dreams, you and I." Sylvia leaned in close to him, her voice lowered to an urgent whisper. "You dream that you will be able to help all the people, so that no children will suffer anymore. I dream that you will be successful in this job, so successful that you will rise in your career. That is all the same, is it not?"

Adam turned his attention back to Sylvia. "Of course, I'm sure it's the same." He tried to sound conciliatory, but he grimaced as he realized his tone was dismissive, not accepting.

Sylvia nodded and said nothing more.

Adam knew she was simply looking for ways to push him up the PPD career ladder. He understood what she wanted, and why. And it wouldn't hurt him to strive to achieve more in his career. He just kept wondering, if it was such a lofty goal, why did it bother him so much? Shouldn't he be grateful that his girlfriend wanted him to succeed in his chosen career?

They stood together, and Sylvia wrapped her arms around Adam's broad shoulders. "You know I am right, don't you?"

"Of course, honey. I know." Adam hugged her back. "And hopefully this will make me look good to the deputy commissioner."

"Good. Then when must you leave?"

"Now… well, soon," he responded. "I'm going to run home and pack a few things, then I'll be on the one o'clock train to DC."

Sylvia kissed him lightly on the lips. "I wish you luck, then. Call me when you get a chance." She paused. "Not if it will interrupt your work, of course."

Adam shook his head, but he smiled and kissed her back.

CHAPTER SIX

ADAM KNOCKED on the door as he pushed it open. A long, dim hallway stretched ahead of him, opening up after fifteen feet into a well-lit room. Adam followed the light and the sound of hushed voices into Jay Kapoor's DC apartment, his shoes tapping on the hardwood parquet floor.

The voices stopped as he walked, and when he entered the living room, four faces turned toward him. Two were silhouetted in the windows that covered the south wall, opening onto P Street below and another apartment block across the street. The younger of these two stayed where he was, seated in an armchair angled slightly away from the window. The older man stood and walked toward Adam, hand outstretched.

"Adam Kaminski?" he asked.

Adam accepted his hand and nodded. The other man continued, "I'm Agent Sam Burke, Diplomatic Security. Pleasure to finally meet you in person." Sam's face was grim, his deep brown eyes carrying a hint of sadness. A man who had seen death before but was still disturbed by it. As he should be.

"Sam, good to see you. Thanks for inviting me over here." Adam turned to look at the two people to his left.

A man and a woman stood in a short, square passageway off the living room. Two closed doors, one on either side of them, kept the space dark. Behind them a third door stood open, offering a glimpse of a bedroom beyond.

"Mr. and Mrs. Kapoor." Sam moved toward them as he spoke. "May I introduce Detective Adam Kaminski, Philadelphia Police Department."

Only Mr. Kapoor shook his hand. His wife stood where she was, her eyes glazed and unfocused, her fingers toying randomly with a man's button-down shirt that dangled from her hands.

"I'm so sorry for your loss." Adam stuck with the standard line, having relied on it so often in his job. He knew how inadequate these words were, but had nothing better to offer the Kapoors.

"Why don't we all come into the living room?" Sam suggested, gesturing toward the open sofa with his left arm while resting his right hand lightly on Mrs. Kapoor's shoulder. She followed his lead, walking stiffly, as if not in control of her legs and not seeing the room in front of her.

Her husband stepped behind her, squeezing his arm around her shoulders as they reached the sofa and guiding her down, his arm still encircling her, offering some protection from the pain that surrounded them both.

Adam glanced at the young man silently occupying the armchair, then balanced on the arm of the sofa beyond the Kapoors. Sam resumed his position on the far wall, leaning back against the windows, his profile dark against the sunlight that caught around the edges of his thick, curly black hair, creating a halo effect.

"Mr. and Mrs. Kapoor," Adam began, but Mr. Kapoor cut him off.

"Detective Kaminski, we are both very glad that you are here. Your commissioner is very kind for agreeing to provide your help."

"Well" — Adam glanced at Sam — "I'm really only here as an observer. Somewhat unofficial." He saw the frown forming on Kapoor's face, so he added, "I am here to do everything I can to find out who killed your son. I promise you, I'm here for him. To seek justice for him. To speak for him if I have to."

Kapoor turned to his wife. Her face had cleared slightly, and she set the shirt she had been holding on the sofa next to her. Turning to Adam, she asked, "Do you believe his death was an accident? A mindless, meaningless…" Her sob cut her words off, and she looked down again, covering her mouth with her hand.

Adam shook his head. A dozen different responses flew through his mind, none that would provide this grieving mother the answers she wanted.

A movement from the armchair caught Adam's attention. The young man had shifted in his seat, sinking even lower into the cushions.

"Adam, this is Todd Heavrin, Jay's roommate." Adam nodded at the young man in response to Sam's introduction. Todd didn't look up, instead continuing to stare at a spot in the middle of the floor.

Adam glanced down to see if there was really something there that could fascinate this young man. He saw only a light stain against the dark wood, visible in the afternoon sun coming in through the windows.

The group sat in awkward silence for a few minutes, Todd continuing to examine the stain on the floor, the Kapoors lost in a world of memory and tragedy. Adam glanced up at Sam, but his face was too dark to read, the afternoon light catching a few white hairs around the edges of his otherwise black figure.

The muffled rattle of traffic four stories down on the street below carried up to the apartment, interrupted occasionally by a sniff or cry from Mrs. Kapoor.

"How long had Jay been working for Senator Marshall?" Sam finally broke the silence. He asked the question to the room, without addressing it to anyone in particular.

Mrs. Kapoor chose to answer. "He had been here for over a year." She smiled. "He was so proud of himself.

And we were, too. It was not an easy position to get." Her face crumpled as she spoke, and she pressed her lips closed. White lines appeared around her mouth as she frowned, standing out against her olive skin.

Mr. Kapoor nodded. "Over a year, yes."

Adam shot an inquisitive look at Sam, and when he nodded, asked, "And this was his first position out of college?"

"Yes, that's right. He had worked before, of course, you know." Mr. Kapoor glanced first at Sam, then focused his gaze on Adam. "We insisted that he have experience working in our stores. He started when he was sixteen, as an assistant in one of the shops."

Kapoor took a deep breath and glanced at his wife before continuing. "He had a tremendous work ethic."

Todd shifted in his seat again. Kapoor didn't seem to notice, continuing, "When he was working, we saw a difference in our profits, in the number of sales. He was a very effective salesman."

Adam listened closely to Mr. Kapoor, but couldn't ignore the shuffling sounds and occasional coughs coming from Todd. He glanced at Sam, who made a slight nod in return.

Adam turned back to the Kapoors. "And did he move right to this apartment, when he took the job?"

"Yes, that's right." Mr. Kapoor answered. "He applied at home. Senator Marshall has an office in Philadelphia, you know? Diya arranged for the interview." Kapoor indicated his wife as he spoke. "Jay was the one who made it work. Not an easy job to get, I assure you. He sold himself to that chief of staff, just as he had sold bracelets in my stores."

Todd's gaze was once more on the floor, but Adam had seen his eyes shift briefly to Kapoor as he spoke, a small smile playing momentarily on his lips.

Adam turned to Todd as he spoke this time. "And have you lived here, with Jay, since he moved here?"

Todd's answer was so quiet it barely carried over the

sounds of the traffic. "I was here first. I let other people on the Hill know I was looking for a roommate — my other roommate moved out, and I can't afford to pay for this place on my own. Jay called me. He seemed like a nice guy, so he moved in." Todd shrugged. "He was…" Glancing at the Kapoors, he finished his sentence. "A good roommate."

Adam looked one more time at Sam, and knew that Sam was seeing the same evasion he was. "Okay." Adam stood. "I think it will help me to look around the apartment, to get a better sense of who Jay was."

Diya Kapoor whimpered, and put her head on her husband's shoulder. "Todd," Adam asked, "can I ask for your help?"

"Oh… uh, sure." Todd pushed himself up from the chair, straightening the legs of his khaki pants as he did so. "What do you want to see?"

"Come on." Adam turned and walked toward the rooms at the back of the apartment. As they entered the small hallway, he gestured to the room straight ahead. "Is this room Jay's?"

"Yeah, mine's through there." Todd tapped on one of the closed doors as they both walked past it into Jay's room.

The windows caught Adam's attention first. Like the living room, one wall was entirely windows. Looking out, Adam saw that they provided a view, albeit at a slight angle, of Dupont Circle. The grassy, circular block created a traffic circle connecting Connecticut, New Hampshire, and Massachusetts avenues, as well as providing a public space with benches surrounding a large fountain.

The Dupont Circle neighborhood boasted artsy bookstores, five-star restaurants, and upscale nightclubs. It wasn't a cheap place to live.

Turning his attention back into the room, Adam cast his glance over the king-size bed, covered in a thick duvet, still wrinkled as if its owner had just rolled out of bed. On the wall opposite the windows, a line of folding doors suggested a large closet that ran the length of the room. A small oak desk held a MacBook and two small speakers, while two tablet computers leaned casually against one side of the bookshelf.

A worn and folded print rested against the books, tucked into a corner of the shelf where it wouldn't get knocked off. Adam picked it up to examine the group of young men and women in bathing suits and shorts, smiling at the camera from the boardwalk of a shore town. He saw Jay's grinning face, his eyes bright. All the kids seemed happy, carefree. It couldn't have been taken too long ago. Adam tucked the print back into the shelf, leaning it up against Jay's high school yearbook, its spine bent from obvious use.

Jay liked to remember his past. His friends.

Pushing open the closet doors, Adam ran his fingers over the suits, shirts, and sweaters hanging there. Cashmere, silk, wool. This young man had good taste in clothes as well as electronics.

"Tell me more about Jay, Todd," he said as he closed the closet doors.

"What's there to say?" Todd asked. "He worked on the Hill, as an aide, like me."

"Was he good at his job?"

Todd shrugged, as if to indicate there was nothing special about the way Jay did his work, but Adam saw that familiar smile playing on his lips once more.

"How did Jay's work compare to other aides'? Or to yours?" Adam pressed.

Todd looked directly at Adam, a flash of defiance appearing, then disappearing once again. He turned his gaze out the window and shrugged once more. "He did his job. He was good at it, I guess. He always found a way to make things work out."

"What kind of things?" Adam picked up a plastic figurine from Jay's desk as he questioned Todd, his fingers running along the surface of the tiny military figure. A boy's toy. A young man's memento of childhood.

Todd glanced nervously at the door to the room. Adam could hear Sam consoling the Kapoors in the living room and knew they needed to have time alone. To mourn their son.

"Look, I get that you don't want to say anything bad about the guy. Especially with his parents in the next room." Adam jerked his head toward the living room. "If there's something you know about Jay that you're not saying, you gotta tell me."

"Why?" The question was simple, but it hit directly on the complexity of this case. "Jay wasn't the guy they were shooting at. Why do you need to know about him?"

Now it was Adam's turn to shrug. "You're right." He shook his head. "It may have nothing to do with this case. That's the way it is with murder investigations. Everyone involved — even the innocent bystanders — suffer for it. We need to examine every possible link, every bit of evidence that could shed light on what happened." He paused, looking at Todd. "Even if it seems like it has nothing to do with this shooting, anything you can tell me about Jay may help."

When Todd's expression didn't change, Adam pushed harder. "What if something you know about Jay relates to his work with the senator? And what if that something ends up being the motive behind why someone would want to kill the senator?" He paused, eyebrows raised.

Todd nodded this time, then stepped toward the windows, away from the open door. "Okay, I could see that. Thing is..." His voice lingered on the air for a moment before fading away.

This wasn't going anywhere fast, but Adam wasn't about to give up. "Maybe we could meet another time — somewhere else?" Adam suggested. "Somewhere we can talk?"

"All right. In Capitol Hill. There's a bar there, I go most days after work. The Capitol Inn. A lot of the aides hang out there. I'll be there tomorrow after seven. Meet me there."

Todd left the room and Adam heard the door to his bedroom open and close. Hopefully, whatever it was Todd wasn't saying could wait until tomorrow.

Adam walked back out to the living room. The Kapoors still sat on the sofa. Sam had moved around behind them and was walking to meet him.

"I'll get more from him tomorrow," he said under his breath while nodding toward Todd's room.

"Got it." Sam voice was equally low. "I gotta get back to my office and check in there. You should head over to the scene."

"That's a good idea. I'd like to see it."

"A DC police officer — Davis — has been assigned to work with you as your liaison."

Adam smiled. "My liaison. I already feel enough of an outsider, that's the last thing I need."

Sam smiled back. "Officer Davis is a good cop, you'll be in good hands."

"Where should I meet him?"

Sam raised his eyebrows a fraction. "Davis is already at the scene. Why don't you head straight over, you can get a taxi right out front of this building."

"Right." Adam shook Sam's hand. "Thanks for all your help, Sam. I don't know how much I can add to this investigation. I appreciate you being so good about my just showing up like this."

"Hey, no sweat. I've been on the job long enough to know that we need all the help we can get. Even if all you do is keep the Kapoors calm, that's a help right there. Listen." He paused, as if considering his words carefully. "Some people don't feel the same way. Be nice to Davis, you'll need a friend in the MPDC."

CHAPTER SEVEN

WAVES OF WATER splashed onto the boardwalk. Actual goddamn waves. Caused by the ducks fighting. The well-dressed man wandering aimlessly along the Old Town Alexandria waterfront shivered.

That couldn't be normal. In all the years he'd been coming here, this was a first. He glanced around to see if other visitors had noticed. A crowd was gathering, as surprised as he was, so he looked back at the ducks. At least he wasn't crazy.

The ducks were. Not him.

Behind him, the historic brick town houses of Alexandria, Virginia stood square and tall as they had for hundreds of years. Tourists lined the parklike waterfront, enjoying the history, the scenery, the restaurants. In front of him, a battle of nature waged.

The piece of bread the ducks fought over grew larger, then started to disintegrate as it soaked up more and more water and the two ducks got more and more violent.

He loved coming down to Old Town when he was tired. Or confused. Or scared. Watching the tourists stroll along the waterfront, stopping for a beer in a local bar, even watching the ducks dive for crumbs tossed to them along the boardwalk helped him relax. Focus.

This was no ordinary day. Scared didn't begin to describe it. Maybe it made sense the ducks chose today to go crazy. He kept one eye on the crowd around him as he watched the ducks, making sure there was no one else around he recognized. No one who would recognize him.

At first it seemed clear the black one would win. It dove in and attacked its competitor with a ferocity rarely seen in these calm, touristy waters. This had to be about more than that soggy piece of bread. Didn't it?

The black duck struck again, its angry squawks drowning out the cries of the brown duck. That would be it, then. He turned to continue his way along the waterfront.

He shouldn't have jumped to conclusions.

The smaller, brown duck wasn't giving up his claim to the bread. The fighting intensified. Other tourists turned away and one young boy ran to his mother. He couldn't look away. He felt drawn to the ducks. He understood their fight. Their need.

If only he could attack the feds that way. Tear the truth out of them. How far had they gotten in their investigation? Did they know the truth yet? Were they toying with him?

Not knowing was the hardest part. He leaned forward and grabbed the wooden rail that separated him from the death battle below with both hands, his fingers digging into the damp wood. He couldn't stand not knowing.

What if he was the next target? You never knew. It was an eat or be eaten kind of world. Just look at those ducks.

He felt the fear of the small brown duck as if he were there in the water with him, fighting for his life. He felt the pain. Felt the need to fight back. The need to survive.

He wouldn't give up, either.

He smiled, then saw the look he was getting from a young mother to his right. She pulled her two children closer to her as they passed him. His grin darkened as he looked at the children. His thoughts flashed to his child. Of course she wouldn't be a child anymore. In her twenties, if he was counting right. He tried not to count.

The family kept moving. A juggler had set up farther down the boardwalk, and the children ran past the fighting ducks, their focus on the entertainment ahead.

He couldn't move forward. He couldn't look away from the ducks. He was in a life-or-death situation, too. He never meant it to go this far. He had no idea how to get out of it. He needed to know more about the investigation.

She would know, of course. The woman who held his heart, who controlled his future. She would scoff at his fears, as she always did. Thrive on them. Grow stronger because of them.

He shook his head, trying to shake the fear out of himself. He squeezed his fingers tighter around the wood, catching a splinter in his finger, then pulled tighter around it, feeling it dig its way in. Deeper and deeper. Just like her.

She would protect him. He was sure of it. She always did. She was always right.

No winner had emerged yet, but there could be no doubt this was a fight to the end. The brown duck was scrappy. Determined. The black duck was bigger. Stronger.

He turned away and walked toward the juggler, wrapping his injured finger in his handkerchief as he walked.

CHAPTER EIGHT

THE BRICK WALL that lined the property of the ambassador's residence rose only three feet high, decorative rather than prohibitive. The iron fence that topped it, a military row of thick, sharp rods, drove the point home.

Adam approached the closed gate and stepped close to see through to the lawn beyond it.

A row of black SUVs blocked the curved drive in front of the stone mansion, stretching from the closed iron gates to twenty feet before the grand entrance. Late afternoon sun glinted off the shining vehicles, then lost itself in the thick dark row of bushes that lined the house.

No yellow crime scene tape marred the elegant landscape, but the drive and yard swarmed with agents. Adam watched as white-suited technicians crawled over the ground around the spot where Jay had fallen and through the bushes where the weapon had been found. One woman in the uniform of the DC Police Department stood near the house entrance, in consultation with a group of men in the uniform of the FBI, the standard dark suit and tie.

The crime scene seemed to have been tagged with an invisible marker. Despite the absence of tape, the other agents, not dressed for the technical work, stayed away from these areas, moving in broad circles as they walked between the house and their vehicles. They didn't need the tape to know to stay away from the scientists doing their work.

Adam picked up voices as radio calls were made to and from the agents, though from where he stood he couldn't quite make out what they were saying.

He stayed on the outside, looking in. Watching. Waiting.

He'd been on the inside enough times, part of the team reviewing the lay of the land, comparing notes, gaining information as the technicians slowly reached conclusions based on minute trace evidence. Standing here, watching from the outside, was a different experience. He let the feel of the scene sweep over him. The heavy scent of the juniper bushes laden with new needles. The hum of bees in the tall stand of tiger lilies off to the side of the lawn, audible over the distant sound of traffic coming from the main street a couple blocks away. The coolness of the shade as the June sun drowned beneath the tall trees that lined the street and dotted the yard.

A fresh-faced young man in a dark blue suit broke away from the others near the door and walked toward him. Adam watched him in the same way that he watched the other actors in this drama, only shaking himself out of his reverie as the young man approached the gate and started to speak. It was time to get in on this investigation.

"Can I help you with something, sir?"

Adam held out his police badge, sticking his arm through the gate. "Detective Adam Kaminski, Philadelphia PD. I'm looking for Officer Davis, MPDC. I'm supposed to work with him on this case."

"Davis?" The young agent's voice made his doubt clear. He examined Adam's identification and gave him a quizzical look. "Philadelphia? On this case?"

"Davis is expecting me."

The man raised an eyebrow as he shrugged and

turned away from Adam back to the house, calling out as he walked. "Davis!" He turned back to Adam, frowning but nodding. "Stay here." Then he trotted back to his side of the playing field.

Adam stayed where he was, standing outside the gate. As if he had any choice.

Officer Ramona Davis turned when she heard her name. Seeing Adam waiting by the gate, she frowned and tucked her notebook into her back pocket. Glancing at the technicians at work as she passed, she covered the distance between them quickly. Her thick black hair was captured in a knot low on her neck, well below her service cap but the requisite distance above her collar. Walking with the grace of a dancer, she seemed to glide over the lawn. Feminine even in the uniform made for a man.

She approached the gate and stopped for a moment, then put her hand out. "Ramona Davis. I've been waiting for you."

Adam shook her hand, his arm bent awkwardly through the gate, her grip firm in his.

Looking at his face, she smiled and shook her head, the laughter that didn't make it to her mouth visible in her brown eyes. "You were expecting a man, I see."

Adam shrugged. "Sorry if I looked surprised, it's really not relevant."

"I know." Ramona smiled again. "Sam likes to poke fun at people. Else he would have mentioned it." She looked Adam up and down as she spoke, and he couldn't help pulling down on his jacket to straighten it.

"It's good that you made it over here," she started to say, then seemed to change tracks. "Though I'm not sure what you think you can learn. It'll all be in the report."

"No doubt. I like to see things firsthand. You understand." Adam said it as a statement, not a question.

Ramona nodded her head once in acquiescence and grinned. "Okay, I'll show you the basics."

She pushed a button on the brick column to the side of the drive and Adam heard the click of the gate unlocking. He pushed it open and walked into the garden.

Ramona turned toward to the house without waiting for him, sweeping her arm to take in the scene in one gesture. She spoke rapidly, as if daring Adam to keep up. "This is the residence of the French Ambassador to the U.S., currently Alain Saint-Amand. It's owned by the government of France. The delegation was coming out of the main house, there" — she indicated the marble steps at the high curve of the drive — "moving toward vehicles parked right in front. The shot was fired from somewhere close to the house, to the right of the entrance. It caught the group as they were approaching their vehicles."

Adam looked out at the scene as he listened to her description, then turned his attention to Ramona. "Someone waiting for the right moment?"

She shrugged. "Waiting. Or someone who knew their schedule."

She touched Adam lightly on the shoulder to indicate that he should follow her, then turned to walk around the perimeter of the yard, keeping up her explanation as they walked.

Adam kept his eyes trained on the scene in front of him, absorbing every detail so he could recall it later as he needed it, trying to ignore the sense of Ramona walking close beside him. The rustle of her uniform as she moved. The light scent of vanilla that lingered on the air behind her as she walked.

She had moved on to saying something about the staff at the residence, but Adam still had some more questions about the scene. "Where was the shooter standing, exactly?"

She bit back what she had been saying and frowned again. "Too soon to know, Detective." She gave his title an inflection that made it sound more like an insult than a sign of rank.

Adam took a breath. He wasn't here to make friends, but he needed her to share information, to let him in to the investigation. "What *do* we know about his location?"

"You can see where the weapon was found, in that line of hedges there. It was thrown there, no evidence so far that he was standing there."

So at least he understood now why the crime scene techs were moving out through the line of hedges and beyond with their equipment and why the techs on the drive were setting up laser range finders, equipment that might or might not work in the shade of the garden.

"They should be able to identify the location of the shooter based on the trajectory of the bullet."

"Pretty close." Ramona shrugged. "You know it won't be exact, but yeah, that will help."

They paused in their perambulation of the yard when the front door opened and a man in a bespoke silk suit stepped out. His was not the standard FBI uniform and he was clearly not part of the investigatory team.

The man paused dramatically on the front steps, one hand over his eyes as if to shade his vision from the few shafts of light that could work their way through the trees' thick foliage. Completing his scan of the yard, he turned toward a group of agents near the front door. One peeled off from the rest of the group and went to meet him.

The agent spoke first. "Ambassador, is there something I can help you with? We are still working on our investigation out here."

"Yes, I can see that, Agent Hennessy." The Ambassador's patrician voice carried across the yard, and Adam and Ramona had no difficulty hearing him. Hennessy's voice was softer, and Adam focused to make out his words.

"I need you to stay inside right now, Ambassador. For your own safety."

"Pshtt." The Ambassador made a sound that on

anyone but a Frenchman would have seemed impolite and waved away Agent Hennessy's concern with a well-manicured hand. "I am not afraid. I know that I am safe here. Look around you, I am surrounded by—" He paused as he turned his own eyes in the direction he had suggested for Hennessy, as if evaluating the scene before continuing. "Protection," he finally finished his sentence, the tone of his voice leaving no doubt that he did not find the presence of the agents comforting. "I must remind you, Agent Hennessy, that this is French property. I cannot have you lingering here any longer than necessary."

Hennessy's mouth firmed, but his response was polite. "I assure you, Ambassador, we will not linger. We need to take a few more measurements of the scene, then we'll be out of your hair."

The Ambassador's hand moved up to his silver mane, though not a hair was out of place. "And I would never dream of slowing that investigation. I simply wanted to assess the current state, so that I could inform my colleagues."

"We only need a couple more hours, sir, then the yard will be yours again. Until then…" Hennessy gestured subtly toward the door.

"Of course, of course. And Agent Hennessy, if there is anything I can offer you in support, please don't hesitate to ask." Ambassador Saint-Amand smiled as he turned away from Hennessy. His eye alighted momentarily on Ramona and Adam, then he turned and continued back into the house, the heavy door closing behind him with a sigh.

Ramona laughed under her breath. "We all have competition, I guess."

"Tell me about Agent Hennessy," Adam asked in a low voice, recognizing an opportunity. "He's not PD?" The words "like us" didn't need to be said.

"Roger Hennessy. He's in charge of the investigation here at the house," she answered, also keeping her voice down and looking away from the front of the house as she spoke. "FBI. He wasn't on the scene when the murder happened. Sam Burke was here. He saw the boy get shot." She paused, and a wave of pain passed silently over her face, then was gone. "FBI took over as soon as they arrived, of course. They're working closely with DS on it, since DS still has chief responsibility for the ambassador's safety."

"Is there French security here?"

Ramona pointed with her chin, her hands steady behind her back. "Just one guy. I don't know his name yet. He's been here for about six months, I'm told. His job is to protect the ambassador. He has no jurisdiction in this investigation. Come on." She once again touched Adam lightly to move him toward the house. He felt the warmth of her touch even after her hand had moved away.

They continued their walk around the yard, staying to the sides so as not to interfere with the crime scene investigators. As they neared the house, their path took them close up against the dark hedge that ran along the front of the house. The weapon had been found in the partner to this hedge, branching out from the far side of the door. Once again, Adam was struck by the coolness of the yard, the damp darkness of the brown and green hedge despite the warmth of the June afternoon.

"You know, I'm actually glad you're here, Kaminski." Ramona glanced at Adam as she spoke.

"Really?" He smiled, moving his hand across his face in a futile attempt to hide his dimples. "I didn't get that impression."

"No." Ramona laughed and Adam could see some of the tension visibly leave her shoulders. "I'm glad that Philly PD sent someone down here." Even as she spoke, she frowned and shook her head. "I mean, not that we need help from Philly PD. Nothing like that — our friends at DS and FBI can work this case better than anyone."

Adam didn't believe the friends idea for a minute, but he let that slide. "Okay, then what's your angle?"

"It's that you need me as your liaison." She shrugged. "Simple self-interest, that's all."

"And you want to be involved."

Ramona raised her eyebrows. "Every time there's a back alley murder no one cares about or an overdose, DC police department gets the case. But a high-profile murder... well, in DC that always means the FBI. I'm looking for a way to get in on a case that doesn't have me running around the Southeast in the middle of the night."

Adam had heard stories about the poorer neighborhood of the city and knew what she meant. "So even though you're assigned as my babysitter, that's still better for you than sitting the case out, is that it?"

"Babysitter, yeah." She put her head to one side. "Don't expect me to sit back and watch."

"I never would."

Ramona laughed again. "I'm glad we understand each other, Kaminski. We'll get on just fine."

Adam remembered a time when he had felt that kind of enthusiasm for his cases, and that level of competition. It hadn't been that long, really, but the years seemed to merge together, one case after another. It was good to be reminded of that kind of purpose and dedication. A focus on catching a killer, no matter what. And it was good that Ramona Davis was finally letting him in.

"Then tell me about Sam Burke," he said out loud. "How'd he get you involved in this? What's your connection to him?"

"Ah, Sam." Ramona paused and seemed to be examining the sky over Adam's right shoulder. "I've known him all my life. At least it seems like that sometimes."

"How so?"

"He was my father's partner."

"Your dad was in Diplomatic Security?"

"No." Ramona smiled. "Nothing so fancy. Dad was a cop. A real cop." She winked with the last statement.

"Sam was DC police? I didn't know that."

"Yep. True blue. For a while, at least. He was a rookie when my dad was in his last years on the force, so they paired up. Dad taught Sam everything he knows." She looked back at Adam, a wry expression on her face. "Including how to look out for me, apparently."

"It can't be that bad having people like that to watch out for you."

"Hey, in this case it's a good thing. I know you were coming down regardless. I hear the Kapoors insisted."

"And apparently have some pull."

"Anyone in MPDC could have been paired up with you. Sam's the point of contact on DS, he made the call to my captain to have me assigned. And here I am."

"And here *we* are," Adam corrected her.

"Right… of course." Her expression gave lie to her words of agreement. "So now you know my story, Kaminski. At some point I might want to hear yours, but how about first we get back to the case at hand?"

Adam pointed toward the spot on the driveway where Jay had fallen, almost cleared now of the technicians that had been covering it. "The shooter couldn't have been too far away. Even once we pinpoint his exact location, there aren't that many places he could have been standing."

Ramona moved her eyes around the yard, across the drive, and to the street. "You're right. No way he was standing on the street, wrong angle. The farthest he could have been was at the edge of the house, firing out toward the drive."

"So how'd he miss?" Adam asked.

Ramona shrugged. "Dumb luck, I guess."

Adam shook his head. "Not for Jay." He put his hand out and focused his eyes, as if taking a shot himself. "Not a chance I would have missed that. You?"

She eyeballed the shot. "Not a chance."

Adam looked back down at her. "So if nothing else, we've ruled out a cop as the shooter." He smiled and she laughed with him.

"You're saying it was someone not used to taking a shot, Detective?"

"Could be, if he was really aiming for Senator Marshall or Ambassador Saint-Amand," Adam agreed. "It's harder to shoot a person than most people realize. Even if you're a good shot, the adrenaline in the moment can pull you off target, shake you up."

"So what's your next move, Detective? How do you want to handle this" — she nodded back toward the group of agents on the yard, half of whom were now packing up their gear and pulling out — "since you're not really part of the investigation?" She looked back up at Adam. "What do you want to 'observe' first?" Her fingers traced the line of the quotes in the air as she spoke, underscoring the sarcasm of her statement.

"I get your point. I guess I'm at your mercy." He put his hand on her shoulder. "I'll look around, but I appreciate your help. I'm going to end up covering the same ground as the FBI. Getting a fresh look at things. You need to let me know when they find something. You know, be the liaison you've been assigned to be."

"Hey!" The call from the young man who'd met Adam at the gate interrupted their conversation. "They want to talk with you, sir. In the house."

As they approached the front door together, the young agent spoke again. "Just Detective Kaminski."

Ramona stopped mid-stride, her eyes widening and a flush growing on her cheeks. "I'm supposed to be his liaison."

"Only him," was all the agent said, then he turned back into the house, holding the door open for Adam.

SILENCE GREETED SAM when he walked into the large office he shared with other agents at the State Department.

He had avoided the main entrances to the building, coming in through a side entrance on 21st Street that only staff could access. Making his way through the warren of security offices that branched off the nondescript entrance, he had seen the usual array of U.S. Marines and Diplomatic Security Agents. Here at the supervisors' desk area, no one was around.

Sam's desk sat across the room, below a high, narrow window that controlled rather than permitted the sunlight into the work space. Unlike the other desks in the room, its surface was clean. All of Sam's ongoing projects were neatly filed away in the metal drawers that lined one wall, securely locked cabinets that also held the hard drives of each computer in the room.

Sam shrugged his worn shoulder bag off his arm onto the desk. He turned toward the cabinets to unlock his hard drive when the phone on his desk rang.

In the silence of the office, its harsh jangle was startling. Sam turned with surprise. Truth be told, he didn't often get calls on that line. People he worked with called his cell phone, and people he didn't work with went through his supervisor — who then called his cell phone.

For a second, he considered not answering. He had two reports waiting for him, reports for two embassies overseas waiting on his review of changes to their security plans. Then more paperwork after that: duty assignments for the local agents under his supervision, staff evaluations, a position description to revise. The paperwork that needed his attention was stacked neatly in the front end of one of the metal drawers, patiently waiting for his attention. Once completed, it would join the other files. Files that filled an entire file cabinet. Files that marked each day of the past ten years of his life.

He knew these reports were important. Lives were at

stake. Security and evacuation plans needed to be top-notch. He had the knowledge and experience to provide an effective assessment, and these people relied on him. But he had gained that knowledge through his time on the streets in DC, not through time spent reviewing reports.

Even thinking about the paperwork that awaited him raised the specter of that familiar fear — fear that he was losing his edge, losing his touch. Losing his ability to be a cop. A good cop.

"Agent Burke," he answered the phone.

THE SIGH OF THE FRONT DOOR closing caught Adam's attention even more than a heavy thud would have. The oak door shut out the front yard, the agents, Ramona Davis waiting on the grass, her frown deepening as the door closed between them.

Inside, the house was cool. Quiet. Calm. Adam followed the young agent across a marble-lined entrance hall heavy with the scent of lilies, perhaps cut from the front garden. Flowers with a beautiful scent, thought Adam, but also the flowers of death. An odd choice.

The young agent opened a wooden door off the main hall and gestured for Adam to step through. He didn't follow and Adam felt the door close behind him.

"Detective Kaminski. Welcome." Special Agent in Charge Roger Hennessy stood and moved around the room's expansive desk to shake Adam's hand. "What brings you down to DC? Someone could have interviewed you in the Philly field office, gotten your take on the planned visit."

"I'm here because of the Kapoors," Adam answered, then not seeing immediate recognition in Hennessy's eyes, he added, "the parents of the dead man. Jay Kapoor."

"I see." Hennessy's brow wrinkled as he walked back around the large desk, its surface stacked with boxes.

"The ambassador sent his aide in here not long after we arrived to pack away any information that could be inconvenient for federal agents to see." He laughed, nodding at the boxes. "Apparently there's a lot of it."

Both men turned their eyes as a shadow passed on the other side of the closed door, then moved on. One side of Hennessy's lips turned up in a wry smile. "He packed up his files, and still keeps dropping by to check on us. Asking for constant updates, as if we have nothing better to do. God, what a scene."

Adam considered the ambassador's position. He might have been the intended target. He also might know more about the situation than he was letting on. "He's giving you full support in the investigation, though, right? Access to the house?"

"Support?" Hennessy grinned. "Yeah, you could say that. Access to the house, no way. This is French property, remember. And this guy seemed to have it in for the Bureau before we even got here."

"The agents in Diplomatic Security must know him."

Hennessy shrugged. "I guess, he seems to talk to them more than to us. But this is our investigation, Detective, not theirs. Which makes me wonder, why did the Kapoors want you here? We got enough agencies involved already, we don't need another. That complicates it even more, slows things down."

"They wanted someone from Philly to work with MPDC, someone who would keep the interests of their son at the front of the investigation."

Hennessy raised an eyebrow. "MPDC isn't conducting this investigation." He paused again, considering, then added, "If you're here to work with MPDC, and they're not involved in this investigation, then I guess that means you're not involved, either."

"I guess you could say that. I was led to believe that Officer Davis, who's outside right now, had been assigned to work as a liaison between the federal investigation and MPDC. In case" — he frowned, raising his hands as if in prayerful supplication — "in case you needed someone who knew DC, knew the criminal element here. In case you needed more boots on the ground in support."

"We always keep a connection with the local PD when investigating an attempted murder." Hennessy's words came out slowly, as if he were calculating the effect of each one. Or controlling his temper. "We rely on their knowledge and their resources. That's all."

Adam kept his voice low, calm. "This wasn't an attempted murder."

Hennessy inhaled sharply, sat back in the leather chair and crossed his arms in front of his chest. Adam leaned forward, sensing the power shift in his favor, just a little. The shadow passed underneath the door again. Light footsteps moved away and up the stairs. In the back of the house, a door banged.

Hennessy's calculations were almost visible in his narrow eyes, his small frown. Finally he coughed. "Good. It will be helpful to have someone keeping the Kapoors happy. Keeping them out of the way, you understand."

Adam nodded his agreement.

"And understand this, Kaminski. I'm not sharing any details that DS doesn't already know. Some things I'm going to need to keep close hold. And I don't want you getting in the way, got it?"

"Understood." Adam kept his face neutral. "I'll help when I can, and I won't overstep my purview."

Hennessy leaned forward in his seat and pulled a manila file folder toward him, flipping it open. "Now tell me about the planned schedule for this trip to Philly. Who made the reservations? Who was your point of contact?"

Adam gave Hennessy all the information he had. About working with Jay to schedule the trip and the various meetings. About the role of Barton McFellan, the lobbying firm in which Jason McFellan was a partner, in covering the bills. About the museums, restaurants, and tours that had been on the planned itinerary.

Hennessy listened, jotting notes occasionally. He said nothing, though an occasional grunt here and there managed to convey his opinion of the value of the trip.

"That's everything," Adam wrapped up his story. "I don't see anything there to shed light on who was taking shots at them."

Hennessy sat for a moment, looking down at his notes, considering the details Adam had offered. "Well, you never know what will prove to be useful. Is it too much to hope you're heading back to Philly this afternoon?"

Adam shook his head. "If you need more about the Philly end, I can make some calls, reach out to friends. Maybe find out more about the people who work at these places, see if there's anyone with a record. Or a grudge."

"That would help."

"I can't look for a motive unless I know more about the intended target. Whoever that was. The senator. The ambassador." He thought for a moment. "Can you tell me who else was here at the time?"

Hennessy sniffed. "You think there was someone else who might have been the target?"

"You never know. Look, it was Jay who got shot, after all."

"True. But we have to work with the odds. Chances are, the ambassador was the target. It's his house. After that, the senator's the most likely intended victim. We can't waste our resources chasing after unlikely leads."

"I understand that."

Hennessy eyes narrowed, but he answered the question. "We had the senator, her husband, and Jay Kapoor, the ambassador and his aide." Hennessy counted people off on his fingers as he spoke. "Jason

McFellan, of Barton McFellan. The drivers — two cars. The servants who were in the house at the time." He stopped, as if he had run out of fingers. "That's everyone."

"They weren't all out on the drive when the shooting happened, were they?"

Hennessy didn't look down at the notes in front of him. "No. Outside we had only the senator, ambassador, two aides, and two drivers."

"So where were the others?"

"Servants were inside, we have statements from all of them. McFellan and Mr. Marshall were still in the morning room, about to walk out and join the others when the shooting happened." He looked down at his notes. "Looks like McFellan was the last out of the room. Standing alone when he heard the shot." He looked at Adam. "Or so he says."

"He clearly knew their schedule. He saw them walk out of the room. Any chance he could have run out and shot at them?"

Hennessy smiled. "If only it could be that easy, Kaminski. Not a chance. Look around you, this is a big place. To get around the side of the house, he'd've had to run down the back hall, out the side door, all the way around from the back yard — that would take over five minutes, just to get in place. Everyone agrees it was a matter of one, maybe two minutes tops from the time the senator and ambassador left the room to the time the shot was fired."

Adam nodded, thinking. "So someone was waiting for them outside. Or inside."

"What do you mean?"

"Are you considering that the shot might have come from inside the house?"

"We don't yet know where the shot was fired from. We're searching the grounds..." Hennessy paused, pursing his lips and frowning. "If we're looking for a place someone like McFellan could get to in a hurry, he's got a better chance of getting to another room in the house than getting outside."

"Would that work? Could someone fire a shot from inside the house?"

"In an old house like this, sure." Hennessy seemed to be warming to the idea. "The windows all open, but don't have fixed screens like more modern houses..." His words trailed off again, but he kept nodding, as if to himself.

Adam knew better than to interrupt. He waited until Hennessy had made the mental connections he needed to make. Finally, Hennessy looked up, a slight smile on his lips. "That would narrow down the list of suspects, wouldn't it?"

CHAPTER NINE

SAM FOLLOWED a young man in a dark blue suit through the rotating doors shutting out the bulk of the rush hour noise on the street outside. Some of the after-work crowd was gathering inside the coffee shop, too, and Sam needed a minute to scan the room to find the man he was meeting.

They were in a chain coffee shop in Foggy Bottom, the type of shop where, once inside, you could just as easily be in Washington state as Washington, DC. The store had the standard decor, standard service lines, even the same music. It was anonymous.

Sam wondered if that was why John Marshall had chosen it.

When he'd answered the call from the senator's husband, Sam's first reaction was to direct Mr. Marshall to the FBI. That's who he should have called in the first place, if he was really looking for an update on the investigation as he claimed.

A movement in the back of the room caught his eye, and he turned to see John Marshall taking a seat at a table near the large windows that fronted onto H Street. Even as he moved back through the room, his pulse quickened, and he remembered what he had missed about investigations.

He knew he should have insisted that Marshall call the FBI. The man's interest in meeting with Sam was questionable. But he was perfectly capable of interviewing a witness. Or a suspect. He had been a good cop once. He still was.

Marshall stood as Sam approached, smiling, patting him on the shoulder as Sam took the seat opposite. He would share any and all information he got from Marshall, Sam told himself. If he learned anything new, the FBI would be the first to know.

Sam smiled back at John Marshall.

"Did you want to grab a coffee?" Marshall asked, raising his own paper mug.

"I'm good," Sam answered, still smiling. "What can I do for you, Mr. Marshall?"

Marshall shrugged, looking down into his coffee. "I don't know. I'm sorry, I know I shouldn't have called you."

"It's okay, Mr. Marshall, but like I said on the phone, you really should have called the FBI if you're looking for updates."

"I know, I know." Marshall glanced around the coffee shop, his eye lingering briefly on a long-haired young man slouching over a laptop at a nearby table, then moved on. "I just... they don't want to talk, you know?"

Sam laughed. "This is a murder investigation, Mr. Marshall." He watched as Marshall's eyes flitted to the door of the coffee shop, following a passerby on the street outside. "I'm not going to share any details with you, either."

Marshall looked back at Sam, smiling. "I know, trust me. I'm not looking for any inside information here."

Marshall's smile was easy, engaging, and Sam found himself smiling in return.

"I wanted to talk with someone else who had been there. Who saw it." Marshall shrugged again, looking sheepish. "It's not an experience you can talk about with other people, you know? Someone who's never seen that kind of violence can't really understand. Lisa's handling it better than I am. She gets the support she needs from her constituents' condolences, from the support of her colleagues. Me? I don't know."

Sam knew all too well what Marshall meant, and he felt bad for the guy. Watching a young man get shot. Die. Marshall needed to talk about the experience.

"The investigation is still young, Mr. Marshall," Sam said. "We're still pulling together information from the scene. Don't worry. The FBI is on this. And they're putting extra manpower into keeping you and your wife safe. I really don't believe you're in any danger right now."

"Thank you." Marshall nodded. "That poor boy… he was so young." Marshall's eyes did another sweep of the coffee shop before landing on Sam. "He was a good kid, you know? Lisa was always happy with his work."

"That's good to know, Mr. Marshall," Sam said. "Is there anything else about Jay that you can think of, that you can share?"

Marshall cupped his hands around his coffee cup, which had to be cooling off by now. He frowned. "Not really. I wish I did. He was good at his job. That's what Lisa said. Good at his job." Marshall looked back up at Sam. "Not much of an epitaph, is it?"

Sam frowned. Marshall was right. They really didn't know enough about Jay, and needed to learn more. Good thing Kaminski was in town to help, since the FBI wasn't looking in that direction.

So what was Marshall's angle? He looked comfortable, relaxed. Sad, of course, but only as much as could be expected in the situation. His eyes never stood still for long. Constantly seeking out the corners of the cafe, glancing at other patrons, catching glimpses of pedestrians passing by.

"Tell me about yourself, Mr. Marshall. What does the husband of a senator do in his spare time?"

Marshall smiled, a wide, open smile that carried up to his bright blue eyes, and opened his hands over the table. "What doesn't the husband of a senator do?

Fundraising. Building relationships. Engaging constituents. Fundraising." Marshall raised an eyebrow. "I wasn't always the husband of a senator, you know."

"Oh?" Sam asked, knowing Marshall wanted him to.

"Time was, Lisa used to be the wife of a small business owner. Construction." Marshall ducked his head modestly. "Then she was the wife of a large business owner. And then she ran for Senate."

"You built up your own business?"

Marshall's face lit up with the memory. "From nothing. I had skills in construction, some experience. I knew people. I knew how to run a business. Only a few years in, I was getting the best business in town, government contracts, that sort of thing."

Marshall's eyes were on Sam, but Sam could tell his mind was far away. Remembering past successes. Past glories. "That's a competitive field, isn't it?" Sam asked. "I'm sure you pissed off a lot of people. Can you think of anyone from your background who may have waited until now to get back at you?"

Marshall laughed, a deep, comfortable sound. "I made millions. I made enough that I could bankroll my wife's Senate campaign." He raised his eyebrows as if surprised by his own accomplishments. "From a school nurse to member of city council in a podunk little town to a United States senator."

"Senator Marshall's background in nursing was always part of her campaigns. A trained medical professional with people's best interest at heart. It's a long way from nursing to U.S. senator, though."

Marshall's smile thinned. "Yes, I made a lot of people angry." He responded to Sam's previous question, ignoring the comments about his wife's background.

Sam waited, hoping for more. Waiting for Marshall to consider his past.

"No one who would do this," Marshall finally said. "Men who sued me, sure. Most lost. Some won." he gave Sam a meaningful look. "I wasn't a monster, Agent

Burke. I was raised to respect the system, follow the rules."

"Strong family values, that sort of thing?"

"Why not? Family's important to me, Agent Burke. I was my parents' only child. I relied on them, then they relied on me."

"I get that, Mr. Marshall. I know the value of family."

"Do you?" Marshall raised an eyebrow then looked away, across the coffee shop. "I did the right thing by my parents, despite… well, we all have some negative memories, too, don't we?" He shook his head as if shaking off the memories and took a sharp breath. "When it came to my business dealings, I followed the same rules. When I screwed up, I admitted to it. I was honest. Always."

"It's not easy being honest once you're involved in politics though, is it?"

Marshall shook his head. "No. Politics is not an honest business." He smiled again, the glint back in his eyes. "I'm still an honest person. We knew how things would look — my connections, my business. My money helped get Lisa her position, sure, but I wasn't going to be part of the game." He swallowed the last of his coffee and grimaced. "I sold it."

"Your business?" Sam asked, surprised.

"All of it. I wasn't so sure when Lisa suggested it, but I'll tell you, it was a good idea. I made a tidy profit and now we don't need to worry about how things look." Marshall dropped his cup on the table. "I don't want anyone accusing me of bias. Of corruption."

Sam ducked as another patron bumped into his chair from behind. He glanced around, but the young man was already moving on to an empty table against the wall. No apologies. He was used to rudeness. It didn't bug him anymore.

"Do you miss it?" Sam asked Marshall.

Marshall shrugged and frowned. "Sure. Of course." He gestured toward Sam with his chin. "You live in DC, you know how things are here. There's only one way to get things done in this town. My wife is doing good. Finally. Changing the world for the better. Influencing people, that's what she's good at." He shook his head. "I wouldn't give that up for anything."

"Hmm." Sam considered Marshall's words, frowning. He was right about the District. Only certain people, in certain positions, were effective. Sam also knew that the most powerful people weren't necessarily those in public office.

A light rhythm cut through the air, and Marshall tapped his hand over his jacket pocket.

"You need to answer that?" Sam asked.

Marshall smiled and shook his head. "That's Lisa. Wondering where I am, I'm sure."

They both sat silent until the rhythm stopped.

"You had a different job before you joined the State Department, too, didn't you, Agent Burke?"

Marshall's expression was innocent, but Sam's eyes narrowed. "Where'd you hear that, Mr. Marshall?"

"I'm the husband of the Chair of the Senate Foreign Relations Committee." Marshall smiled. "I hear a lot of things."

Sam nodded, considering. If Marshall knew that much about him, then he knew that Sam still had connections within the PD. Is that why he wanted to meet?

"I may have been off the streets for a few years now, Mr. Marshall, but I'm still a cop. I'm good at my job." He paused, then added, "And I know how to keep information close."

"Of course you do. Sorry, I didn't mean to imply otherwise." Marshall stood. "I think I need to move on. It's been a pleasure speaking with you, Agent Burke. Thanks for meeting me, I really appreciate it."

"No problem." Sam shook his hand, still frowning. "Any time you need to talk, you call me."

Marshall pulled his phone out of his pocket as he walked away, and Sam saw his smile fade as he looked at it. A much darker expression crossed his features as he stepped out onto the sidewalk.

ADAM SHOOK Hennessy's hand as they stepped into the residence hallway. "Thanks for talking with me, Agent Hennessy."

Hennessy's grip tightened. "Remember what we talked about, Kaminski. I have my job. You have yours."

He was about to answer, but turned his head at the sound of a gentle tread on the stairs. He was surprised to see Ambassador Saint-Amand heading towards them. The sound had led him to expect a woman.

"Agent Hennessy," Saint-Amand's silver voice called to the agent about to head out of the house. "A moment, if you please."

"Yes, sir?" Hennessy stopped where he stood, a picture of a man in motion interrupted.

"You promised me an update. Do you have that for me yet?"

"Ah... yes, of course. We can go back into the office."

"No, no..." The Ambassador frowned into the crowded office. "That won't be necessary. Please join me in the drawing room." He gestured vaguely down the long hall. "And perhaps your friend?" Saint-Amand turned an inquisitive eye on Adam, and Adam had the impression his self-worth had just been assessed. Accurately.

"Right. Det—" Hennessy corrected himself quickly, "I mean, Ambassador Saint-Amand, may I present Detective Adam Kaminski, from Philadelphia. Detective Kaminski, this is Ambassador Saint-Amand, French Ambassador to the United States."

"Ambassador," Adam said as he shook the other man's hand. "It's a pleasure to meet you."

"And you, too, Detective, of course." The Ambassador had a way of speaking that made every word sound sincere. "What brings you to DC?"

"I'm here on behalf of the Kapoors, Ambassador. The parents of the dead man," he added to clarify, but the ambassador was nodding even before Adam spoke.

"Of course, of course. Yes. I am aware of them. I understood they would be in town." He drew a gray silk handkerchief from his breast pocket and held it loosely between his fingers, giving it only the slightest of rubs. "How distressing. How terrible for them."

Adam thought he saw a glimmer of moisture in the other man's eyes. "Did you know them, sir?"

"What?" The Ambassador started as if broken out of his train of thought. "No, no. I have a child. I can imagine what they must be feeling."

Adam nodded silently. Hennessy checked his watch.

"I am very pleased that you are here, Detective," Saint-Amand continued. "It is good to know that all available resources are being used on this investigation." His eyes slid sideways toward Hennessy. "I'm sure the Federal Bureau of Investigation needs all the help it can get."

"We are on top of this, Ambassador," Hennessy responded, his words clipped. "Shall we?" He gestured toward the back of the house.

Saint-Amand didn't move. "Detective, a dear friend of mine is hosting a reception tonight. Perhaps you would like to attend?"

"Ambassador!" Hennessy's voice carried an edge Adam hadn't yet heard, but Saint-Amand simply smiled at Adam.

"I appreciate the invitation, sir, but I don't think that would be appropriate. I'm only here to help with this investigation." Adam watched Saint-Amand as he answered. Was he really trying to help, or intentionally riling Hennessy?

The ambassador's expression was inscrutable. "I believe you might find this gathering interesting, Detective. Of course I had not planned to attend, since I was to be in Philadelphia. Now I am in town, I am obliged to attend, it would be rude not to. And I have been asked to invite anyone I choose."

Saint-Amand couldn't have missed the red splotches growing on Hennessy's cheeks, but he kept his smile cool, focused on Adam. It must be unintentional, Adam told himself. Saint-Amand couldn't know that Hennessy wanted Adam back in Philly. Unless he'd overheard… perhaps there was a reason he'd suggested the FBI use his aide's office.

"Detective Kaminski can't make it tonight, Ambassador, he has other obligations." Hennessy spoke. "Shall we go, sir?"

Saint-Amand let his eyes run over Hennessy the same way he might assess a basket of turnips in the market, but he nevertheless turned toward the back of the house and Hennessy followed. Adam had just put a hand out to open the front door when Saint-Amand called to him.

"Detective."

Adam turned, the oak door held open, Ramona still standing outside.

"I will give your name to the host for this evening, in case you change your mind."

Adam tried not to look at Hennessy. He could think of no better way to figure out what Saint-Amand's game was. He caught Hennessy's glare and knew he might regret this. "Thank you, Ambassador, I'll think about it."

Saint-Amand's eyes fell on Ramona, who stood in the shadow of the front porch. "And please, do bring a date."

CHAPTER TEN

ADAM MOVED his hand up to straighten his tie one more time. Ramona grinned, and he slid his hand back to his pocket.

She leaned toward him, her words carrying on the soft melody coming from the string quartet in the corner. "If you're so uncomfortable all dressed up, why did you come tonight? And why did you bring me?"

Adam glanced over at her, her four-inch heels bringing her eyes level with his. "You're not complaining, are you? The way you clean up, I'd say you were a regular at posh events like this one."

Ramona smiled. "Stop teasing. I had all of thirty minutes to get dressed. A little more advance notice would be nice next time."

"You look gorgeous, and you know it." Adam dragged his eyes away. "This is all about work. I don't know why Saint-Amand invited us, maybe just to piss off Hennessy. Maybe because he wants to show us something. Or someone."

He glanced around the room, groups of two or three people each clustered around the bookshelves to his left stacked with gilt-bound volumes, around the plush armchairs facing the marble mantle, near the mahogany end tables spread with lace and silver candlesticks. Through the French doors he could see more guests gathered on the brick patios and walkways, wandering through the dimly lit garden paths. Adam couldn't help but wonder what books he might find on the shelves here, but brought his mind back to the investigation.

"You're right." He nodded without looking at Ramona. "I do hate events like this."

"I don't know." She shrugged. "I could get used to this." She selected a prosciutto-wrapped shrimp from a passing waiter. "Not bad…"

"It's not real." Adam shook his head. "Not the place, not the people… everyone's putting on a show, trying to cover up who they really are with a false front. An act."

Ramona turned slowly to look around the room, then brought her eyes back to Adam. "Then who are you pretending to be?"

"Tonight, I'm pretending not to be a cop. It's an act, like everybody else."

"I know, you're here to work."

"Places like this, even with everyone playacting — no, especially with everyone playacting — this is the best place to learn the truth about people, better than any interview room. This is where the truth slips out. The truth about their characters, their self-perception. By learning who someone wants you to believe they are, you learn a lot about who they really are."

Ramona stared at him for a moment before speaking. "That's pretty deep, sensei."

Adam shook his head and rolled his eyes. "Go. Mingle. Learn something. We'll compare notes later."

"Aye aye, sir." Ramona smiled and winked as she moved away from Adam toward the bookshelves. Adam watched her back for a second, smooth caramel skin exposed beneath black lace, before turning his attention back to the bookshelves on the far side of the room.

Senator Marshall and her husband stood there, apparently engrossed in conversation with a short balding man in an impeccable gray suit. The senator said something — Adam couldn't hear what — and the man smiled and nodded eagerly. His eyes focused on her face.

The senator seemed about to speak again when her husband put his hand on her back and leaned in to whisper something to her. She stepped back as he leaned in, but inclined her head to hear his words.

She put out a hand to shake that of the balding man and together the two Marshalls moved on. Adam leaned up against the doorway, drink in one hand, hors d'oeuvres from passing waiters in the other, watching them move.

They moved as a couple, from one group of people to the next. A few words here, a laugh and a smile there, then on to the next small audience. The conversation must have turned to the morning's shooting on several occasions. Each time, Adam could see a look of concern, of regret, on the speaker's face. Followed by a look of acceptance on the part of Senator Marshall. She clearly appreciated the support. He couldn't have handled such public grieving. If he lost someone he worked with — if Pete were shot, God forbid — Adam would curl up in a dark room and work through it on his own. Not in public. Not like this.

After each of the couple's interactions, Mr. Marshall would take the lead, letting his wife know when it was time to move on, occasionally introducing her to the people they approached. Dictating their schedule.

When they approached Ambassador Saint-Amand, their mood became more serious, no doubt once again discussing the tragic events of the morning. He moved in toward the ambassador as the Marshalls were pulling away.

"Ah, Detective Kaminski, is it not?" Saint-Amand smiled graciously and shook Adam's hand. "I am so pleased you were able to make it this evening. May I introduce Mademoiselle Cormier." The Ambassador indicated the tall woman next to him, elegant in a dark gray evening gown that hugged her gentle curves on its way down to hover above the floor. Her eyes matched her gown and seemed to be laughing as she put her hand in his.

He inclined his head, pausing for what he knew was a little too long to appreciate her beauty, then turned back to the ambassador. "Thank you for the invitation, sir. It's a wonderful way to spend my first evening in DC."

"Detective, have you met our host yet?" Saint-Amand asked even as he waved over the balding man Adam had noticed earlier. "Mr. Andrew Kendall, may I present Detective Adam Kaminski, from Philadelphia."

Adam shook hands with his host. "I hope I'm not intruding on your hospitality, sir. I was with the ambassador earlier today and he suggested I join this gathering."

"Of course, of course," Kendall spluttered. "Any friend of Alain is a friend of mine." Saint-Amand flinched as Kendall pumped him on the back.

"Detective Kaminski is in town to investigate the shooting this morning, I'm sure you heard about it."

"Oh, yes, I was chatting with Lisa and John Marshall about it." Kendall bobbed his head up and down. "What a shock. You must have been terrified."

"I'm off the clock tonight." Adam raised his glass as if in a toast. "For now, I'm here to meet some interesting people and learn a little bit about this town."

"Of course you are, Detective." Saint-Amand smiled and raised an eyebrow. "I'm sorry, you will excuse us. Madame Cormier and I must talk with Mr. Kendall for a moment." Saint-Amand's voice dropped and he leaned his head toward Adam. "For me, tonight is about business. You may have heard of the riots around the suburbs of Paris recently?"

Adam nodded. He'd seen something in the paper, hadn't he?

Saint-Amand continued, "We are struggling, my country, with our past. To have been a colonial power means that many different peoples now consider France their homeland. Many French are not willing to accept this."

"That's not a problem unique to your country, Ambassador."

"No, perhaps not. Mr. Kendall is in a unique position to offer his assistance. Please, excuse us."

As Saint-Amand led Cormier and Kendall toward the French doors, a third man lurched toward them, almost knocking the drink out of Kendall's hand.

"Ah, sorry, sorry," the man mumbled, pushing his glasses up on his nose. His hair shook as he moved, loose curls and waves cluttering his forehead. "Oh, Mr. Ambassador, sir," he continued, his voice high and tight, "I was hoping to speak with you. About Senator Marshall."

"Mr. Towne." Saint-Amand's voice was low. "I am not free at the moment, I am sorry. Have you met Detective Kaminski yet?" Saint-Amand gestured toward Adam.

Towne turned to wave a hand vaguely in Adam's direction, but when he turned back to Saint-Amand, he saw only his back retreating through the French doors.

"Ah, well." Towne turned back to Adam.

"Adam Kaminski." Adam put his hand out and the other man took it in a limp handshake.

"Yes, hello. Greg Towne."

"And are you a friend of the ambassador? Or our host, Mr. Kendall?"

"Kendall?" Towne looked around the room, surprised. "No, no, I haven't met him yet."

"You were invited to his party?"

"Ah, no, not exactly. I mean, yes, yes, I was invited." He giggled nervously. "I'm not a gate-crasher or anything."

"No." Adam said nothing more, waiting for Towne to continue.

"Right. I'm a historian, you see. Art historian. Well, architectural sometimes. I specialize in structural art, you see — the built environment." Towne pulled down on his jacket with his free hand. The movement shifted the line of the jacket, transforming a well-made, well-fitted suit into something that looked as awkward as Towne did.

Adam nodded noncommittally. He had no idea what Towne was talking about. "So what brings you here this evening, Mr. Towne?"

"Ah, I'm on the HPRB, you see. We were all invited. By the senator. Senator Marshall, that is."

Adam glanced around the room to see where Ramona had wandered off to. He spotted her perched on a gold-upholstered chaise-lounge, smiling engagingly at the man across from her. A cough from Towne brought him back to his present conversation.

"Please, go on," he said, having no idea what Towne had been talking about.

"The HPRB — the Historic Preservation Review Board, you know?" When Adam didn't respond, Towne continued, "Very prestigious, very important. Senator Marshall chairs our committee, you see. So we work with her personally on a number of matters."

Adam looked at Towne again, this time with a frown. "You told the ambassador you wanted to speak with him about the senator. Why was that?"

"That?" Towne coughed, putting his glass down on the glowing wooden surface of a nearby table, oblivious to the condensation dripping onto the polished surface. He extracted a handkerchief from his trouser pocket, holding it in front of his face as he collected himself. "That, oh, that was nothing," he concluded finally. "Nothing, really." He shoved the handkerchief back into his pocket.

"I see." Adam continued to watch Towne closely. The man seemed to wither under Adam's gaze. Adam felt a twinge of pity for him. He looked like a fish out of water, a man who could have been confident in a different place, at a different time. Perhaps in jeans and an old sweater tucked into a good book. Adam could relate.

"No, in fact I came here this evening specifically to talk with the senator, you see. She simply hasn't had a chance yet." Towne shrugged, trying to look casual. "She has a lot of people here she needs to see, you understand."

"Of course," Adam agreed, noticing that Ramona had now moved over to talk with a tall blond man.

"It's about work, though, it wouldn't interest you." Towne waved his hands in front of Adam, and Adam couldn't help but think of a little wizard, trying desperately to make himself disappear. It didn't work. Towne still stood there.

"And does the senator want to talk with you?" Adam asked casually.

"Of course she does." Towne's voice rose even higher with anger. "Of course, she invited me tonight, didn't she?"

"She invited your board, you said," Adam reminded him.

"Yes, yes, whatever. Look, Detective, uh… I'm sorry, I don't recall your name."

"Kaminski."

"Yes, Detective Kaminski, I'm not sure why you're asking me all these questions. Why are you here tonight?" If Towne had meant the question to sound aggressive, he failed.

"I was invited by the ambassador," Adam responded. "I believe he thought I could learn a few things at this gathering."

Towne caught himself in another fit of coughing, picking up his drink again to calm himself. It left a ring on the wooden surface.

Towne finally got his breath back. "I'm sure that's true, Detective. There are many accomplished people here. Is there anything in particular you are interested in?"

Adam thought about it for a moment, then answered with the truth. "Murder."

"I see." Towne's frown deepened. "Well, that's nothing I can help you with, of course."

Adam smiled. "Thanks for clearing that up."

Towne frowned again, then turned abruptly and moved away, bouncing off the table as he turned. He flinched, but kept moving, heading toward a short, stocky woman standing alone in the corner. A safe target, perhaps.

Adam turned to scan the rest of the room. There was someone here Saint-Amand thought he should meet. Who was it?

THE MAN IN THE SILK suit shut his eyes for a minute. Just for a second. The love of his life, standing next to him, nudged him and he opened his eyes. She was smiling, talking to a man who stood in front of them. He'd already forgotten the man's name. He produced a charming smile anyway.

The room glittered around him. The sparkle of diamonds around a woman's neck. The gleam of gold watches, rings, cuff links. Light catching in champagne flutes and crystal chandeliers. Even the air seemed to glisten, the scent tantalizing, perfumed but undefinable.

God, this was exhausting. Smiling. Shaking hands. Smiling more. Pretending he cared. Thankfully, it was almost over — the party, the day, everything.

He wanted this day over and behind him. Far behind him. Then he could relax.

He risked glancing around the room at the other guests. A few caught his eye and smiled at him, raised their glasses in mock toasts. Were they mocking him? Did they know?

He frowned and turned back to the large woman in front of him. Her massive figure was stuffed into a deep green gown at least two sizes too small for her. She looked liked the slugs he used to fight with his grandfather in their ongoing efforts to protect their small garden of Savoy and romaine.

He pictured throwing salt on her and grinned. Then caught himself when he realized she was saying something about foreign debt. He wasn't sure how much he missed. He nodded and tried to look concerned. Aggrieved, maybe. Determined to fix the problem, certainly.

He felt another nudge as he was nodding, frowning. He didn't turn around, just reached his arm to the side, placed his hand against his partner's back.

His true love smiled up at him, then turned her attention to the large woman in front of them who was still talking about foreign debt. He didn't care anymore how boring it was. *She* was up to something. He could see it in her smile. Feel it in the minute vibrations that carried through her thin cocktail dress.

He felt the familiar thrill. Excitement. Fear. Love. Surely this was love.

Whenever he was with her, his world turned upside down. He didn't understand, didn't trust his own thoughts. He didn't know what to expect. Trying to control things only made her mad. Made things worse. All he could do was blindly follow.

Sometimes she hurt him. Once, he had been devastated. Usually she was kind. Tender. Caring. She took care of him. She always would. Wouldn't she?

He glanced around again, this time with confidence. The detective from Philadelphia was still here. Talking with the chief of staff for Congressman Waldmann. What a bore. That man could talk the bark off a tree.

He couldn't believe the policeman had come tonight. Had had the gall to show up. Maybe he was looking for a way up, like everybody else here. Rubbing shoulders. Sharing compliments and secrets like they were worth something. But they weren't.

He knew better. He knew the truth.

He smiled to himself. The cop wasn't going to get

anywhere. He couldn't believe he had been nervous about him. He was going to muddle around for a few days, find nothing, then hightail it back to Philadelphia.

Let's play another round, he thought. He smiled at the large woman and excused them, then turned in the direction of the detective. His love followed his lead, as she always did.

The detective saw them coming. Turned towards them. Smiled. He smiled in return. Shook his hand. A strong handshake. They exchanged pleasantries, words that meant nothing. He kept up his act. Concerned. Determined to fix things. Sometimes aggrieved.

He was getting good at aggrieved, surprising how easy that one was.

They shook hands again. Parted ways. He guided her toward another guest. As if they were floating. High above everyone else there.

As long as he was with her, he could fly.

ADAM FELT HER presence behind him before he felt her touch on his arm. He turned to face Ramona.

"Did you get what you came for?" she asked, her eyes following another group of guests heading toward the door.

Kendall stood near the door, shaking hands, sharing kisses in the air, patting shoulders. Very congenial.

"I don't know," Adam admitted. "I'm not really sure what I was looking for."

She moved back toward the French doors, and Adam followed the trail of vanilla scent that hung in the air behind her.

"Mr. Marshall, he's a character," Ramona started.

Adam nodded. "It's almost as if he were directing the senator tonight."

"Where to stand. Who to talk to. What to say. When to smile." She pursed her lips. "He's someone to watch."

"And then there's Ambassador Saint-Amand

himself." Adam frowned as he saw the ambassador making his exit with Madame Cormier, clasping his host's hand enthusiastically.

"Why was he so eager to have you here this evening, Kaminski? What did he want you to see?"

"I still haven't figured that out," Adam responded slowly. "The FBI think he was the target, you know. Of the murder."

"Attempted murder, as they like to call it." Ramona shook her head. "Do you think the ambassador was the target?"

"Could be." Adam shrugged. "He mentioned to me that he was here to talk to Kendall about some problems in France right now. Problems with immigrants, I take it."

Ramona nodded. "Sure, I've heard about what they're going through."

Adam nodded too, wondering why he hadn't seen anything in the papers about it. Maybe he was reading the wrong sections. "What do you know?"

"Just that there have been some riots. Youth getting angry over what they see as disparate treatment. Even people who become French citizens are treated differently. Unfairly, some would say."

"That's tough," Adam murmured.

"And it could be related, you know," Ramona added. "Part of the problem seems to stem from the narcotics trade."

"Drugs." Adam wasn't surprised. In his world, the drug culture was always only a step away.

Ramona nodded. "Cocaine, lots of it. Makes its way through Africa to France, then on to the rest of Europe."

"So the racism against the immigrants is presented as a drug war. An attempt to stop the trade, not the people."

"You got it," Ramona said. "All above board. But not doing well so far, from what I've heard."

"Maybe the French drug war made it to the States," Adam thought out loud. "FBI's searching for a lead domestically, when this could be a crime with an international motive."

Ramona smiled grimly. "A drug killing, pure and simple. We know about those, don't we?"

Adam didn't respond to her question, instead asking who else she had talked to that night.

"Jason McFellan was here," she answered. "He was at the shooting too, remember?"

"Sure." Adam nodded. "Not too surprising he'd be here, I guess. It's his sort of event."

She smiled. "He probably bankrolled it. Same as he was going to pay for the senator's trip to Philly. Always willing to help out — and always willing to remind someone when they owe him something in return."

The room was gradually emptying out as the guests headed for their next engagements, dinner parties, business meetings. Only a handful remained. Those who were most comfortable here. Or those with nowhere else to go.

Towne stood by a bookcase, looking decidedly nervous. He glanced around the room as if still waiting for someone to arrive. His glass was empty, but he held onto it, clutching his hands around it.

"Do you know him?" Ramona asked, seeing where Adam was looking.

"We spoke. A couple of times."

"And? Anything interesting there?"

"Definitely interesting." Adam smiled at her. "Though probably not related to this case. He's a weird one though."

"Who is he?"

"An art historian. Or architect — I'm not sure which. He's on some sort of architectural board chaired by Senator Marshall," Adam explained.

"The HPRB?" she asked. "That's pretty prestigious. A highly connected group of people." She looked back at

Towne, a new expression on her face.

"You don't say…" Adam considered this information. "Then why does he look so uncomfortable here?"

She shrugged and frowned. "I don't know. I'm sure he goes to a lot of these things. Kind of part of his job."

She watched as Towne tried to put his glass down. He hit the edge of the table and the glass started to go over. Towne caught it just in time, crying out as he did so. A few other people turned to look at him, then looked away. He stepped even closer in to the bookcase.

Adam shook his head. "I guess he's one of that type."

"What type is that?"

"The type that doesn't fit in anywhere."

"Maybe." Ramona frowned. "To me, he's acting like a man with a secret. A man with something to hide. Look at him." She gestured with her hand. "He's nervous."

"Huh." Adam inclined his head as his eyebrows went up. "You're absolutely right. I shouldn't dismiss him so easily. In fact, Ambassador Saint-Amand is the one who introduced me to him."

Both cops watched Towne for a minute longer, then Ramona turned to Adam. "So, what's next this evening? Can I tempt you to join me for a late dinner?"

CHAPTER ELEVEN

TRAFFIC WAS LIGHT, for DC, and Adam enjoyed the short ride through the clear night. Lights from the city dimmed any stars he might have seen, but Georgetown provided its own starlight, gas lamps and street lights beckoning along the brick-lined streets.

Adam knew better than to accept Ramona's offer. She looked far too good in that cocktail dress. He had to keep his mind focused on the job at hand.

As the taxi turned onto the Key Bridge, Adam could see Foggy Bottom to his left along the river. The Kennedy Center glowed along the riverbank, lit up for the evening's performances. Farther south, beyond the Tidal Basin and the monuments, the river darkened as it ran up against the Anacostia Freeway and bordered the southeastern part of the city.

He ran through the evening's conversations again in his head. Ambassador Saint-Amand. The Marshalls. Greg Towne. Jason McFellan. There must be something there, something that tied one of them to Jay Kapoor.

Or maybe he was looking for a connection, hoping for a connection. Maybe the FBI was right, and this shooting didn't have anything to do with Jay at all.

He let his thoughts wander as they headed toward the square dark buildings of Arlington, where his cheap — by DC standards — hotel was located.

After the glitz and warmth of Georgetown, Arlington

seemed bare. Only one street he passed was lined with restaurants and coffee shops, heavy with pedestrians. His hotel room as he entered it stared back at him, equally bare and unappealing. He was here to work, not to enjoy himself.

He kicked off his shoes, loosened his tie, and picked up his cell phone. He tapped the screen once and the phone dialed the familiar number. It rang. And rang. No answer.

Adam hit redial.

After six or seven rings, he heard Sylvia's voice. Not talking to him, talking to someone else. "Just a sec, sorry. I think I have to take this."

"Sylvia?" Adam spoke into the phone, "you there?"

"I'm here, darling, sorry about that." Her voice became muffled once again. "One sec, I'll be right back."

Adam heard the sound of footsteps. A door closing.

"I can't talk long, Adam, I'm working."

"A cocktail party with donors?" Adam asked, thinking of Sylvia's job in development for a local university.

"That's right. Some good potential here. It's important."

After coming to the U.S. from Poland, Sylvia had tried to complete the master's degree she had started in Warsaw. During her first semester, she had befriended a number of people in the Office for International Students and become active in their programs.

It didn't take long for her to realize that the diplomatic skills she'd honed while working in Warsaw worked just as well in development situations. After a few cocktail parties with potential donors — where Sylvia and other international students were trotted out to showcase the school's international appeal — it became clear that this was the field for her. The school hired her the following semester, and she was now working full-time for them.

Adam recognized the sounds carrying over the phone

from Philadelphia to DC. The same voices, the same laughs. It could have been the same party he'd left. Different players, but the game was the same.

"I wanted to call and say I love you. It looks like I'll be down here for a few more days."

"Oh, dear, is it not going well?" Sylvia asked, and Adam was relieved to hear the concern in her voice.

"Too soon to tell," he answered. "Nothing wrong yet, just seems like it might take some time."

"Good, good." Adam heard a door opening, a man's voice in the background. "Look, Adam." Sylvia spoke again. "I do need to get back to this. As long as things are going well, the deputy commissioner will be happy."

Adam should have known that would be her concern. Not the fact that they would be apart for a few more days. Her field meant she spent a lot of time mingling with folks who made a lot more money than Adam did, from graduates of the university who had succeeded in their chosen field to heads of foundations and research institutes who might be interested in supporting the university's programs. Introducing her boyfriend, the cop, didn't help her efforts, and she had long since stopped inviting Adam to join her at the various events she was required to attend. Maybe if he were a captain — or commissioner even — it would be different.

"Sure," Adam conceded. "He'll be happy. As long as I give the Kapoors what they're looking for."

"And what's that?"

"Justice for their son." Adam lay down on the bed as he spoke, yawning. The bedcover was worn and rough, a dull brown made duller through washings too numerous to count.

Sylvia laughed. Not at him, he realized. At whoever else was with her.

"Sylvia? You still there?"

"I really have to go now, Adam. This is a good party."

He sat up again on the bed, that familiar sensation tickling at his mind. "This will be good for my career, honey. You can trust me on this." His right eye twitched as he said the words, but he ignored it.

"Good. That will help you, Adam. It will help us."

Adam nodded at the words, even though she couldn't see him. "I'm glad you're having fun."

"You know I love my work, darling. It is work, though, believe me."

"I know, I'm sorry. I didn't mean to suggest…"

Sylvia cut him off. "Call me tomorrow? I love you."

The line went dead.

CHAPTER TWELVE

"I DON'T APPRECIATE the implications of your question, Detective Kaminski," Towne spluttered. Drops of creamy coffee fell onto his Brioni tie, and he dabbed daintily at them with a paper napkin before turning back to Adam.

"I didn't mean to offend you, Mr. Towne," Adam said. A few phone calls had led Adam to this food court in the Old Post Office Pavilion, where Towne was known to take his morning coffee.

"Dr. Towne." Towne's voice was sharp. "I ignored your slights to my title last night because we were in a social setting, but if you're here to question me…"

"Of course, sorry, Dr. Towne." Adam nodded his head once in acquiescence. "I was wondering what brought you to the Kendall's cocktail party last night."

"I don't see how that's any of your business. What are you investigating? A stolen champagne goblet?" Towne sniggered, then played nervously with the cuff of his shirt, adjusting it to an even half an inch below the sleeve of his tailored jacket. His fidgeting revealed a slight fray in one cuff, but he seemed not to have noticed it.

"Murder, Dr. Towne. The murder of Jay Kapoor."

Towne frowned and looked down, chastised, his fingers tapping against his coffee cup. "Yes, of course. I heard about that."

"Through your connection with the senator?"

"No, I was.... that is, I mean I read about it. Online, Detective, like everybody else. It's on the news, on the blogs. You know, politics.com, Senate Central, Political Dish…"

Adam blinked and shook his head. "I think you follow different news outlets than I do, Dr. Towne."

"Hmm. No doubt." Towne pursed his lips and narrowed his eyes as he answered.

"Did you know about their planned trip to Philly?"

Towne shook his head roughly but didn't speak. Was he as nervous, as uncomfortable in his own skin as Adam thought? Or was Ramona right, his attitude the result of keeping a deeper secret?

"Where were you yesterday morning, Dr. Towne?"

"Oh, that's rich. Very rich." One side of Towne's lips drew up. "I was at a staff meeting, Detective. You can ask any one of my colleagues."

"So then, tell me. Why were you at the party last night? Really."

Towne frowned into his coffee before looking back at Adam. "Look around you, Detective."

Adam looked up.

Arched beams high above them bound hundreds of panes of weathered glass, forming an elegantly angled roof high above the public arcade. Cheap restaurants and tourist shops lined the ground level, with tables set out in the middle under the glass. Each level up from where they sat held office space, each level another step up toward the exposed sky. The grandeur of the nineteenth century architecture showcased carved columns and tiled frescoes. Arched windows on the higher levels opened up to the indoor courtyard below.

He imagined this was what it would feel like to be on a Parisian boulevard, as if the table where they sat stood not in the middle of an enclosed courtyard, but instead along a bustling street, the smells of coffee, gyros, and pizza mingling with the sounds of children's calls and office workers' hushed conversations.

"It's a beautiful space," Adam acknowledged. "I understand you come here a lot. I'm surprised, seems a little touristy, having to wait in line to get in, going through security."

"Me?" Towne laughed mirthlessly. "I don't 'go through security,' Detective." Towne's voice mimicked Adam's. "Not with my HPRB identification. Hah, security." He shook his head as he took a sip of coffee. "I won't be coming here for much longer. It's been sold, you see. To convert to a hotel." Towne's mouth turned down as he almost spat out the last word.

"I take it you're not in support of the change in use?"

Towne simply raised an eyebrow in response, his disdain for the proposed project clear on his face.

"Sounds to me like you're in a position to stop something like this, with your place on the HPRB," Adam said. "Why didn't you?"

Towne inhaled deeply before responding. "I tried. It's not only this space, Detective Kaminski, though it is impressive in its own right." He nodded slowly, then took another sip of his coffee.

Turning his face skyward once again, Adam looked up toward the Old Post Office Tower, which soared more than three hundred feet above where they sat. He had been up the tower in the past, stopping at the observation deck to take in the grand view of the city around it.

"Tell me about it," he prompted Towne.

At first Towne was confused, not understanding Adam's question. Then his eyes lit up as he realized it was an opportunity to boast about the historic building. "Nancy Hanks was a great woman," he said.

Adam frowned at the change in topic. "Who's Nancy Hanks?"

Towne's eyes widened and he pulled his head back as if to create space between himself and the offending question. "She saved this building," he explained. "I thought you would have known that. She was the person responsible for recognizing the architectural and historical significance of this building and ensuring its preservation. Saving it for the next generation. For people like my daughter, you see, and other young people who don't yet realize how important it is. And she was successful. Until now, that is."

"And you're trying to get Senator Marshall to change her mind, to renege on the sale of the building?"

Towne nodded, frowning. "Are you familiar with the Bells?"

Adam shook his head.

"The Bells of Congress," Towne explained, unable to hide his enthusiasm. "They're on display. If you go up, you can see them. Replicas, you see, of the bells at Westminster Abbey, in London. They were a gift for our nation's bicentennial."

"Doesn't the sale include some provisions for preserving the historical elements of the building?"

"Yeah, sure," Towne dismissed the idea. "As if historical preservation will ever trump the almighty dollar." He jiggled his coffee cup, his coffee long since cooled. "No one cares about DC because no one really lives here. They just pass through. They don't care about the city, about its resources."

Adam frowned. "The District has a large local population, Dr. Towne."

"Well, no one important, anyway." Towne waved the topic away with his coffee cup, and Adam heard the liquid sloshing about. "It's a national park, you know. The tower. And the bells. Does anyone care about that?"

"It seems like you care," Adam said slowly.

"Of course I do. I made it my mission to protect this building. To prevent the committee from approving the sale. I worked tirelessly, using every connection, every angle I could think of." He shrugged. "I failed."

"Did you blame Senator Marshall for approving the sale?"

Towne shook his head impatiently. "You don't understand. This isn't over. I will find a way to talk to her, to get her attention. It's not too late. The building still stands. The tower still stands. I need her to see reason. Her and the others on the committee."

"Why is this so important to you, Dr. Towne?" Adam asked with honest curiosity.

Towne looked at him thoughtfully. "Don't you have something in your life that's important to you, Detective? Something worth fighting for? Something that inspires you to do what you do?"

Adam thought of Sylvia, urging him to move forward with his career. He thought of Julia, struggling to make it as a photographer in Philadelphia, relying on his help. And he thought of the funeral. A funeral for three children cut down cruelly by a drive-by shooting. Children he was supposed to protect as their teacher, but couldn't.

"There are things that are important to me, Dr. Towne, things that motivate me. But I know where to draw the line. Is this project important enough for you to kill to keep it?"

Towne considered the question, then shrugged. "I don't know, Detective, I really don't. Thank God I've never had to find out. It is important." His eyes roved the seating area around them, then turned up toward the glass ceiling. "I'm not going to let this go, just walk away."

"It's already sold, Dr. Towne. It seems to me the opportunity to stop it has already passed."

"Bah," Towne said dismissively. "This is Washington, Detective Kaminski. Nothing is ever done. There is nothing that can't be changed, rewritten, amended, or simply undone."

"Except murder, Dr. Towne."

Towne's eyes narrowed, his lips pulled into a straight, taut line. "Yes, of course, Detective. Except murder."

SAM TAPPED on the open door as he stuck his head into the room. Ramona waved him in without looking up from the computer monitor. "Come on in, Sam, grab a seat."

He dragged a chair over, sitting across the desk from her.

"You just missed Detective Kaminski," she said. "He's on his way to track down Dr. Towne."

"Makes sense. He seems like a man with something to hide. And a problem with Senator Marshall."

He leaned forward to flip through a pile of papers lying on Ramona's desk next to her computer. "Is this what you found on Marshall?"

"So far," she answered, her eyes still on the screen. "Let me print this one up, too, and I'll show you what I have."

She clicked her mouse, and a printer across the room whirred to life.

The work space Ramona shared with her fellow officers was empty except for the two of them. Three other desks filled the room, piled with files, photographs, pens, and papers. From the open door, sounds of the busy precinct carried in, along with the scents common to all squad rooms — stale coffee, sweat, worn leather, and a faint hint of smoke embedded in someone's clothing. Sam smiled. He felt right at home.

Ramona brought the printed sheets back to her desk, then moved her chair closer to Sam's so they could look through the files together. "Remembering your glory days?"

Sam laughed. "Yeah, sorry, the squad room does bring back memories."

She glanced over at him, then looked away, smiling. "You've moved on, Sam. You succeeded. I'm jealous. Why're you wasting time thinking about the past?"

"Ah, the ambition of youth. I remember it well. Let's focus on what you found, shall we?"

"Everything I've found so far backs up what he told you yesterday," she said. "Construction. Built up his company, then sold it. Been working since then in support of his wife's position."

"So why did something seem off with him yesterday?" Sam wondered aloud. "Don't know what it was, but he was definitely not telling me everything."

Ramona looked up at Sam and shrugged. "Everyone has secrets, Sam. There's probably a lot he wasn't telling you."

"I know, I know." Sam furrowed his brow as he shuffled through the papers in front of him, looking for something. He didn't know what.

"The general impression seems to be he's the one in charge of that relationship. And of her," she said, tapping the file in front of her and looking up at Sam.

"You got that from his file?" he asked.

"You're not the only one with contacts, you know. I made a few calls before you got here."

"Working on building your connections, huh?"

Ramona shrugged. "I'm not planning on being stuck in this squad room forever, you know that. It's why you helped me get on this case, isn't it?"

She was right, of course. Sam only worried that if she moved too fast, pushed too hard, she'd regret where she ended up. That was a conversation for another day. "All right, he bought her Senate seat with his millions, so now he thinks he can call the shots."

Ramona shrugged and raised her eyebrows, acknowledging the inevitable truth to the assumption. "Why shouldn't he? They're a team, after all. The voters knew about him when they elected her. Politicians' private lives aren't private anymore, are they? You vote for a candidate and you're voting for her whole family, warts and all. In their case, I'm sure he was trying to help her forget about their daughter."

"Daughter? I thought they didn't have kids."

"They don't. Anymore." Ramona lowered her eyes and frowned as she explained. "The child died, at quite a young age. Six years old."

"Oh, God." Sam shook his head. "I can't imagine going through that."

"Looks like she's been focused on her career ever since. And he's been helping her keep that focus. She got elected mayor of their town not long after the death, and she's never stopped to look back."

"Or never let herself stop long enough that she has to look back. She must've put all her energy into her work after that. She really moved up fast."

Sam turned back to the sheets in front of him. Printouts showing everything from Marshall's driving record to his credit score. Old bank accounts, business deals, newspaper clippings about his successes. And occasional failures.

"That explains her drive—"

"And his, too," Ramona interrupted him.

"Sure." Sam kept reading as he spoke. "I'd really like to know more about him, his background. Maybe before they got married. He came from somewhere, and he built up a small empire for himself. He's gotta have baggage. People who have a grudge against him."

Ramona nodded as she continued to focus on the papers in front of her. "There are a lot of sources. This could take awhile. Websites and blogs from Pennsylvania, others from here in DC. Or at least, about what goes on in DC… who knows where these are really being written, you know?"

"I know, don't believe everything you read online. Some of these anonymous blogs are probably bored teenagers in Kansas making stuff up."

Ramona laughed. "Or worse, politicos in China intentionally misleading Americans, riling them up." She frowned, pulling out a piece of paper and waving it at Sam. "Who writes this nonsense? SenateSecrets.

Political Dish. The names are funny, but the information shared through these blogs is potentially really damaging."

"Yeah? Anything about the Marshalls?" Sam looked over her shoulder.

"A little. This one in particular." She tapped the paper. "Like you said, I need to dig into this some more. Figure out the truth from the BS." Ramona smiled and looked up. "What about Adam, Sam?"

"Adam?" Sam looked sideways at her and smiled. "Detective Kaminski?"

"Stop it, you know what I mean." She punched his arm. "What's his story?"

Sam shrugged. "I don't know a whole lot about him. I only started working with him on this trip for the senator. We haven't had a lot of time for girl talk." He grinned and she hit him again, this time harder.

"Ow… okay." Sam frowned and rubbed his arm. "He hasn't always been a cop. He mentioned that he used to teach history, then switched careers. I know he lives with his girlfriend, he's mentioned that. And there's another woman in his life — Julia. I'm not sure who she is, but I overheard his partner mention her, that he supports her somehow."

"Huh. Multiple women. Quite a guy."

"Hey, I'm telling you what I've heard. Don't jump to any conclusions. I have no idea who Julia is or why he's supporting her. She could be his old, infirm aunt or something."

"So he's a gallant kind of guy, is that what you're saying?"

"Maybe." Sam frowned. "It's not all peaches and cream with him. There's a reason he left teaching."

"That is an odd career choice, teacher to cop. What happened?" Ramona asked, unable to hide her curiosity.

Sam shrugged. "I dunno, like I said, he hasn't shared a lot. That's his business, nothing to do with me."

"Hmm…" Ramona had turned back to her monitor, clicking through more screens of information about John Marshall.

Sam couldn't help but wonder if her mind was on the information in front of her, or somewhere else entirely.

CHAPTER THIRTEEN

"WE ARE A RELATIVELY small staff, you understand," Elise said as she handed Adam a cup and saucer. Adam held the delicate saucer while taking a sip, then turned to place the cup on the wooden surface to his left.

"And you run the household staff, is that correct?"

"*Oui*, that is correct. I have been the house manager here at the ambassador's residence for three years." Elise gave a sharp nod as she spoke. "I manage the household staff, supervise the contract for the gardens, and of course we also have Tomas." She gave the name a French pronunciation and used her prominent chin to indicate the young man sitting across the table from Adam.

"Call me Tom." He smiled weakly and shrugged, then lowered his face to his coffee.

The kitchen in which they sat was testament to the effectiveness of Elise's leadership. Stainless steel work surfaces shined next to spotless granite countertops. Cooking knives, mixers, bowls all showed neatly from behind glass-fronted cabinets. It was an elegant, well-equipped kitchen, ready for the chef to prepare a light dinner for two or a dinner party for thirty, depending on the ambassador's needs for the day. The chef himself had left the premises, out for his daily visits to the grocers and butchers.

"Can you tell me who from the staff was working yesterday morning?" Adam turned his question to Elise.

She shrugged and her frown was quintessentially French. "*Les femmes des chambres*, of course, were upstairs tidying the rooms." Adam nodded. Sam was upstairs right now with one of those maids, hopefully getting her perspective on the shooting. And hopefully not getting caught, since he didn't have the right to search the premises. "Tomas had a quick bite here in the kitchen, but then went out to the cars, oh... what time, Tomas?"

"Oh, I — I was out there for a while. Before the senator's car even showed up."

"Yeah, I was going to ask about that," Adam stopped him. "Why were the senator and her husband here?"

"Well... because they were going to Philadelphia?" Tom's words were more question than statement.

"Yeah, I know that. Why were they meeting here?" He glanced first at Tom, then Elise.

Tom simply shrugged, but Elise volunteered a response. "It was very gracious of Senator Marshall to agree to start their journey here, with the ambassador. They had a civilized breakfast together. Then they could start the drive at the same time, to arrive at the same time." She raised her eyebrows as she offered the explanation, as if for a brighter man it wouldn't have required an explanation.

Adam smiled in response. "And that was it, the only people here that morning?"

Elise shook her head and lowered her eyebrows. "I do not understand the question."

"In the house that morning." Adam spoke slowly. "You, Tom, two maids, plus the ambassador, the senator and her husband, and Mr. McFellan. Was that it?"

"And the chef, of course." Elise sounded surprised. "And M. Toulard, assistant to the ambassador."

"Of course." Adam nodded again. "Anyone else I've missed?"

"Well, the police." Tom spoke up. "I mean, there was

the Diplomatic Security here for the ambassador, and Secret Service for the senator."

"Right." Adam picked up his coffee cup, though he could tell without tasting it that it had long since grown cold. "And you can vouch for all of the staff? You trust them?"

"I did not hire all of them, if that's what you mean." Elise's words were simple, but her tone made it clear that some of the staff didn't meet up with her standards.

Adam made a mental note to revisit the staff's background, then shifted tacks. "Did either of you see anything that could be helpful to our investigation? Anything at all."

Tom shrugged and raised his eyebrows. Elise frowned. "I see many things, Detective. What specifically are you asking?"

Adam considered the question as he placed his cup back on the table. What was he asking? If she had seen someone running through the house with a smoking gun, perhaps. Or if the chamber maid had come to her in tears having just killed a man. Adam smiled as he considered the options, then turned his gaze back to Elise.

"Anything at all, ma'am. Even the smallest details can prove useful, things that may seem insignificant to you. I'm sure you notice everything that goes on here," he added.

Elise nodded in agreement. "I do. I am aware of everything that takes place in this house."

"And nothing struck you as odd that morning?"

Elise gave her head a single shake, her lips tight together. "I run an organized house, Detective Kaminski. If anything had been out of order, I would have known."

Adam had to agree. If something unusual had happened that morning, Elise would have known. He glanced out the window to the landscaped back yard that stretched an easy fifty yards before ending at the hedges that lined the property, dividing it from the equally grand house on the next street over.

"I have told you who was here when the young man was killed. I have told you I saw nothing unusual. I have nothing more I can add."

Tom glanced at his watch as Elise spoke, then jumped up. "I gotta get out to the car. The ambassador'll want to go in ten minutes."

He gave a quick nod toward Adam, a more obsequious look to Elise, then headed out a side door that led to the garages.

"I appreciate your time, and the accuracy of your memory, Elise." Adam rose as he spoke. "If you are sure there's nothing else you've left out, no one else who was here."

Elise moved toward the door as she spoke. "Not by the time the senator arrived, no. That was it." She made as if to step through the door, but the sharpness of Adam's voice stopped her.

"By the time the senator arrived. What does that mean? Was someone else here earlier?"

Elise glanced over her shoulder, then turned back to the hall when footsteps sounded, moving from the room next to the kitchen toward the front door. "No one that matters, I assure you. I am needed elsewhere now. You must excuse me."

Adam watched her stiff, black-clad form as she marched up the hall toward the foyer, ready to see the ambassador off on his afternoon's appointments.

Shit, Adam thought to himself, trotting after her. *Why isn't Sam back downstairs yet?*

"IT'S FINE, BETH, nothing to worry about," Sam reassured the young woman in front of him, giving her his best smile. "If you can't trust a cop, who can you trust?"

That, at least, elicited a reaction from her, though not

the one Sam had been hoping for. "*Merde*. You're all the same, aren't you?" She snapped her dust rag against the bookshelf as she spoke, her French accent revealing her status as an African immigrant.

"Cops?" Sam asked, confused.

"Men." She gave him a cold look, then turned back to her dusting.

Sam smiled and shook his head. At least she was talking now.

"I can't talk to you," she continued as if reading his thoughts. "I have work I must do while the ambassador is out." She looked at him out of the corner of her eye. "And I am sure you should not be up here." She wagged a finger at him as she spoke. "This is a French residence."

Sam shrugged. "Like I said, it's fine. And I won't take you away from your work for long, I promise. I need you to tell me about yesterday morning. What happened, what you saw, things you noticed. Anything."

Beth stood upright, hands on hips, and put her head to the side. Her black hair, pulled into a tight twist at the back of her head, looked almost toffee brown as the light hit it.

"I was upstairs when it happened. What could I have seen?"

"Okay." Sam looked around the room they were in, thinking about his next question. Floor to ceiling bookshelves left no doubt as to the function of this room. Books of all shapes and types filled the shelves. Sam was surprised they weren't all leather-bound tomes. He saw paperbacks as well as hardcover books tucked away on the shelves. A few volumes lay on the shining oak table in the middle of the room, a few more on the end table next to the red leather couch. A comfortable room to sit and read, no doubt. He turned back to the maid in front of him.

"What other rooms are on this floor?"

She shrugged, then turned toward the door, waving

for Sam to follow her. "Come on, I'll show you."

He followed her to the main hallway on the floor, where she stopped and pointed at each door as she spoke. "The ambassador's office. Mme. Saint-Amand's office." She turned back toward the doors on the front of the house. "Two guest rooms, not currently used. And of course the library." She gestured back to the room behind them, which took up most of the west wing on the second floor.

"Can I look in those guest rooms?" Sam walked toward a closed door even as he asked.

Beth said nothing, though she managed to express both her disapproval and recognition of her own inability to stop him through a simple harrumph.

"Come, show me the rooms." Sam had one door open and looked back at Beth. She followed him in.

"Do you clean all of these rooms?" Sam asked.

"Of course, who else do you think does it?" Beth moved over to the windows as she spoke, glancing out at the front yard. The forensics team had cleared out, but divots in the grass, deep treads in the gravel, remained as evidence of their examination of the grounds. She shook her head and turned back to Sam.

"I clean all of these rooms, this floor and the one above. There is a second maid who does the ground floor and the attic rooms."

"You didn't happen to be in this room yesterday morning, did you?"

Beth frowned and looked away, shaking her head so slightly Sam wasn't really sure it was an answer.

"Where were you when the shot was fired?"

Beth shrugged again, this time running her rag over the chest of drawers that stood against the wall next to the window. "I am not sure exactly... I can not know where I am every minute." She stopped moving and looked at Sam. "I was not in here. No, that I know. I would have seen something then, no? And I saw nothing."

"You still might've seen something. Wherever you were." Sam didn't push her more than that, waiting for her to share whatever it was that was making her nervous. He watched as she picked up a brush and mirror set from the top of the dresser, idly wiping the back of the mirror with her rag, then placing them back on the dresser. In the exact place they had been before, Sam noticed.

"You take great pride in your work, don't you?"

"Of course I do. What kind of question is that?"

"It's clear. From the way these rooms look. I don't think anyone would doubt that. No matter what you're hiding. I don't think you need to worry."

Sam walked over to her, to put his hand on her shoulder in what he hoped would be a reassuring gesture. She stepped away from him as he reached out, moving back toward the door of the room.

"Right. Fine." She shrugged. "I stepped outside for a minute. Just a minute, I promise." She looked up at him, and for the first time Sam saw doubt in her deep brown eyes. "Do you have to tell Elise?"

"Of course not." Sam shook his head reassuringly. "Your secret is safe with me." He paused, then added, "Unless it has something do with the murder." He raised one eyebrow, and Beth laughed.

"Murder. Hah. I could murder him, though…" She glanced out, back down the hallway, then turned back to Sam. "Look, people are moving around downstairs. I really must get back to the library before Elise catches me." She looked meaningfully at Sam. "Or catches you, right?"

Sam shrugged. "Where were you? Where did you go?"

"I stepped out the back door. Just for a minute. Maybe two. I was definitely back up here within five minutes."

"Why did you go outside, Beth?"

"It does not matter now." She looked down at her hands as she spoke. "It really does not matter." She looked back up at Sam, the defiance he had seen earlier back in her eyes. "I did not see anything. Or anyone. Well, anyone involved in the murder. No one sneaking around with a gun, that sort of thing."

"Someone could have come up here while you were downstairs, right?"

Beth took a step back at the question, as if she hadn't considered that. "Well… I suppose so. I was not gone for long, I swear it." She shook her head as she spoke, her eyebrows raised. "If someone came up here, then it was someone who knew the house, knew where he was going. It was not much time."

This time Sam heard the footsteps downstairs, too. With only a final glance at Sam, Beth turned and ran down the hall back to the library. Sam started toward the main staircase, but the voices carrying up made it clear the ambassador and his house manager were in the foyer.

Stepping as quietly as he could, Sam turned back toward the small door at the end of the hall, next to the library. He was pretty sure there was a back staircase here somewhere. The lords of the manor wouldn't want the servants running up and down the main staircase.

AMBASSADOR SAINT-AMAND didn't glance at Elise, but stood in the front hall looking through the contents of his portfolio. As Adam watched, Elise stepped past him to the left of the front door. She opened a door that blended so well with the walls Adam hadn't even noticed it before, reaching in and extracting a long black umbrella. This she handed to the ambassador's assistant as he stepped out of his office, closing the door behind him. The ambassador hadn't looked up to see either of them.

With a nod, the assistant took the umbrella, then moved toward the front door. Only after the front door was open, the assistant standing waiting next to it, did the ambassador look up.

"*Bon, allons-y.*" He stepped out of the house, his tread as soft and delicate as Adam remembered. The assistant glanced at Elise, then followed.

A noise from the kitchen behind him caught his attention, and Adam turned as Sam approached him.

"Hey, I was getting worried about you," Adam spoke under his voice.

"Came down the back stairs." Sam gestured toward a plain panel door with his head. "I figured a place like this had to have a servant's staircase, right?"

"I suppose so, though I gotta admit, I wouldn't really know." Adam grinned. "Any luck?"

"Come on, let's compare notes out in the car."

Adam glanced back up the hallway, where Elise was closing the front door, then turned and followed Sam back out the side door toward the garages.

Pale paving stones marked out a path from the side door toward the garage that stood about fifty feet away from the house, closer to the street. Adam and Sam hung a right as they passed by it, Adam glancing in through the small windows. The garage looked like it could easily hold four cars, maybe more.

Sam's car was parked down the curved drive, away from the house. Once they were out of earshot of anyone in the house or garage, Sam spoke first. "The upstairs maid admitted she went out back that morning. Right around the time of the shooting. To meet someone, she says."

"Who?"

"She didn't tell me. Not yet, anyway. She gave the impression it was a boyfriend or something. And that it didn't go well. We need to check that out."

"Elise let slip that someone else was here yesterday morning. She wouldn't say who, either. Maybe that was it."

"Huh." Sam frowned as he pulled the driver's side

door open and slid in. "That's a surprise. Beth seemed sure Elise didn't know about her visitor — she wanted me to promise not to tell her."

"Elise is a tough cookie. She may well know everything that goes in that house, as she claims." Adam got in the passenger side, pulling the door shut behind him.

Sam started the engine, then turned back to Adam. "So a mystery man comes to the house to meet the maid. Maybe Elise knows about it. Or maybe there was someone else here that morning that Elise hasn't mentioned."

"Was it a coincidence that Beth was out back when the shot was fired? Or was she drawn away from that room at that time intentionally?" He glanced up at the second floor windows as he spoke. "Which window is it?"

Sam leaned forward to look out the front window, then pointed. "Three to the right of the front door."

"She would've had a great vantage point to see the whole thing."

"Yeah…" Sam let the word hang in the air for a moment before continuing. "It could also be the room where the shot was fired. I checked the window. It opens smoothly, removable screens. It would only take a few seconds. Look." He pointed again. "The shooter just had to lean forward out the window and he'd have had a perfect target."

"That's kind of bold, don't you think? Good chance of being seen."

Sam shrugged. "I don't know. Who's looking up?"

Adam glanced over at Sam. "You? Secret Service?"

Sam sighed and looked down at the steering wheel in front of him. "Yeah, theoretically. Maybe we weren't."

"Come on." Adam pulled his seatbelt across his chest. "You had your eyes peeled, I'm sure of it. If the killer did use that window, then he couldn't have been seen. Or you would have seen him. Got it?"

"Or" — Sam looked up at the window, then back at Adam — "or she never left the room. She was there when the shot was fired. Maybe she let her mysterious visitor in, then showed him up to the room."

Adam nodded as Sam pulled the car down the drive toward Kalorama Drive. "Lots of questions still." He looked back at the mansion as they pulled away. "Drop me at Barton McFellan. I'm meeting Ramona there." He laughed at Sam's expression. "Apparently she doesn't trust this unsophisticated Philly cop to talk to your K-Street lobbyists on his own."

CHAPTER FOURTEEN

ADAM SPUN AROUND to find the source of the sound, the sirens boomeranging off the glass and brick buildings surrounding Franklin Square. He exhaled when he saw the ambulance, felt the tension drain from his shoulders.

Why he routinely tensed at the sound of sirens was beyond him. His partner, Pete, claimed it was normal, that it came with the territory of being a cop. Maybe. Adam wasn't convinced. Not having a radio, with the constant update of activities in the area, made it even tougher. Not knowing was never good.

He slid back on the bench, no longer perched on the edge but still tensed. He glanced at his watch one more time. He was still early. He could hardly blame Ramona for that.

He let his eyes drift over the square, benches filled with business women and men in drab suits grabbing a quick bite from the food trucks parked along the curbs. A group of children from a local day care center had taken over a patchy area that had once been grass but was now worn down to firmly packed earth. Even as he saw the people around him, he thought again about what he had learned that morning. Elise was keeping something back, that much was clear. And who was the unknown visitor that neither she nor Beth would name?

A movement to his left caught his eye, and he turned

as Ramona came around the bend in the walkway toward him. She wore plain clothes today, probably recognizing they would serve her better in their meetings that afternoon. She walked with an unconscious grace, more noticeable because of the radio clipped to her belt and the weapon Adam knew was tucked into the holster around her shoulders. When she saw Adam she smiled, her skin glowing under the noon sun.

Adam blinked and shook his head, looking away. She was his partner as long as he was down here. He had to keep this professional, no matter where his libido was pointing him.

Ramona stopped next to his bench but didn't sit. "I got a call from Agent Hennessy this morning."

"Anything interesting?"

She ignored his smile. "They got the ballistics results back. They're not one hundred percent sure…"

"They never are," Adam prompted her when she paused.

Ramona nodded and continued, "It looks like the bullet was fired from inside the house."

Adam frowned. "That sounds about right. Sam and I were thinking the same thing earlier. Second floor window, right?"

"Probably. They aren't being exactly forthcoming. Hennessy said they had the results late yesterday. He didn't bother calling me 'til this morning. And even then not a lot of details."

Adam shrugged. "It's the name of the game, nothing new there."

Ramona raised an eyebrow, but let it drop as her radio crackled to life. She stepped away, pulling the two-way microphone away from her waist and holding it close to her ear.

Adam turned his attention back to the square and this time didn't notice her approach from behind him.

"Did you learn anything new this morning?" Her question startled him out of his reverie.

"A bit." Adam grimaced with the recognition of how little they had learned, but filled her in on what he had. "The most interesting lead seems to be the unknown person — or people," he finished his explanation.

Her lips turned down at the corners as she considered his report, not quite a frown, not quite a pout. He waited, watching her think, tucking the information into an internal file cabinet. "Sorry I couldn't join you," she finally said. "I would have liked to see Elise and Beth for myself."

"I wouldn't mind getting your take on them, either. Maybe we can head back later, after our meeting."

"Maybe." Ramona inhaled through her teeth. "But I don't think so."

"Why? What's up?"

"Two things. I did dig up some more background on Marshall — Mr. Marshall, that is. I shared it with Sam earlier, he may have told you."

"He didn't mention it. Go on."

She leaned forward, her arms resting on the back of the bench. Adam turned in his seat, partly to face her, partly to pull back from her, to distance himself from the tempting scent of vanilla that surrounded her.

"He seems to be the man in charge." She looked out over the square as she spoke, but Adam could tell her mind was focused on what she had found that morning, not the children playing a few yards ahead.

"Seems to be?"

She shrugged, her head to one side. "I guess. That's what Sam thinks, anyway. His money. His plan. He lets people know that if they want the senator's support, they need to get his first." She squinted and tilted her head again. "It's just…"

Adam watched her, waiting, wondering what was going on inside her head.

She finally pushed herself up from the bench with a shake of her head. "I'm not so sure. Women aren't as easy to push around as men like to think." She turned to Adam and smiled.

"And the other thing?" Adam asked.

"The car—" Her radio cut her off again, though this time she didn't walk away, just held up a hand to silence Adam while she listened, then nodded.

Turning her attention back to Adam, she said, "You know, I told Hennessy what I'd found when he called this morning, but he didn't seem too impressed. Or interested."

"How do you mean?"

"He's running with the evidence from ballistics. He thinks it was an inside job. One of the staff, maybe. Related to the narcotics problems, maybe." She shrugged. "And it could be."

Adam frowned. "Or someone who had access to the house. Someone who'd been there before."

"Like most of the people who were there that morning," Ramona agreed.

Adam pursed his lips, thinking. "The senator. Mr. Marshall. Mr. McFellan." He glanced at Ramona. "And our unknown guests."

She smiled at him. "So Hennessy isn't thinking that, or he isn't sharing. Either way, he's focusing on the staff for now."

"Then I'm glad Sam and I made it over there this morning — and out again, without getting warned off by Hennessy."

Ramona frowned. "You think he'd do that?"

"I don't know." Adam turned to look at her. "You said yourself he's not being overly forthcoming. You know he doesn't really want me — or you — on this investigation. Was there a second thing?" Even as he asked, he glanced at his watch. "Shit." He jumped up. "Weren't we supposed to be at Barton McFellan five minutes ago?"

Ramona shrugged. "Yeah, you ready for this?"

"You've done this before, right?"

She stopped walking and turned to face Adam. "What the hell do you take me for, a rookie?" She smiled as she spoke, but it failed to lessen the aggression in her tone.

"Sorry." Adam held his hands up. "It's just this will be our first suspect interview together, and we don't really know each other. How we work, or at least how we work together."

"Don't worry about me, Detective Kaminski, I know these people and I know how to talk to them."

"Then lead the way, Officer Davis." Adam gestured gallantly with his arm, stepping next to her as she passed by him.

Even crossing with the light, they had to dodge cars stuck in the consistently heavy DC traffic. Walking up to the glass front of the building that housed the firm of Barton McFellan, Ramona turned and flashed a smile at Adam. "This should be interesting," she said as she pulled the door open.

CHAPTER FIFTEEN

RAMONA'S HAND snapped out, grabbing onto Adam's knee. He raised his eyebrows as he turned toward her, but her wink stopped the question forming on his lips. She smiled and withdrew her hand.

A few seconds later, Adam realized he was bouncing his knee again. For all of Ramona's confidence about this interview, he knew better. It wasn't a question of being a good cop or even being experienced. The question was, how would they work together.

He and Pete had spent years fine-tuning their technique, letting questions bounce back and forth between them, knowing exactly what the other would want to ask next and leading the witness in that direction.

It was like playing bridge. The game was won or lost by how well you read your partner's signals. It was difficult and it was intimate. And without it, the job could be deadly.

Adam realized he was staring at Ramona, and blinked. He turned away, but not before he saw her smile to herself.

The young man who entered the lobby of Barton McFellan carried more than his own twenty-five years' worth of importance. He walked with his back ramrod straight, his chest out. When he stopped in front of Adam and Ramona, he spoke down his nose rather than lowering his face.

"Officers." He nodded at each of them. "I am Michael Ward. I can answer any questions you have. Mr. McFellan is not available."

Ramona glanced at Adam and grinned, then rose from her seat in a single slow movement. After that first glance, she kept her eyes on the young man in front of her, and Adam felt the waves of disdain coming off her.

Ward must have felt them, too, for he took a step back.

Ramona took a step forward. She stood toe to toe with Ward, her eyes only fractionally below his. "We're here to talk with Mr. McFellan." Her voice was calm, quiet.

"I… I told you, I can answer—"

Ramona cut off Ward's stumbling answer. "Mr. Ward, we made an appointment with Mr. McFellan as a courtesy." She put her head on the side. "This interview is not optional. We're going to talk with Jason McFellan."

Ward took another step back, Ramona still matching his stride. His arms flailed at his side for a moment, and Adam didn't know if he was going to brace himself against the wall to his left or slap Ramona across the face. Though he was pretty sure he knew what would really happen next.

Ward nodded. Coughed. Turned back toward the door through which he had entered. Adam and Ramona followed him through the door to the back rooms of Barton McFellan, Advocacy Consultants.

THE ASH in the crystal ashtray that sat on the walnut table next to the window surprised Adam. He could smell no trace of the cigar, and surely most buildings these days were strictly nonsmoking.

He glanced at Ramona. She had settled into one of the plush chairs facing McFellan's desk. The chair stood only a few feet in front of the desk, but when combined with the expanse of polished walnut that made up the desk's surface, she seemed yards away from McFellan, who leaned back heavily in his leather chair.

The wide window behind him gave an open view onto Franklin Square and let rays of light in to shine on McFellan's desk and chair. A line of shadows cut across his face as he turned to look at them or leaned back farther in his chair.

McFellan was an impeccably groomed man of indeterminable age. Somewhere between thirty-five and fifty. Adam couldn't tell if his confidence was making him look older than he really was or if tailored suits, tailored workouts, and weekly facials were making him look younger.

"Would you like to wait until your lawyer arrives?" Adam asked as he took the chair next to Ramona.

"That's not necessary." McFellan waved the suggestion away with a confident smile. He had sent his assistant off to call his legal counsel as soon as he understood that Adam and Ramona would be interviewing him that afternoon, regardless of his preference. "As you know, I have nothing to hide." He grinned. "And I am perfectly capable of keeping secrets."

Ramona smiled and inclined her head in agreement, which McFellan seemed to appreciate. He opened a drawer to his left and pulled out a cigar, then dropped it again when he saw Adam's look.

"What can I do for you, officers?"

"We'd like to get your take on the shooting yesterday." Ramona took the lead, smiling as she asked the question. "What you saw… what you heard… anything that would help the investigation."

McFellan frowned. His brow furrowed as if in deep thought, he moved his head slowly up and down. "Yes, I see. But then" — he looked up at them — "isn't the FBI investigating this attempted murder? Why is MPDC interested?"

"It wasn't an attempted murder, sir." Adam spoke calmly, quietly. Ramona's hand tightened on the arm of her chair. "We're here investigating the murder of Jay Kapoor."

"Who?" McFellan's look of confusion lasted only a second or two, enough for Adam to form a strong sense of the man. "Oh, yes, of course. I'm so sorry." Now McFellan's face registered compassion. Sorrow.

Adam's lips turned up into a mockery of a smile, and he said nothing more, waiting.

McFellan turned his eyes to Ramona. She simply smiled in response.

"Ahem," McFellan cleared his throat. "Well." When neither Adam nor Ramona spoke, he continued, "I must admit, I do believe this was an attempt on the life of the senator, not Mr. Kapoor. The poor young man was in the wrong place at the wrong time."

"A place in which he often found himself, though," Adam pointed out, "next to the senator."

"Well, yes. Of course." McFellan shrugged. "But that's his job. Was his job, I mean."

"You have a background on the Hill yourself, Mr. McFellan. Isn't that right?"

Adam glanced at Ramona, not expecting the question. This is what he had been worried about.

McFellan inclined his head. "That's right. It's no secret I started out in the Senate as well."

Ramona laughed. "In the Senate. You make it sound like you were elected. You were a staffer, weren't you?"

McFellan's smile broadened. "I apologize if my answer sounded evasive, officer. I certainly didn't intend it to. I'm very proud of my background. Yes, I started as an aide, like Mr. Kapoor. I worked my way up to Chief of Staff."

The line of shadows fell across his face as he leaned back in his chair, linking his hands over his chest. "At one time I thought I'd run for office myself one day. It didn't take me long to realize the real power is held by those behind the scenes."

"Senate Chief of Staff wasn't enough for you?" Adam asked.

McFellan laughed under his breath. Shook his head and looked down at his hands as he answered quietly, "I had complete power over the political positions of the senator from Wisconsin, without ever having to run for office. To expose myself to public scrutiny. I could do what I wanted. Run the country the way I thought it should be run." He looked up again at Adam and Ramona. "What can I say?" He shrugged. "I saw the path before me and I took it. I moved even deeper behind the scenes. With even more power."

"With the quaint title of advocacy consultant." Ramona raised an eyebrow.

McFellan leaned forward, only slightly closing the gap between him and Ramona. "I don't make the rules, I just know how to follow them. You'd be amazed what you can do once you really understand the system. It's what everyone should do — learn the rules, take care of yourself. We'd all be better off." He rolled his eyes and waved a hand as he spoke, disdain competing with arrogance on his face. "It's not my fault if the great unwashed don't even understand the rules they vote for. Or how to work them to their advantage."

"Do you know the senator well, Mr. McFellan?" Ramona's voice was friendly, inquisitive as she posed the question, her eyes showing nothing but curiosity, as if she hadn't noticed McFellan's attitude.

"Oh, yes." McFellan leaned back in his chair again, folding his hands over his chest. "She works very closely with us, you know." He looked back and forth between Adam and Ramona, then continued, "We've had an arrangement in place, oh…" McFellan pursed his lips as he thought about it. "Oh, for almost two years now."

"Two years?" Adam asked. "What arrangement was that?"

Ramona glanced at Adam, but McFellan answered, "Her position here, of course. That she would be moving her offices here, from the Hill."

Ramona nodded. "And since that arrangement was made, you've been spending a lot of time together."

McFellan shrugged. "Sure. Nothing unethical, of course." He smiled at Adam. "We offered her financial support for a number of her priorities. Those that served the needs of our clients, you understand."

"How does that work, Mr. McFellan?"

McFellan seemed confused by Adam's question. "Well… we offered her certain gifts — hotel rooms, the use of our jet, constituent dinners… oh, um… maybe some cash now and then, donated to her campaign fund."

"Her campaign fund? Given your arrangement, surely she wasn't running for reelection?"

Ramona and McFellan both smiled at Adam's question. "No, detective," McFellan answered. "No, I suppose not."

"Why did she need these gifts from you, sir?" Adam asked. "I understand that her husband had bankrolled her campaign and still provided financial support to her work."

McFellan shrugged, raising his hands in acquiescence. "Is any amount ever really enough?"

"Or did she have other expenses?" Ramona asked. "Expenses she didn't want him to know about?"

"My dear" — McFellan grinned at Ramona — "That's really not for me to say, is it?"

Adam watched the transformation as Ramona's face grew hard, her eyes narrowed. "The 'arrangement' you're describing is hardly legal, Mr. McFellan." She raised her eyebrow as she spoke the word, making clear her disdain for the idea. "If we report this to the Select Committee on Ethics, she could be brought up on charges."

McFellan's grin dropped. "I suppose you could," he said drily, "but since she'll be working here by the end of the year, she'll be out of their jurisdiction before they even convene a meeting to discuss the alleged transgression."

"SO… WHAT? McFellan thought Jay was in his way somehow and decided to take him out?" Adam asked as he pushed the button for the elevator.

"That doesn't fit with his personality, does it?" Ramona smiled as she looked sideways at Adam. "He's more likely to find some way to get Jay fired, not shoot him. And it probably wouldn't be too hard for him, based on some of the stuff I've seen about him online."

"Like what?"

"He uses his money and his power to get whatever he wants. Budget line items for pet projects. Congressional votes suddenly shifting his way. You should check out some of the dirt posted on Political Dish."

Adam smiled, thinking about the last thing he had read. A biography of the Black Count, the father of Alexander Dumas. Fascinating, but probably not relevant to this investigation. "I don't follow political blogs, sorry. So maybe Senator Marshall realized what she was getting into and wanted a way out?"

"Doesn't work." Ramona smiled again. "He was still inside when the shot was fired."

"And how could she have done it, when she was standing right next to Jay?" Adam finished the thought for her.

Ramona smiled. "You read my mind."

"Just because she couldn't do it herself, doesn't mean she didn't set it up."

"John Marshall has something he's not telling us, Sam's sure of it. But how could he have done it, either? He was in the house with McFellan."

"McFellan admits that Marshall left the room first. We've been thinking that left McFellan without an alibi — but it leaves Marshall without a witness, too." Adam was warming up to this idea when his thoughts were cut off.

"Excuse me. Yes, you. Hello." The woman's voice was high and sharp, almost as sharp as the stiletto heels that dug little holes into the carpet as she marched toward them.

"Can we help you?" Ramona turned toward the woman as she spoke.

"You can leave, that's what you can do. I don't know what the hell you thought you were doing, interviewing my client without me present, but it's all garbage. You can't use any of it." She glared at Ramona, then turned her attention to Adam. Her eyes moved down from his face to his legs, and her glare softened. She almost smiled.

Adam smiled warmly, his dimples on full display, and put out his hand. "Detective Adam Kaminski. I'm here from Philadelphia, investigating the murder of Jay Kapoor."

She took his hand limply. "I know who you are and why you're here. And why you're leaving."

"We're leaving because we're done here." Ramona's smile was saccharine sweet.

"You, my dear, are leaving because I just spoke to your captain. You'll be hearing from him any minute now, I imagine." The lawyer's smile was triumphant. "And you." She turned to Adam. "I don't know why Philly PD is here, but you have no jurisdiction here. And no right to talk to my client. Again. Period." She emphasized each word with a tap of her alligator-skin heels.

The three of them stood in the plush and polished hallway, the lawyer glaring at the two police officers. The moment was broken by the soft chime of the elevator.

"It was a pleasure meeting you, ma'am." Adam turned to the opening doors.

Ramona waved at the lawyer as she stepped onto the elevator behind Adam. Just as the doors closed,

Ramona's radio chirped. "Damn, I hope she didn't hear that." Ramona mumbled as she reached for the microphone. "I really don't want to give her the satisfaction."

Adam waited as Ramona finished her call with her dispatch center. She turned to him with a grin as she clipped the microphone back to her belt. "So I guess you're used to dealing with women, huh?"

Adam shook his head. "What are you talking about?"

"Don't tell me you didn't notice the way she was looking at you."

"Hey, that's her problem, not mine."

Ramona shrugged and put her head to the side. "I guess. I've heard you manage to get along very well when it comes to women."

She was smiling as she spoke, but it didn't take the accusation out of the words as far as Adam was concerned. "I don't know what you're talking about, or where this is coming from. Or what business it is of yours, frankly, Ramona."

Her smile dropped and she turned to stare at the elevator buttons.

As the doors slid open, Adam said, "Look, I gotta be somewhere."

"Fine." Ramona's voice was tight. "I gotta check in with my captain anyway. I thought that interview went well." She looked at him, then looked away. "I'm surprised you didn't."

"It's not that." Adam saw that she was confused. Probably hurt. But he was here to investigate this murder, that was all. He needed to work closely with her — but not too close. "That went fine. I'll see you later, okay?"

She gave him a quick nod and headed out onto K Street. Adam watched her go, hoping he was right about her.

CHAPTER SIXTEEN

"SO HOW'S she doing?"

"Ramona?" Sam looked at the round face of the man sitting next to him on the porch. The bright eyes that Sam knew saw everything were now settled deep into a weathered face. Hair that had been salt and pepper when Sam first met Howard Davis now lay in tight white curls around his head, and the quick smile Howard had been known for had etched thick grooves around his lips and across his forehead. "She's doing great, thanks to you." Sam smiled.

"Huh," Howard grunted without smiling. "She needs to come and see her mother more often. Then she'd be doing great."

Sam looked out at the neighborhood around them. Each house along the block had a similar front porch. Sam didn't see anyone else out front, though voices from the alley suggested a few neighbors were out back tending to their tiny gardens. Across the street, an American flag jumped with the slightest breeze, its bright stars and stripes hiding the paint peeling on the wooden column it hung from, distracting from the warped panels of the porch floor.

Howard's own house showed subtle signs of decay. The post stamp sized front yard looked clean and well kept, but the porch steps sagged from years of use and pockmarked brick walls cried out for repointing.

The porch seemed to brighten as Tish stepped out of the house, carrying a tray laden with two tall glasses of iced lemonade and a small pot of the colorful daisies she grew in their back yard.

"She was here just last week, and you know it," she chided Howard as she put the glasses down in front of the two men. Carrying the daisies over to the porch railing, she placed them in a patch of sun, then turned back to her husband. "She comes over more than most of the other girls from the neighborhood. She's a good daughter."

Sam smiled his thanks for the lemonade and took a slow sip, watching Howard over the glass.

Howard grumbled, but Sam saw the familiar twinkle in his eyes. "She's a good cop, anyway. I'm proud of that." He took a sip and replaced his glass. "So, really, how is she doing? I hear you got her involved in a pretty high-level investigation."

"She's serving as the MPDC liaison for the FBI, they have the lead." He followed Tish with his eyes as she snaked between the men and back into the house. The screen door banged shut behind her. A second bang let them know she had joined the others on the alley that ran behind their house, weeding her cozy plot of land, listening to the gossip of the alley.

"This is the shooting up at that ambassador's house?"

"That's right." Sam nodded. "We don't really know who the real target was. A young man was killed. An aide to Senator Marshall. So we think she or the ambassador might have been the intended victim. The killer missed."

Howard's lips pulled tight into a thin line. "They always seem to miss, don't they? Hitting us, instead."

Sam smiled to himself, struck again by the similarities between father and daughter. "Actually, I came by to ask for a favor."

"Oh, really? So this isn't a social call?" Howard smiled.

"I'm always happy to see you, Howard, you know that. But yeah, you might be able to help with something."

"Shoot." Howard waved his hand in Sam's direction. "Metaphorically, I mean."

"It looks like there might be a drug connection in this case. We're not sure what, it just keeps coming up."

Howard was nodding as Sam spoke. "And if they come into the conversation, they're probably at the heart of the case. I know."

"I'm trying to find out about a couple of the staff who work at the ambassador's residence, where the shooting happened. It seems the ambassador was trying to tighten restrictions on immigration to his country—"

"All in the name of fighting drugs, right?" Howard interrupted him.

"Of course. His staff might have been involved in the shooting. So we're wondering if they have any connection, either to the immigration war or the drug war."

"How can I help?" Howard's brow furrowed. "I'm not involved in that. And it's been a long time since I did any legwork."

Sam shrugged. "I know, I know. I thought if I gave you a few names, you might have some friends you could call... see if they came up in connection with any old investigations."

"Humph." Howard shifted in his chair, grabbing his right knee as he did so, his arthritic fingers digging into his leg as if to catch the pain and tear it away. Sam stayed quiet until Howard had resettled himself, then Howard continued, "I think Ramona's in a better place to get you those answers. She's still on the force, she can look up any records."

"I know, and she is. I wondered if this went back a bit. And since it's French territory, some of it won't be in the records..." His voice trailed off as he watched a young man sauntering along the sidewalk in front of the house. The young man didn't look in their direction as he passed, simply kept walking, hands in his pockets, jeans hanging well below the top of his black boxer briefs.

"How's Troy?" Sam asked as the young man walked out of earshot.

"Him? Ha." Howard resettling himself again, grunting a little. "He's moved out, anyway."

"That good?"

"Maybe. Who knows. He's living with some friends. A few blocks away. In the wrong direction." Howard indicated with his head. While Howard and Tish had set themselves up in a sturdy old brick row house near the Frederick Douglass National Historic Site, a worn-out but well-kept block with good neighbors and a vibrant community, other streets deeper into Anacostia weren't as nice.

"He can take care of himself," Sam encouraged Howard. He wasn't so sure himself. Troy had been in and out of trouble his whole life. Unlike his sister, he hadn't yet settled down. Or found a full-time job. He knew Ramona worried about Troy as much as Howard did. And Sam shared that concern.

"Look, I know I'm pulling at straws here." Sam brought his thoughts back to the reason for his visit. "Maybe this was an excuse to see an old friend." He smiled.

"Hey, I understand digging everywhere you can, hoping to find something." Howard shrugged. "Back in my day that's what an investigation was. Turning over every bit of dirt, trash, and old rags you could find, in case you found a rat. Hell, sometimes even a rat dropping would do." Howard grinned with the memory of his old job, the deep lines of his face dancing around his eyes and mouth. "You're not asking to make me feel like I'm still useful, are you?"

Sam laughed as he stood, handing Howard the list of names he had prepared. "You don't need me for that, old friend." He glanced inside the house. "Give Tish my best, will you? I gotta get going."

He toyed with his car keys as he walked back to his car, parked up the street. Maybe there was nothing to this drug story. It could be a false lead. But he couldn't risk ignoring it, and anything he could learn about the people involved could prove to be the key to the case.

CHAPTER SEVENTEEN

ADAM STEPPED BACKWARDS as the exhausted waitress squeezed past him, a tray of beers, whiskeys, and martinis clutched against her chest, her face pale and drawn. From the outside, the bar looked like a quaint, traditional inn. A whitewashed wood house with green trim, a front porch that ran along the full front of the house. On the inside, it was dark, crowded, all the small rooms now connected to each other, each packed with tables and stools. At this time of day, it was standing room only.

All around him, young men and women, only a handful over the age of thirty, gathered in clumps around dark oak tables, some standing, some sitting. Waitresses moved through the crowd with difficulty, carrying orders of Martinis and single malts.

Adam scanned the crowd in the front room. Todd wasn't there.

Turning to his left, away from the dome of the Capitol barely visible through the west window of the Inn, he moved into the next small room. Identical to its neighbor, this room boasted more of the same crowd. Adam couldn't help but think that it *was* the same crowd. Everyone dressed the same, ordered the same drinks, even laughed the same, he noticed, as another short staccato broke out in the corner.

Adam had armed himself before coming to this

scheduled meeting. Not with a gun, but with information. His first call to his partner had been short, perfunctory. Pete had called back within the hour, and the second conversation took a little bit longer.

"Sorry that took awhile, partner. I found what you need," Pete said as soon as Adam answered his phone.

Adam had just made his way to the Capitol Hill neighborhood, and took Pete's call from a street corner near the Inn where he was scheduled to meet Jay's roommate, Todd Heavrin. "Not a problem, Pete. I needed the time to get over here anyway. What'd you find?"

"On the surface, he's a good kid with an interest in politics. He worked on the senator's campaign team. She hired him full-time once she was elected. A fairly common story."

"I'm guessing there's more than meets the eye with our friend Todd?"

"There always is, isn't there, partner? At least with all the folks who fall into our radar."

Adam nodded at the truth of this as he glanced around. Leaning against the side of a brick apartment building that stood opposite the Inn, Adam had a clear view of the entrance and he watched with interest as more and more young people filed into the bar.

He spotted Todd as soon as the aide turned the corner from 3rd Street NE. Todd walked with his hands in his trouser pockets, his head down, as if scanning the sidewalk ahead of him for traps. He chewed on his lip as he walked, and Adam wondered what he was so nervous about. Meeting with him?

He watched the young man hold the door to the Inn for a couple of women who had approached from the other direction, then follow them in. "He's here now, Pete, I shouldn't keep him waiting for too long."

"This won't take too long, partner," Pete assured him. "It's worth hearing."

And Pete had filled him in on the fairly detailed

background information that was available about Todd
Heavrin.

With this information tucked away, Adam now
continued his search for the young man, moving into the
dark rooms further beyond.

"I DON'T KNOW why I'm talking to you." Todd
shook his head and wiped the back of his hand across
his mouth as he put his beer back on the round table
between them. "This is none of your business. You
pressured me yesterday, made me think I needed to tell
you everything." The hand that Todd returned to his
glass shook ever so slightly, and beads of sweat started
reforming along his top lip.

Adam took a sip of his own beer before he answered.
"It's all important, Todd. Like I told you before, that's
the thing about a murder investigation. Everything has
to come out." He lowered his head to make eye contact
with Todd. "Everything."

Todd gave a quick grin and shook his head. "Hey, I'm
not a suspect, am I?"

"Of course not. I need your help understanding Jay,
that's all. Who he was. What sort of thing he was
working on. You know."

Todd returned his hand to the table to toy with his
beer glass but didn't take another drink. He glanced over
at the group of people he had been with when Adam
first found him, then glanced away again. "This was a
stupid place to meet. Now everyone will be talking about
it, wondering what I said to you. Wondering why you
want to know." He looked up at Adam. "Hell, it'll
probably be online by the time I get home tonight.
Latest gossip on Political Dish, 'exposing the secrets of
the people behind the power.'"

Todd used his fingers to draw quotes around the last
few words, what Adam could only assume was the
tagline for the website. He ignored the sarcasm. "Look,

Todd, let me make this easier for you. I checked you out before meeting you tonight."

"What does that mean? What are you talking about?" Todd's eyes darted back and forth between his untouched beer and Adam.

"It means I know you've got a criminal record, Todd. It means I know you have information you want to keep hidden — from your boss, from your colleagues." Adam swept his hand to capture the scene around them. "From your friends."

Todd jerked and ducked his head. He picked up his beer and took a long drink, placing the half empty glass back on the table. "That really is none of your business. Nothing to do with Jay's death."

"How do you know that?" Adam asked, curious.

Todd grinned, and for the first time took a deep breath. "Because Jay was too smart for that." He tipped his head to the side, assessing Adam. "Jay wasn't the great guy his parents say, you know?"

Adam nodded, waiting for Todd to say more.

Todd shrugged and took another sip of beer before continuing. A bark of laughter from a table across the room caught his attention, then he turned back to Adam. "I still don't know why I should talk to you. Since you seem to know everything I have to say anyway."

"Not everything, Todd. Far from it. But look." Adam leaned in, conspiratorially. "I understand why you're worried. Why you need to keep your past secret." He shrugged and looked down, as if deep in thought.

"I have a sister a little bit older than you," he continued. "I take care of her — she relies on me. It's tough trying to get by when you're starting out."

"Tell me about it." Todd's face screwed up. "There's too much competition. Not enough jobs to go around. And now they're cutting everything — cutting budgets, cutting positions, cutting contracts." He paused, considering. "All I ever wanted was to work in politics.

That's why I broke into that office in the first place, you know."

Adam didn't respond, hoping Todd would add more. Instead, Todd turned to him. "Tell me about your sister. What does she do?"

"Julia? She's a photographer."

"Artist type, huh?" Todd seemed dismissive of the career choice. "That's asinine. It's hard enough getting a job in a real field."

"Like politics, you mean?"

"Sure, why not?" Now Todd was getting defensive, not at all what Adam had hoped for.

Adam changed tracks. "Maybe you're right. She's just one more woman in my life I have to look out for. Between her and my girlfriend, they keep me busy, I can tell you. How about you, do you have girlfriend, Todd?"

"Nah, not me. I'm not ready for that type of commitment. Believe me" — Todd tried to look knowing but failed — "there are plenty of girls out there for a guy who wants to have a good time."

Adam smiled. "I'm sure there are. How about Jay, did he have a girlfriend?"

"Jay?" Todd laughed. "The only person Jay cared about was Jay. Trust me on that."

"Why do you say that?"

Todd's beer glass now sat empty between them and he was warming to his story. Adam sat back and listened, knowing better than to interrupt.

"Jay knew about my past. At first he said he didn't care." Todd laughed mirthlessly. "Yeah, right. He cared, believe me. He cared when it came time to pay the rent. 'Oh, Todd, you can front me this month, right? We wouldn't want Lisa finding out about your record, would we?'" Todd's voice rose as he mimicked Jay.

"Was he often short of funds?" Adam asked.

"Jay?" This time Todd's laugh was real. "That man was never short of funds. He was rolling in it."

"Your job doesn't pay that well, does it? Do you think

he was getting support from his parents?"

"Not from his parents. No way. He was getting it from somewhere, though. Maybe other people he had dirt on?" Todd looked directly at Adam. "Maybe those thugs he thought I didn't know about?"

"Thugs?"

"You know, dirtbags. He'd meet up with them on the corner a couple of blocks from our apartment, in Adams Morgan."

"Why would Jay be meeting with shady characters on a street corner?" Adam smiled even as he asked it, at the absurdity of what Todd was describing.

"Fine, don't believe me. Whatever. Like I said, this is none of my business anyway. Or yours."

Adam put both hands out to calm Todd down. "Okay, okay. Sorry. I do believe you, and I appreciate you telling me." He waited until Todd's breathing had slowed back to normal before continuing. "Tell me more about your work. What do you do for the senator?"

Todd shrugged. "We answer constituent mail. Work with other offices to develop language. Write up briefing statements on issues she's considering."

"How does she choose what issues she's going to focus on?"

Todd shrugged again. "I don't know. Whatever interests her, I guess. Oh, and we run interference when she's trying to avoid someone." Todd smiled as he spoke.

"Anyone in particular you're thinking of?" When Todd didn't answer, Adam pushed. "Greg Towne, maybe?"

Todd laughed out loud. "So you've met Towne, huh? Yeah, he's a character. Lisa wouldn't have met with him if he'd camped out in the hall outside her office. Which he came pretty close to doing, by the way."

Adam smiled with him. "What's his story?"

"Ah, I don't know. Sad old guy, really. He wanted to

save some building, and she refused. Voted for tearing it down and replacing it with a hotel." He looked back at Adam, his eyes and voice completely serious now. "We need that hotel, you know. We need the jobs, we need the tourists it will bring. This is no joking matter. Historical buildings are all good and well, but the economy is more important." He shrugged. "To Lisa, anyway."

Adam took another sip of his lager as he considered what Todd had told him. The room was slowly emptying out now, the after-work crowd moving on to their various dinner plans or heading home for the evening. Todd shifted on his stool and Adam knew he wouldn't keep his attention for much longer.

"Thanks for sharing all this with me, Todd. What you've told me about Jay, that's going to help. A lot."

"You won't tell his parents, though, will you?"

Adam's opinion of Todd moved a step up as he saw real concern in Todd's eyes. "Not if I can avoid it. They deserve to keep their memory of their son."

Todd smiled. "You're in it now, though, Detective."

"How do you mean?"

"Like I said, everyone will know I met with you. And they'll wonder what I told you. You might not believe me about them, but those guys Jay met with, they did not look like nice guys. They looked dangerous."

"And now they'll know I know about them?"

Todd shrugged. "Maybe. Who knows. Maybe no one else on the Hill knows about them, and they'll never hear that I met with you. Maybe they don't even know I know about them."

Adam nodded. "You're right." He smiled. "That's how I know I'm getting somewhere in an investigation."

"How?" Todd asked, his brow furrowing.

"When people start getting worried. And start making mistakes."

CHAPTER EIGHTEEN

SAM FINISHED CHEWING before asking, "So your captain didn't have a problem, did he?"

Ramona wiped the pizza grease off her hands. "Nah. He's cool. Passed on the complaint, like he has to. He gets why MPDC has to be involved. He wants me to keep digging." She picked up her slice of pepperoni and took another bite. Grease pooled on the paper plate in front of her.

"Good." Sam looked around. "Kaminski should be here soon. He said he'd meet us."

Ramona shrugged. "Probably still finding his way around."

They sat in a booth toward the back of the narrow pizzeria. The counter that ran along the other wall stopped a few feet short of where they sat, and the booth behind theirs was unoccupied. With only the doors to the restrooms and utility closet near their table, it was a good place for a private conversation.

Sam watched Ramona dig into her slice and smiled. Her appetite, the smell of pepperoni, garlic, and dough, the clank of pizza oven doors opening and closing… it all brought back memories of the many evenings he had spent on patrol with Ramona's father. Learning everything he could from the older man.

He had just turned his attention back to his own dinner when he felt a hand on his shoulder. Adam slid into the booth next to him, the weight of his large frame shifting the cushion underneath him.

"Adam, glad you could make it." Sam slid over to make room. "I figured it made sense for us all to touch base, see where we are. Ramona was filling me in on your meeting with McFellan today."

"Great." Adam smiled at Sam, then stood, barely glancing at Ramona. "I'll grab a coupla slices and join you."

Ramona watched him walk away, her face a mask.

"So tell me," Sam nudged her.

By the time Adam came back with his pizza, Ramona was wrapping up the story. She paused, glancing at Adam. A tentative smile touched her lips, then fled as Adam looked away. Adam focused on his dinner while Ramona finished her report.

Sam knew she had given him all the details of their interview, including their exit interview with McFellan's lawyer. But she'd definitely left something out. The story she'd shared shed no light on what was causing the tension between her and Adam.

"I spoke to the Kapoors," Adam said, then took a bite of his first slice.

Sam nodded, waiting for Adam to finish chewing. "How are they holding up?"

"Like you'd expect. They need answers, I don't have any yet." Adam looked across the table at Ramona, the first time they'd made eye contact. "How about you, did your captain really give you grief 'cause of that lawyer?"

Ramona shook her head as she took a sip from her paper cup.

"So what do we know?" Sam looked at his friends. "I got some stuff on Marshall — the mister, I mean. A lot of it I think you already know. She ran on his money, seems to rely on his ideas."

"I still think there might be more there," Ramona said, frowning. "Just because they agree on stuff doesn't mean she's blindly following him."

"Okay, you're right." Sam held up his hand. "I won't rule anything out."

"Any problems in their past?" Adam interrupted them.

Sam frowned, surprised. "She's a politician. So, yeah, definitely." He ran his hand along his chin as he thought about what he'd learned over the past two days. "Let's see, there were accusations of corruption, but that's not unusual and they came to nothing. There's always a lot of muckraking in any campaign." He stared at Adam for a moment, thinking. "They lost a child. That's bound to have some effect on their behavior. Their outlook on life."

"No kidding." Adam frowned and looked like he was going to say more, then shut his mouth.

Sam waited, then added, "It almost derailed her political career. She announced her retirement from City Council right after."

"The people spoke," Ramona said.

"She was already popular with the voters, and this made her even more human. The way she handled it, the way she and her husband stood together as a family despite the tragedy." Sam shrugged. "She accepted their support, thanked them for their condolences. And she kept working. Her career really picked up after that."

Sam glanced at Adam, and watched as his eyelids dropped, his eyes darkened, his lips pulled tight. "Sorry, man. You okay?"

Adam gave one nod, his attention apparently focused on a spot across the restaurant. "Bugs me, that's all."

Sam and Ramona looked at Adam, then exchanged glances. "What's bugging you, Kaminski?" Ramona asked the question.

"It hits too close to home, that's all." Adam shrugged and dragged his eyes back to his friends at the table. "I lost some kids once. In a drive-by." The muscles in his cheek moved as he talked, his jaw tight. "They never caught the guy."

"Your kids?" Ramona asked in whisper.

Adam moved his head to one side. "My students. I was a teacher then."

"Ah." Ramona smiled and bit into her last slice as if trying to cover it up.

Sam toyed with his napkin, waiting for Adam to get his control back.

Before Sam could speak, Ramona spoke again. "And here I thought you became a cop for the thrills."

Sam sat up straight, expecting Adam to respond with anger. His response was quiet, a simple question. "Why'd you think that?"

Ramona shrugged. "I guess it's a stereotype. God knows I'm the last person who should be falling for those." She raised an eyebrow as she looked at Adam.

"What kind of stereotype?"

"You know, the tough guy, the kind of guy who likes to have a woman on the side. I guess I jumped to conclusions."

Sam cringed, but Adam said nothing more, only frowned.

"We need to know more about Ambassador Saint-Amand," Sam jumped in before Ramona could say anything else. "We've got the background on Lisa Marshall, but there's too much we don't know about Saint-Amand. And I should be able to dig something up fairly easily."

"Sounds good. I want to learn a little more about our friend Towne, too."

"Towne?" Adam's eyes wrinkled with the question. "You taking him seriously as a suspect?"

Ramona shrugged. "His name keeps coming up. It seems he was a regular at the senator's offices. I'll see what I can find on him."

"Good." Sam slapped his hands on the table. "That's it for me tonight, then. I gotta get home. Call the kids. Kiss my wife."

He grinned widely at Adam, who slid out of the way.

"Take care, you two," he said as he turned away. Then throwing a significant glance at Ramona, he added, "Don't do anything I wouldn't do."

Ramona laughed as Adam slid back into his seat, grabbing his paper cup and draining it.

Sam paused in the doorway, turning back to watch Ramona and Adam before heading out. Ramona's hands played with her napkin as she looked at Adam. "You know, up to now I would have said that reading people was one of my strongest skills, Detective."

"Best skill a cop can have."

Her lips turned up into a fraction of a grin. "So why can't I get a good read on you? I seem to keep getting you wrong."

Adam smiled back at her, running his hand across his face as he did so, then stood. "I gotta go, too. I got a call to make."

Sam stepped out onto the sidewalk, his hands in his pockets, a frown on his face. He hoped he hadn't made a mistake pairing those two up together.

SYLVIA'S VOICE came on the line after only three rings. She never answered his calls that fast, so Adam wasn't surprised to hear the familiar message.

He waited for the beep before he spoke. "It's me honey, calling to say I love you. Give me a call if you get in at a reasonable time tonight."

He tapped the screen to end the call, then tossed the phone next to him on the worn bedcover. With a grunt, he adjusted the pillows behind him and sat back, staring at the wall across the room. A bland image of beige, white, and red swaths of paint hung on the wall, covering faded wallpaper.

The pain in his gut returned, and he shifted on the bed, trying to get comfortable. "Should never eat pizza late at night," he chided himself, though he knew it wasn't the food that was bothering him.

He shifted his eyes, staring at the dark phone next to him, running the day's events over in his mind.

His meeting with Towne. That was a man on a mission, and fanatics could be dangerous if they lost sight of their ethics in pursuit of their goal. But killing Senator Marshall didn't serve Towne's purposes. Unless there was something else he wasn't sharing.

He thought about McFellan, but his mind kept seeing Ramona — standing down the assistant, smiling sweetly at the lawyer.

Adam shifted on the bed again and picked up the phone. He tapped the screen to life, willing it to ring.

Ambassador Saint-Amand's staff was another angle. Maybe Hennessy was right on that, maybe this was all a drug deal gone wrong. That had definite promise. And meant he'd be heading back to Sylvia sooner rather than later.

He touched his phone again. No message from Sylvia. With a frown, he dialed a new number.

"Hello?" Julia's voice was soft, pleasant.

Adam smiled into the phone. "Hey, sis, how's it going?"

"Adam." He could hear her answering smile in her voice, picture her eyes wrinkling up in pleasure. "How you doing? Where are you?"

"Back at my hotel. It's been a long day. The case is getting kind of interesting, though."

Julia took a deep breath. "I hope so, interesting enough to make it worth focusing on death."

"I know, I'm sorry. I won't burden you with the details. It is sad." Adam's brow lowered as he nodded. "I'm on a good team here. Some smart people. We'll figure it out."

There was a pause on the other end of the line, and he heard the sounds of running water, then the click of a gas range coming on. "You at home?"

"Yep," Julia answered. "Just putting on some water for tea. Want some?"

He laughed. "That sounds great. Wish I could come over." He pictured her in her loft apartment, the kitchen open to the living room, steps up to the raised bedroom beyond. Not large, but open and airy. And filled with images, with paintings from Julia's days at art school, with work given to her by friends trying to make a living as sculptors and painters, and with Julia's own photographs, hanging on her own walls while waiting patiently for a chance to hang on a studio wall.

Some of her work had sold. Not at great prices, but she was slowly building a name for herself in the art community in Philly and New York. Slowly. Until then, she filled in the gaps with jobs doing weddings and parties. And with the occasional loan from her big brother.

He heard a shuffle as the phone moved against her shoulder and he could imagine her brushing her strawberry blond hair back off her face, pulling it to the other side of her neck.

"How's your work going?"

"Mmm, okay." A spoon clinked against a ceramic mug. "I have a wedding this weekend, so that's good."

"Heard anything from Woodley's yet?" Adam asked about a local gallery that had hinted at some interest in carrying her photographs.

"Not yet, but it's early days. They're planning their winter showcase now."

Adam nodded to himself, impressed as always with her optimism.

"All right, then, just wanted to check in. Make sure you're okay."

"How's Sylvia?" Julia's question was quiet, simple. Adam knew what it implied.

"She's fine. I spoke to her yesterday. She's busy with work, that's all."

"Uh-huh."

Whenever Adam felt the urge to advise Julia about her choice of career, he remembered her opinions of his choice of women. And kept his mouth shut. He didn't want to start that conversation again.

"Okay. Take care of yourself."

"You, too, Adam. Stay safe."

Adam hung up and looked back at the mass-produced image hanging on his wall, wishing it was Julia's photograph. Julia's photograph of him and Sylvia at the flower show this past spring.

Wishing it was Sylvia.

CHAPTER NINETEEN

THE ANGLE OF THE SUN turned the windows into mirrors, revealing nothing from inside the apartment. Adam shifted on the bench and turned his head. It didn't help. He counted the windows up from the bottom, fairly certain he was looking at Jay's bedroom windows.

It was two days since Jay had died. He wondered if Todd had started looking for a new roommate yet.

Ramona nudged him as she sat next to him on the bench. "Here." She handed him a paper cup of coffee. "I didn't know how you liked it, but I figured you for a cream and sugar type of guy."

He smiled as he took the cup. "You figured right, thanks."

"Finally." Her smile grew, then she turned her eyes to see what he had been looking at. "Jay's apartment?"

"Yep." He took a tentative sip, then a bigger one. He looked around Dupont Circle. Every bench was taken, with business men and women sipping coffee and looking at their phones, students in groups, or solitary figures reading, listening to music, talking on phones. Pedestrians filled the paths, moving quickly around the fountain in the center of the square as skateboarders took over one side path. A tall black man in a leather jacket stood on the far side of the fountain, flipping through a magazine. "Busy area," he commented.

"Mm-hmm." Ramona nodded as she sipped her coffee. Adam wondered how she took hers, but didn't ask. "This is a great neighborhood," she said after she had swallowed. "Center of town, close to everything, a Metro stop." She looked around as she spoke. "Restaurants… cafes… bars." She frowned. "Pretty good location for an aide."

"No kidding. Todd said Jay always had extra money on hand. Though he wasn't always willing to use it to pay the rent."

A skateboarder came within arm's reach of them. Adam felt the wind as the boy zipped by.

Ramona stood, wiping off the legs of her brown suit with her free hand. "Come on, let's walk."

Adam followed as she led the way north out of Dupont Circle toward Connecticut Avenue. "This is the way to the ambassador's residence, isn't it?"

"A little farther up, to the west. Not too far, really. Walking distance."

Adam considered this as he sipped the last of his coffee. "And how far is Adams Morgan?"

Ramona looked sideways at him. "Adams Morgan? It's up there"— she gestured with her coffee cup. "Farther up, off to the east a bit. Why do you ask?"

"Something Todd said last night." He glanced at Ramona and caught her eye, then looked away. "Todd said Jay used to meet sometimes with a couple of shady characters on a street corner in Adams Morgan."

Ramona frowned and raised her eyebrows. "Hmm. That doesn't sound good. Did Todd know why?"

"Uh-uh." Adam shook his head. "Just that he knew they met a few times. I'd like to know more about that."

"I can see if I can find anything, but I'm not sure where to start on that one." Ramona stepped to the side, around a young woman walking the other way, to toss her empty cup into a trash can. Adam watched the way her suit jacket clung to her body, pulled tight around her hips. She turned and caught him looking.

"You're not in uniform again today," he said.

She shrugged. "Figured we'd do better if I was a little less conspicuous, you know?"

Adam smiled. "So did you find anything more on our friend Towne?"

"I did, actually." Adam caught the white glint of Ramona's teeth as she flashed a smile. "He doesn't have an alibi for the murder. And he has a licensed firearm."

"Towne?" Adam asked, confused. "He definitely didn't strike me as the type. And I thought he was working that morning."

"He was. He was also late. I checked with his department chair. They had a staff meeting, he showed up about halfway through. And that's not typical for him, either." She pointed with her chin. "Up there, to the right. That would take us up to Adams Morgan. A few blocks up."

Adam looked the way she indicated. Store fronts lined the street, little shops with awnings and A-frame signs. Stores selling books and beads, gourmet coffee makers and scented candles. He caught a whiff of incense from one as they passed close, and knew it was only being burned to block other, less legal smells.

"Huh. That's interesting. You know, I spoke to the senator's scheduler earlier. I have an appointment with the senator later this morning."

"Sure."

"I asked her about Towne. Since Todd mentioned the man practically camped out in front of the senator's office."

Ramona stepped sideways to avoid a young man running past them, racing for a bus that was pulling away from the curb. Adam grabbed her arm as she moved past him, then dropped it.

"Thanks." She smiled up at him. "So did you learn anything else about Towne?"

"He was pretty insistent on seeing the senator. Before she left for Philly." Adam answered Ramona but his eyes were still on the tall man in the leather jacket, who had turned to walk up the street toward Adams Morgan. The same man who had been in Dupont Circle earlier. He shook his head. It was a coincidence, surely. He turned back to Ramona.

"Hmm. Now that's interesting." Ramona narrowed her eyes as she considered this information. "Had he managed to schedule a meeting with her?"

"Nope. The scheduler said the senator's calendar was booked, there was nothing she could do."

"And I assume Towne didn't take that too well." Ramona's lips narrowed into a tight line.

"You assume correctly. She said Towne kept insisting he had to see her — before she left town. He finally said if she couldn't help him, he'd find another way to see the senator."

"That's even more interesting."

"It doesn't place him at the scene," Adam pointed out.

"No, that's true." Ramona frowned, furrowing her brow. "I can check it out. I wanted to meet this Elise anyway, you know?"

"Good." Adam tossed his empty cup into a trash can as they waited at the corner for the light to change. "I want to get your take on her, too, see if you can pick up anything else about her."

"If Towne was there, he wasn't alone," Ramona added.

"How do you mean?"

"Well, Sam said the upstairs maid — Beth?" Adam nodded, and Ramona continued, "If Beth stepped out to meet with a young man, I seriously doubt it was Greg Towne."

Adam laughed. "No, you're right about that. I don't see him romancing the help."

Ramona grinned. "So we know there was someone there to see Beth. And we know Elise is hiding something, or someone, else."

"If that someone else is Towne, then he was one of only two unknown men at the residence that morning," Adam finished her thought.

She stopped walking to look up at him. "So I'll stop back at the residence, then. I know Sam is planning to meet you up on the Hill later—" She cut herself off, following Adam's eyes.

A black SUV had pulled up to the curb a few feet ahead of them. Adam watched as two men in navy blue suits got out, one from the front passenger side, the other from the back. The driver stayed in the car.

"Detective Kaminski?" one of the suits asked.

Adam nodded.

"Got a sec?" The man smiled, but Adam was quite sure this wasn't a friendly invitation.

He glanced at Ramona, who stepped back. "We'll catch up later," she said as she turned away.

Adam followed the two men into the SUV.

"THANKS FOR JOINING US, Detective Kaminski." The younger of the two agents, seated next to Adam, spoke first. The driver hadn't turned around when Adam slid into the back seat.

"I didn't get the impression I had much of a choice." Adam kept his voice low, hiding his irritation.

"Well" — the young agent grinned — "we wanted to touch base, that's all. I'm Special Agent Fitzpatrick, that's Special Agent Liu. FBI."

Liu turned around in the front seat. His black eyes blinked, but he didn't smile. Or speak. He stared at Adam.

"And what can I do for you, gentlemen?" Adam smiled.

"We wanted to hear how you were doing. And how much longer you'll be in town."

Adam shrugged. "I don't know. Is there anything you know that would affect my schedule?" He raised an eyebrow as he asked the question.

Fitzpatrick smiled, and Adam realized how young he really was. Practically a boy himself. An armed boy, he reminded himself.

"Look, I'm still looking into Jay Kapoor." When the young man didn't respond, Adam added, "The dead man? I'm meeting up with Sam Burke, Diplomatic Security, later this morning, over at Jay's office."

"You mean Senator Marshall's office?" Fitzpatrick asked the question, but Liu turned and glared at Adam again.

"Yes, Senator Marshall's office," Adam answered slowly, nodding. "Do you have a problem with that?"

Fitzpatrick turned his lips down as he shrugged. "We're getting the impression, Detective, that you're not showing a whole lot of respect for the process, for the way we handle things here." He raised an eyebrow at Adam. "Are you?"

"What are you talking about?"

"We got a call from Ambassador Saint-Amand. It seems you were in his house. Talking to his staff. Without his permission."

So that's what this was about. Turf. And maybe international relations, he had to admit, since he had technically conducted an investigation on foreign soil without permission. Adam shifted in his seat as he glanced first at Fitzpatrick, then at Liu, then back to Fitzpatrick.

Fitzpatrick grinned. "I take your silence as admission, Detective."

"Okay, I was there." Adam nodded. "Now what happens?"

"Nothing. Yet," Fitzpatrick answered, but Liu snorted as Fitzpatrick spoke, making his disdain for the situation clear. Fitzpatrick glanced at Liu and grinned, then continued, "Apparently the ambassador doesn't want to make an international scene out of this. Yet."

He looked away from Adam, his attention on the

pedestrians swarming along the sidewalk, moving to and from Dupont Circle. "He seems to like you, Detective. Though I can't imagine why."

Adam let his breath out. "That's good. I'll bear that in mind."

"That's not good, Detective. We don't think there's a lot you can add to this investigation." Fitzpatrick turned back to face Adam and smiled broadly. "Especially if you're going to run roughshod over the law. We appreciate you coming down, but perhaps it would be better if you wrapped things up here and headed back to Philadelphia."

Adam looked at the man sitting next to him. Young. Bold. Cocksure of himself. Adam grinned. "I'm here on the instructions of my deputy commissioner, at the request of the DC police commissioner. I'm here to help, and I'll share whatever information I can with you, but I'm not leaving until I have an answer for two grieving parents."

Fitzpatrick grinned at this. "Of course, we're happy to hear any information you have." The way he spoke made it very clear he didn't expect Adam to be able to provide them with anything they didn't already know.

Adam simply nodded, but Fitzpatrick wasn't done yet. "I think Special Agent in Charge Hennessy is going to have a conversation with your deputy commissioner, Detective. Just to make sure he still wants you down here."

Adam bit his lip and his eyes narrowed. "You do what you have to do." He pushed the car door open and stepped out into the traffic lane. A Volkswagen swerved to avoid him, its tires squealing. Adam looked back at the three agents in the car and slammed the door.

CHAPTER TWENTY

SAM SHIFTED HIS WEIGHT, leaning back against the low stone wall. The white dome of the Capitol loomed behind him, but he kept his back to it, ignoring the flow of visitors who passed him heading in that direction.

To his right, the tip of the Washington Monument peeked over the top of the trees lining Constitution Avenue. If he turned left, he could follow the line of the street moving farther north into the residential area of Capitol Hill.

He checked his watch again, then slid his hand back into his pocket. One of the blue-jacketed armed guards from the Russell Senate Office Building stepped out from the entrance and made his way down the marble steps. His eye caught Sam standing there, and he paused. Even in a suit, a black man hanging on a street corner still managed to draw attention. Sam shook his head and looked back toward the Mall.

When he glanced back at the building, the guard had moved on. Adam was coming down the street toward him, along Delaware Avenue from Union Station.

Sam pushed himself up. When the light changed, he jogged across the street to meet Adam at the bottom of the steps. "You're late."

"Sorry about that." Adam followed Sam through the thick double doors of the building's main entrance as he answered, "Ramona's back at the ambassador's residence, talking to the staff again. We think Towne may have been at the residence that morning after all." He cut himself off as they approached the guard's station and showed their IDs.

The oldest of the Senate offices, the Russell Senate Office Building opened up before them into long hallways running the length of the building and surrounding an internal courtyard. Sam had been here before for other meetings and he led Adam through a maze of side hallways to a staircase.

"I've known Ramona for a long time now, you know?" He looked back at Adam, following him up the stairs. "Her dad was my partner. And my mentor. In MPDC."

"Yeah, she mentioned that. Good guy, huh?"

"The best. I still go to him when I need help. Or guidance." Sam glanced at a directional panel then turned left. "I talked to him yesterday, to see if he can find us anything on the ambassador's staff."

Adam frowned. "Good thinking. I'm sure he'll keep Ramona in the loop."

Sam grinned. "Those two are like peas in a pod. Even if they didn't look alike, you'd know she was a second version of him, I'll tell you. She's a great cop, like he was. And a strong woman." He stopped walking and turned back to Adam. "She's important to me, you see? I'm responsible for seeing that she's okay, and I take that seriously."

Adam stopped short, a step away from Sam. "What are you trying to tell me, Sam?"

"Just to be careful of her, that's all. Look" — he looked up and down the hallway, then back at Adam — "I don't know what's going on between you two, and I don't care. Don't let it interfere with the job. And don't let it put her at risk. That's all."

Adam smiled. "I'm one hundred percent focused on the job, Sam. And I'm too old to be taking any risks.

You don't need to worry about her, I promise."

"Hmm," Sam grunted as he turned toward the senator's suite.

The oak door off the main hallway opened into an old office that now served as the entrance to a warren of connected rooms running along the side of the building. The original layout for this building had included two offices for every senator, but these had long since been redesigned and connected, creating suites with series of work spaces, each opening off the other.

A young woman sat at a paper-strewn desk against the far wall. Her pale, peaked face was surrounded by a wave of light, almost white, hair. Behind her, a row of windows looked down over Delaware Ave. She looked up as they entered. "May I help you?"

"Detective Adam Kaminski, here to see Senator Marshall. She's expecting me."

The young woman shifted some papers on her desk to reveal an oversized calendar. "Detective Kaminski, yes, you're on her schedule. And you are?" She looked expectantly at Sam.

"Sam Burke, Diplomatic Security. We're working with the FBI on Mr. Kapoor's murder."

"Oh." The woman frowned and shifted more papers across her desk. "I'm not sure, Mr. Burke. Are you also a constituent of the senator's?"

"A constituent?" Sam grinned. "I'm an investigating officer, ma'am. We're here as part of that investigation."

"I'm sorry." She shrugged, though she didn't look particularly apologetic. "The senator agreed to see Detective Kaminski because he is a constituent and it was at the request of the Kapoors, themselves prominent constituents."

"And donors, right?" Sam's grin had hardened. "Look, don't trouble yourself. I'll wait while Detective Kaminski speaks with the senator. How's that?"

The young woman smiled and stood from her desk. "Then you can follow me, sir."

Adam glanced back at Sam as he followed the woman through one of the doors to the right. Sam shook his head, eyebrows raised. Adam nodded and kept walking.

Walking over to the window, Sam glanced down at the park across the street. The cherry blossoms had long since faded, the leaves on the trees now a dark green. He turned back to the space in front of him. He wasn't about to poke through anyone's desk, he knew better than that, but he saw no reason not to look around. He headed out through one of the doors to the left.

"WITH HIS ATTITUDE toward immigration, I'm surprised no one has taken a shot at him before now." Senator Marshall smiled sweetly as she spoke, one hand resting gracefully on her lap, the other holding a small china cup. She took a sip of the coffee, then replaced the cup on the low, round table in front of her.

Sitting across from her in her office in a matching leather armchair, Adam frowned. "So you're fairly confident Ambassador Saint-Amand was the intended target, then?"

Lisa Marshall's smile faded, her bright red lips puckering, the creases in her forehead sparkling slightly from overly applied powder. "I suppose that must be it. Cold comfort to the Kapoors. I feel so badly for them, I really do."

Adam nodded, doubting her sincerity more with every word. "Losing a son is never good, whether he was an innocent bystander who got in the way or if the killer was aiming for him." Adam was about to say more, but the expression on the senator's face stopped him cold.

"Don't." She shook her head, one time, very slightly.

"Senator?"

Her face was a mask. A parody of the lies parents tell their children to stop them from making funny faces. As if she had tried to stop herself from frowning, then froze halfway through. "Don't talk to me about losing a child,

Detective." The words forced their way through her tight lips.

"Senator, I'm so sorry. I didn't mean…" There was nothing more Adam could add to that. He stopped talking.

She sat and stared at him. Adam could only imagine the turmoil going on inside her. If it was there, she covered it up. Nothing of her inner struggle showed through the mask her features had become.

A cloud passed over the window, dimming the light for a moment. A phone somewhere rang, ignored. Lisa Marshall sat still.

Then everything changed. As if someone had snapped their fingers or a veil dropped, her muscles released. She reached a steady hand out and took another sip of her coffee. "I don't believe Jay was the intended target. Not Jay. Absolutely not."

Adam pretended to ignore the transformation he'd just seen. "And how about you, ma'am? How can you be sure the shooter wasn't aiming at you?"

Senator Marshall smiled, as if completely relaxed. "I'm a politician, Detective. If someone doesn't like me, he can always vote me out of office."

"If he's your constituent, that is," Adam said. "I have noticed you're not quite as accessible to people from outside your legislative district." He pulled his lips into a tight smile.

"Well, of course, I focus on the interests of my constituents. That is what I'm paid to do, you know."

"And you'll be leaving office at the end of this year, I understand?"

"Yes, that's right." She was still smiling, replacing the cup. "I have an offer from Barton McFellan. An opportunity for me to get more closely involved in the issues that are most important to me, without getting bogged down in all the rest of the legislative calendar, as I do now."

Adam realized she was treating this interview exactly

as she would an interview with a local journalist. Everything was on the record. And nothing could be taken as truth.

"Tell me about Jason McFellan," he asked. "I understand he was there that morning, as well. Was he on the trip to Philadelphia?"

"Jason? Oh, no. He rarely chooses to leave DC. Except of course to go to Maryland, for social reasons." She smiled again, nodding. "He did join us for breakfast, however. I think he saw it as an opportunity to get to know me a little better, in a casual setting. Getting to know John as well."

"What was your husband's role going to be while you were in Philadelphia? Was he just along for the ride?"

"Hah." This was the first time she had shown true amusement. A real laugh. "As if he could offer any other assistance."

"Your husband?" Adam let his confusion show through.

She shrugged. "My husband. McFellan." She shrugged. "Any of them."

"So McFellan was there to have breakfast. And to talk with Ambassador Saint-Amand?"

"I suppose. It's always good to know the right people."

Adam put his head on the side, his brow furrowing. "What is the ambassador the right person for, Senator?"

"Well…" She spread her hands wide. "As I said earlier, he's involved in a lot of things. Not much that would interest Barton McFellan, I did tell Jason that. But" — she exhaled deeply — "he insisted on coming. Thought it would be quite a treat, apparently."

"What kind of things?" Adam repeated patiently.

"Immigration reform. The drug war. You know how it is. He wants his country to take a firm line, as we have. To root out the problem before it gets worse. And, as I said, he's made a lot of enemies in the process."

Adam nodded, sipping his own coffee. It was

lukewarm, without sugar. He grimaced and replaced the cup on the coffee table. Senator Marshall's office was easily three times the size of the linked offices leading up to it, offices Miranda had led him through on their way here. One wall held a row of windows looking out onto the small park across Delaware Avenue. Adam could see dark green leaves moving in the breeze. The main door was behind him but another door stood to his left. He wondered where that led. A secret escape route, perhaps. He grinned to himself, and Senator Marshall frowned.

"Tell me about Jay, ma'am," he said. "Was he working on anything that involved the ambassador?"

"No." She shook her head. "Jay served as my Director of Constituent Services. He worked with Pennsylvanians who came to me for help or support."

"Did he spend most of his time in your Philadelphia office, then?"

"No, he was based here. I have two other aides who work at the Philadelphia office. They report to Jay—" She grimaced. "Sorry, I should say reported. They reported to Jay, who managed all constituent relations for me."

"And you were happy with his work?"

"Absolutely. He was a good worker, a good man. He had a very promising future, Jay Kapoor." She shook her head as she shifted in her seat. "This is a tragic loss."

"I am sorry to have to make you think about it, Senator."

"No, no, not at all. I've been getting some wonderful support from my constituents. It's been heartwarming." She smiled. "It's even made me reconsider my retirement from public service."

"It was a very close call for you, too, Senator. I know how scary that is."

"Do you, Detective?" She smiled wider, her ruby lips glimmering. "I suppose in your line of work, you do. Yes, indeed, I think people appreciate how difficult this has been for me."

"Can you tell me anything more about what Jay was working on?" Adam leaned forward as he asked the question.

Senator Marshall shifted back in her chair. "I don't understand why you're asking, Detective. As I said, I'm sure the killer intended to shoot Alain Saint-Amand, not Jay. You really need to assure the Kapoors of that."

"We don't want them thinking that working for you got him killed, is that it?"

Senator Marshall's face sharpened. "What a horrible thing to say, Detective." She stood. "I believe you are done here."

"I'd like to take a look at Jay's work area, if you don't mind."

She frowned, so Adam continued, "The Kapoors specifically asked me to offer them some insight into Jay's work here."

She picked up her phone. She didn't speak, but within a few seconds the young blond woman was back in the office.

"Miranda, please show Detective Kaminski to Jay's desk. He'd like to look at some of Jay's work." Her displeasure was evident in the tone of her voice, but Adam would take what he could get. "Don't let him simply poke around, though."

"Of course, Madame Senator." Miranda gestured to Adam to follow her.

Adam turned back to the senator. "Ma'am, was there anyone else there that morning that you're aware of?"

"What do you mean? You have all the reports, you know who was there."

"I've gotten unsubstantiated statements from two witnesses that there was at least one other person at the residence that morning. Maybe two. I'd like to know if you're aware of that."

"I... well" — a frown flitted across her face, quickly replaced with the stock smile Adam was beginning to recognize — "I can't help you there, Detective, I couldn't confirm anything like that."

"There was someone else there, is that what you're saying? Someone you can't confirm?" Adam stepped forward and Miranda took a step after him. Adam stopped and glanced back at her. Did she think he was about to attack the senator? And would she throw herself in between them if he did? He smiled and looked at the senator.

"I'm not in the business of spreading rumors, Detective." Senator Marshall stepped behind her desk, her back to the windows. "If there was anyone else there that morning who is not included in the FBI reports, I cannot confirm that. And I will not speculate to please you."

Adam felt a light touch on his arm, then Miranda jerked her hand back. She looked nervous, uncertain. Adam smiled at her, thanked the senator for her time, and followed Miranda out to Jay's desk.

SAM FOUND his way back to Jay Kapoor's work area in time to see the blond woman they had met earlier stepping between Adam and Jay's desk, sliding a sheaf of papers into an open drawer.

Adam glanced up, saw Sam, and smiled. "Hey, Sam, just looking around." He glanced at the woman and winked. "Not too much though, right, Miranda?"

"Is it okay for us to look through here, do we have permission?" Sam addressed his question to Miranda.

"Yes, the senator approved this. But she specifically told me not to let you simply poke around. Is there anything in particular I can show you?"

Her face pulled even tighter as she spoke, and Sam felt bad for her. Even with her hovering over them, they were bound to come across information the senator wouldn't want them to have. Surely Lisa Marshall knew that. She had set Miranda up with an impossible task.

He leaned on the desk across from Adam, his arms

crossed against his chest. "Tell me what Jay was working on — as much as you can, I mean. I know you can't discuss any personal matters. He did work directly with constituents, right?"

"He was the Director of Constituent Services, yes… we had other staff in Philly and Harrisburg who really worked directly with constituents. Jay more… kind of… oversaw all that." Miranda stepped closer to Sam as she answered, turning her back on Adam, who still stood at the front of Jay's desk.

Adam moved silently, leaning over the desk, reading through everything that was visible, occasionally gently nudging a paper out of the way to read something below it.

"How was he to work with? Can you give me a sense of who he was, what kind of person he was?" Sam asked, smiling at Miranda encouragingly.

"Well… you talked with Todd already, didn't you?"

"That's right, but you might have a different impression than Todd. Did you work closely with Jay?"

"Not really." Miranda shook her head, in the process glancing back at Adam. He stood exactly where she had last seen him, against the desk innocently watching her and Sam speak. She turned back to Sam. "Jay worked more closely with the senator, to be honest. I'm her scheduler, so I report to the Chief of Staff, not directly to the senator."

"Will losing Jay give you an opportunity, then? A chance for promotion?"

Miranda gasped. "That's a horrible thing to say. I would never want Jay to die. And I would never want to get a promotion because someone was killed. Even someone like Jay." At her last sentence, her hand flew up to cover her mouth and she turned her back to Sam, her eyes now on Adam.

"Tell me about Jay." Adam spoke softly. "Don't worry, what you say to us won't be shared with Jay's parents. Or the senator."

Miranda nodded, pulling out the chair next to Jay's desk. She perched on the chair, her elbow resting on the surface of the desk. Adam took the chair behind the desk, presumably Jay's chair, bringing his hazel eyes closer to level with hers. Sam stepped back to let Miranda focus on Adam.

"He knew a lot," Miranda started, then paused.

"A lot about politics?" Adam encouraged her.

"No, no." Her hair seemed to float around her face as she shook her head vigorously. "About people. About our lives. Our private lives." She chewed on her lower lip as she pulled her words together.

She looked up at Adam, her eyes begging him to understand. "He would remember things. Little things, little details. And bring them up again. Months later sometimes. Like… like I had a bad night one night. I got drunk…" She closed her eyes as she spoke. "Spent the night with a guy I hardly knew."

"I'm sure that happens." Adam smiled encouragingly at her.

"Of course, yes. It's just… Jay brought it up again. Months later. Like he thought I owed him something."

"Like what?" Adam asked.

"He needed to get someone in to see the senator. And I asked him" — she stared at Adam, her eyes wide — "Why not go to the senator? You work with her, I said. He smiled… that creepy smile of his. And said he didn't want her to know he was involved." She furrowed her brow. "Which doesn't make any sense at all, because he's the Director of Constituent Services, of course he's involved."

"Who was the person?" Adam asked.

She shook her head. "I never found out. I didn't make the appointment." She shrugged. "I have no idea what Jay was thinking, that bringing up that night would make me want to schedule this appointment."

"And did he ever mention it again?"

"No… no, he didn't. Sandra did."

"Who's Sandra?"

"She's our legislative director. The senator's, I mean. She's on the staff."

"What did Sandra say?"

Miranda shrugged. "Just that I should be careful what I tell Jay. What I let him know. I guess he had been saying some pretty mean things about me, about that night. It didn't matter." She turned her confused eyes back to Adam. "No one cared. It happens. I don't know why he was being so mean about it. Sandra was right. I watched what I said around Jay after that."

CHAPTER TWENTY-ONE

"ANYTHING INTERESTING on his desk?" Sam asked after they had passed the guard's station on their way out of the building.

Adam looked up and down the street before answering. "A few things. He had a collection of letters from constituents, complaints about everything from tax rates to local noise violations."

Sam grinned. "All good things to write to your senator about, right?"

Adam laughed. "He also had some news clippings, looked like he was organizing them into a photo album. Stories about local elections, crimes, crazy hospital fees, break-ins, a hit-and-run, that sort of thing."

"News clippings? Isn't everything online these days?"

"Well, if I wanted to make sure I could put my hand on something when I needed it, maybe years in the future, I'd keep a hard copy. Web pages change, get removed..."

"Even get edited. You're right. So he's stockpiling news. But why?"

"Look, we know from Todd that Jay was involved in some kind of shady dealings—"

"The drugs, right?" Sam interjected.

"Yep, could be." Adam nodded as they crossed the street toward the Capitol grounds. On this beautiful June day the sidewalks teemed with pedestrians, some visitors to the nation's capital, others locals with business on the Hill. "I get the sense he liked to use information. To avoid paying the rent... to get people in to see the senator..."

Sam whistled. "You're talking about blackmail."

Adam shrugged. "That's a dirty word, I know, but if it fits..."

Sam looked up at the Capitol in front of them. "I got a call from Ramona's dad while you were in with the senator."

"Oh, yeah?" Adam asked as his phone started to chirp. He pulled it out of his pocket, glancing at the name of the caller. "Listen, Sam, sorry, I gotta take this."

"I'll see you later, then?" Sam asked, but Adam was turning away, phone to his ear, a deep frown creasing his forehead. He watched as Adam started walking toward the Mall, his pace picking up as he moved.

"CALM DOWN, Julia. Say that again." Adam's feet moved without his control, his steps getting faster as he absorbed what his sister was telling him.

"A break-in, that's all. It's just... I don't know. I was here, you know? Sleeping." Adam could tell Julia was doing her best to stay calm, but even so her voice shook as she described what had happened.

"Where are you now? Are you safe?"

"I'm safe, Adam. I'm here at home, the thief's long gone."

"What's missing?"

"It's... oh."

"Julia—" Adam's voice broke and he took a deep breath, tried to control his thoughts. He needed to help, not freak out. "Talk to me, Julia."

"Some artwork. Some is gone. Some is..." Julia sniffed. "Destroyed."

"He vandalized things? Is that what you're saying?"

Julia took a moment to respond and Adam knew that

she was nodding. "Yes." She was struggling to keep her voice in control. "Ruined them. I can try to fix some, but..." He heard the sound of something hitting the ground over the phone, Julia dropping a piece she had given up for lost. She inhaled sharply, the tears loud in her cry.

He could almost feel her shudder through the phone, and his pace picked up even more as his feet turned into the grounds of the Capitol. "How did they get in?"

"The police said the thief jimmied the front door. I guess the lock wasn't good enough. I guess you were right."

"This isn't about right or wrong, Julia. You were at home, you deserved to be safe. You did nothing wrong, you hear me?"

Silence again, probably Julia nodding again.

"And you didn't hear anything during the night?"

"I did." Julia was crying steadily now and Adam bit his lip. "I did," she continued, "I heard something. I..."

"You're safe, Julia, that's what's important here, don't forget that. Now tell me, what did you hear?"

"A noise, something soft. I woke up, with a feeling, you know?"

"Sure, I know what you mean. Did you check it out?"

"No... I didn't. I sat up. I didn't hear anything else. I convinced myself I was dreaming, imagining it."

"That's probably a good thing, Julia. God knows what could have happened if you'd confronted him."

Julia made another sharp inhale, and Adam regretted having said that.

"And the police are there, right?"

"They were. They came, took my statement, looked around. They said they weren't optimistic, Adam."

"Damn." Adam held the phone away from his mouth for a moment, his jaw working hard. "Okay, I'll call in, see what I can do."

"Adam..."

His steps had continued as they talked, but the tone in

her voice now brought him up short. "What? What else is it?"

"It's just a feeling."

"That's okay, sometimes gut feelings are important."

"When I woke up… I felt…" Julia took a deep breath.

"Go on," Adam encouraged her.

"On my face… I felt it on my face."

Adam gripped the phone tighter. "Felt what?"

"I think he licked me, Adam. I think he licked my face. While I slept."

Adam said nothing. There was nothing he could say. He felt his own breath coming fast, his eyes clouding with rage. He took a deep breath and felt the anger shuddering through him. The helplessness. The same helplessness he knew Julia was feeling, too.

"How could I have slept through that, Adam?" Her voice faded into nothingness.

"Bastard," Adam swore under his breath. A woman passing by turned and gave him a look. He turned away, down the slope of the hill toward the Capitol Reflecting Pool. Blurred lines shaped and reshaped the outline of the Capitol dome as the water in front of him moved in the growing breeze. A symbol of freedom and democracy forming, then breaking apart, then taking shape again, warped and unclear. Then gone again.

He tried to focus on the details of his sister's story, trying to recognize something that would give a clue to the perpetrator. That would keep Julia safe.

"You got the lock fixed?" he asked.

"I called. I'm waiting for the locksmith now."

"Are you alone?"

"No, Danny from next door is here with me."

"Okay, good." Adam took a deep breath. Danny was hardly the man Adam would turn to for help — unreliable, unemployed — but in a pinch, he would do. At least Julia wasn't alone. "Listen," he continued, "I'm gonna call Pete, see if he can come over, take a look around."

"Isn't he in homicide, like you? No one was killed here, Adam." Julia tried to make her voice light, but to Adam her laugh sounded more like a cry.

His little sister was scared. And he was mad.

"Don't worry about that, he'll come over. He'll take care of you." And find the bastard who did this, he thought to himself as he hung up the phone.

Pete answered on the first ring. Adam had stopped walking and was now standing, his eyes staring, unfocused, at the giant statue of Ulysses S. Grant that loomed over the reflecting pool.

"Hey, partner. How's DC?" Although he was speaking as fast as always, Pete's voice was calm, quiet.

Adam took a breath. "I need your help, buddy. It's Julia."

"Okay. She need a loan again?" Adam could hear Peter shuffling papers in the background. He must be sitting at his desk, Adam thought, completing the interminable paperwork owed by every homicide detective.

"Her place was broken into last night. While she was sleeping."

The sounds on Pete's end stopped and Adam could picture him sitting up in his chair. "What happened, tell me."

Adam related everything Julia had told him. The broken lock. The stolen and vandalized artwork. The lick.

"She reported this to the District? I haven't heard anything yet. How valuable were the pieces that were taken?" Adam could hear the scratch of a pen as Pete jotted down the details.

"She's still piecing together what was taken. She didn't exactly keep an inventory of all her works and the gifts from artists she knew."

"I get it..." Pete let his voice draw out, presumably as he jotted the last few notes. "You want me to see who's on the case?"

Adam exhaled. "Yeah, I do. And I want you to work it."

"Buddy, I'm here to help. I'll go over and see her. But you know I can't take over the case."

Adam looked up at the sad, green face of Grant, looking with determination out over the reflecting pool, his back to the legislature, his gaze on the city of Washington, DC. "I know what the rules are, partner, but I'm asking you to do this."

Pete took some time before responding. Adam felt a trickle of sweat pooling in his lower back, and shifted his shoulders, letting the fabric of his shirt rub it away. "Will you watch out for her?" he finally added, when Pete hadn't responded.

"Of course, partner. No problem. I'll take care of it."

"Call me as soon as you know anything more, will you?"

"You got it." Pete's voice was calm again, in control.

Adam dropped the phone back into the inner pocket of his jacket, feeling it weigh his jacket down, destroying the line of the suit. He turned to follow Grant's gaze, looking out over the city. Did he really want to be here, solving the murder of a man he didn't know? Or should he be back at home, taking care of his sister when she really needed him?

He needed to do what he could, offer what help he could, then get out and get home. He turned back to Constitution Avenue and the nearest bus stop.

CHAPTER TWENTY-TWO

"PARDON ME." The elegantly dressed man gave a curt nod, but kept walking.

He hated the crowds. Hated having to rub shoulders with people like this. Messy. Ignorant. Tourists.

He walked quickly, pushing his way past slow-moving tour groups and families pulling crying children, quivering with disgust when he accidentally brushed up against one of them.

Another fat man in stained sweatpants rubbed up against him. He shuddered and stepped to his right, barely avoiding tripping up a tour guide who was walking backwards as she led a group toward the rotunda.

He pulled the red silk handkerchief out of his breast pocket and dabbed at his forehead. It was the tourists making him hot. It must be. He stuffed the handkerchief back in his pocket. A second later he pulled it out again, folded it, and placed it back as it should be, its tip protruding from the top of the pocket.

He took another shallow breath. It was too hot in here. Too crowded. Not enough air. Damn these nobodies, breathing his air.

They do nothing, only come and watch the people who have real power. He glared around the room as he strode through it, shifting his eyes if anyone made eye contact.

Not him, of course, he corrected himself, glancing side to side as if nervous someone had heard his thought. No, no, not him. Her. The love of his life was the powerful one, not him. He respected her for that. Loved her for that.

He would never challenge that.

Would he?

He kept a light tattoo going on his pants pocket with his fingers, waiting for the vibration that meant she was ready for him. Ahead, a marble railing ran at waist height, enclosing a circular opening. He stepped forward to look down into it. Tourists below stared back up at him. He grimaced and stepped back.

He had reached his destination. Her designated rendezvous site. There was nothing he could do now but wait for her. He turned, his eyes darting from tourist to artwork to tour guide to child, never landing long enough to make an impression. To make a connection.

Giant oil portraits stared down at him from each wall. No matter which direction he turned, he came face to face with images of dark streets, marble domes, stone and brick cathedrals.

The aged paintings were a mockery of the city that existed today just outside these walls. This was no Roman capital, filled with wise men honestly debating the merits of government, working to improve the lot of the people.

Hah. That's a laugh.

This city — his city — was a town of dealmakers and deal breakers. Of bankers, lobbyists, and money launderers. The kind of place where you needed someone to watch out for you. Someone who knew how to work the system. Someone powerful.

He pulled the handkerchief out of his pocket again without realizing he was doing it, dabbing at the beads of sweat that pooled once again on his forehead and at the back of his neck.

He had paid an exorbitant price for his silk suit. Its

thin, gentle folds lay elegantly against his muscular frame. Silk was beautiful, but still so hot.

Why wasn't it cooler in here? Didn't they know the people who were supposed to be here, the ones who belonged, were dressed in suits and ties? Who cares if a stupid tourist gets a little cold?

He folded his handkerchief carefully. Slid it back into place in his pocket.

He wasn't nervous, he told himself. He had no reason to be.

He had taken steps to save a piece of the past. To hide it. He should have trusted her, trusted his love for her. God knew she was always right. She'd be proud of him when she found out, right? It didn't hurt to have some memento.

He laughed out loud as he recognized the absurdity of that thought. A passing child stopped in surprise, put his hand up to take his mother's. He raised a lip in a snarl at the child, and it hurried on.

He shook his head and turned back to the railing. Leaning on it heavily, he saw a bead of sweat fall from his face, launching itself into the space below to land on some hapless tourist.

She was never happy. Especially when he made his own decisions. Took initiative. That's not what she wanted. He stood. He legs were shaking, his hands gripping the railing as if holding on for dear life.

Surely she'll be happy this time. The young aide was just a warm-up. He could be next. He had to be safe. They had to be safe.

He saw her approaching out of the corner of his eye. He stood up straight. Took another shallow breath. Smiled and walked toward her.

CHAPTER TWENTY-THREE

*DEMARCHE TO USEMB PARIS: Immigration ...
industrial espionage suspected ... Update to previous reports on
FR ed system ...*

The subject lines of the cables scrolled across his screen as Sam moved his mouse, scanning the topics for anything that could shed light on this investigation. Something about Saint-Amand would be nice. He grinned to himself as he looked for the cable with the subject, "Alain Guerin Saint-Amand linked to narcotics trafficking."

Not one he was likely to find.

He kept looking. His phone calls that morning had been equally unhelpful. If Saint-Amand or anyone on his staff were involved in something illegal, they were doing a good job running under the federal radar. He hadn't checked with the State Department's Bureau of Intelligence and Research yet, only the law enforcement arm of Diplomatic Security. INR was his next destination, if nothing else turned up.

The chirp of his cell phone brought his mind back to his desk and the office around him. He glanced up at the tiny window as he pulled his phone out of his jacket pocket. The sun hadn't quite made it around to his little portal yet. Blue sky showed clear through the window, just turning that pale shade of turquoise that meant the sun would be pulling into view within the hour.

"Agent Burke," he answered his phone.

"Burke, it's Jackie from the Comms Center. You put out an alert for the name Troy Davis? Well, it came up today."

The legs of Sam's chair screeched against the floor as he stood with force.

Communications technology was still a problem in law enforcement, particularly when it came to federal and local law enforcement agencies sharing information. The problem wasn't the will, it was the technology. To address the problem quickly and cheaply, Sam had simply requisitioned a DC police radio, set up in State's Communication Center. It was a standard practice whenever DS had to work with a local force.

And as he always did whenever his comms was tracking DC police calls, he asked for an alert if any particular names came up. Some because they were wanted. Others because he wanted to keep an eye out for them. Like Troy.

"What's the context?"

"Suspect one of three… chase still underway for other two…" Jackie read off the incoming message, her voice calm. "Probable drug bust." Her voice changed, and Sam knew that this time she was speaking to him in her own words. "Looks like they got the guy, now they're trying to grab his friends. Anacostia. Twenty-fifth and Wagner southeast. You interested in this guy?"

"It's personal, Jackie, thanks for the call." Sam was packing up even as he got off the phone with Jackie, thanking her for the heads-up. He held his breath and counted the seconds as the computer slowly shut down. As he pulled out the hard drive. Spun the combination lock on the filing cabinet.

No way he was going to let Howard's boy down, not without at least trying to help. Not after everything Howard had done for him.

Not willing to wait for an elevator, he took the stairs

down to the underground parking garage three at a time, almost tripping as he turned the last corner. The slam of the door reverberated against the concrete walls as he threw himself into it, out into the vehicle pool parking area.

"Josh, need a car now," he shouted the greeting, checking his watch. Four minutes since Jackie had called. They'd already had Troy in custody at that point. It wouldn't take them long to book him, and then there'd be nothing he could do to help.

"You got it boss, number 10 is fueled up and ready to go."

He held his hands up for the keys, but instead of tossing them, Josh jogged over. "Need to sign for it, you know that."

"Yeah, whatever." Sam scrawled an illegible signature across the bottom of the page and grabbed the keys.

He knew better than to race out of the State garage with tires squealing, rubber burning. He resisted the urge to punch the gas, guiding the car swiftly but carefully through the short maze of the garage out to the C Street entrance. Fingers tapping on the wheel as he waited for the security check. Holding his breath as the security gates lowered into the ground, moving at their usual glacial speed.

Troy was in trouble, that much was clear. He knew Troy was a good kid. He also knew the boy had problems. Knew Ramona and Harold were kidding themselves, blind to Troy's attitude. His hostility. His anger.

That's why he had given Comms Troy's name. Every time he had worked a case with MPDC over the past couple of years, he had given them Troy's name, in case it came in over the radio. In case Troy ran up against the MPDC. Because when that happened, Sam wanted to be there. To help. If he wasn't too late.

He checked the clock on the dash. Six minutes since

he'd got the call from Jackie. He needed to get to Troy while there was still time for him to intervene.

He hit the gas.

ADAM SHUT HIS EYES, frowning. He couldn't get the picture out of his head of someone evil in Julia's apartment while she slept. When he opened his eyes again, Ramona was watching him. He didn't want to bring her in to his troubles. "So tell me how it went this morning at the ambassador's residence."

"Hennessy's confirmed everything Senator Marshall told you about Ambassador Saint-Amand," Ramona started. "He's a big player back in Paris, apparently. Pushing hard for tougher immigration laws and tougher drug laws."

"And not making any friends in the process, I assume."

Ramona nodded her agreement. "Is that what's bugging you? The ambassador's political position?"

Adam tightened his lips and shook his head. "Don't worry about me, focus on the job at hand."

Ramona's brow furrowed but she said nothing. The waiting room at Barton McFellan looked the same as it had the day before. Same plush gray rug, same orange accents on the doors and chairs. Same ghastly art on the walls. Adam thought of Julia and frowned.

Ramona checked the clock on the wall. "How long does it take her to get here?" she mumbled.

"Got here fast enough last time." Adam smiled, remembering the lawyer's anger at them for talking to her client without her. Apparently, McFellan wasn't making the same mistake again today. They were waiting until the lawyer arrived.

"Jay may have been involved in drugs in some way. Probably was. I don't see the connection to the ambassador — or his staff," Adam thought out loud.

Ramona picked up the thread of his thought. "He was

the type to grab opportunities as they presented themselves. Maybe somehow, in Senator Marshall's dealings with the ambassador, Jay picked up a connection he could work."

"Only if the ambassador's crooked, and a complete hypocrite."

Ramona raised an eyebrow and gave Adam a look he couldn't argue with. "Point taken." He smiled. "So Jay gets his drug connection from the ambassador's connection. Now he's got his own link to the stuff the moment it hits the street. If he was working as a low-level middle man, he'd be raking it in."

Ramona's face darkened, her fingers beating out a fast rhythm on the arm of her chair. Adam wondered what she was getting so angry about.

"Then who shot him?" Ramona raised her hands in a gesture of despair. "The ambassador, because he didn't like Jay profiting off his own connections?"

"Or because Jay was blackmailing him," Adam pointed out. "We know Jay liked that particular revenue stream."

"Doesn't make sense." Ramona shook her head. "Saint-Amand was on the driveway with him. He couldn't be the shooter." She stopped, her head to one side. "Unless he paid one of his staff to do it." She shook her head in frustration. "Then why was he so eager to be helpful? He invited you to that cocktail party, encouraged you to be part of the investigation, didn't complain when you interviewed his staff."

"That's a good question. The staff certainly had access that morning. Beth. Or Elise." Adam looked at Ramona. "You spoke with them this morning, do you think that's possible?"

Ramona thought about it, examining the piece of art on the far wall, then shook her head. "No, I don't. I don't know why, it doesn't sit right with me."

"No, me either." Adam nodded. "If someone from that house is involved, there's gotta be something else, something we're missing."

The double glass door at the end of the room opened, and the young assistant who had tried to put them off yesterday came into the room. As he was about to speak, Ramona's phone bleeped. She nodded at Adam, held a finger up to the assistant, and turned her back on both of them, her ear to the phone. "Hello?"

Adam turned to the assistant, who stood gripping a leather notebook in front of his chest. His knuckles turned white as he gripped the notebook even tighter, his eyes on Ramona's retreating back. "Well. I came out here to tell you that Mr. McFellan is ready to see you now. If you're no longer interested…" He let his words fade away, blinking in irritation.

"Let's wait 'til my partner gets off the phone, shall we?" Adam asked in a quiet voice, reclaiming his chair. He sat back and crossed his legs, his right ankle lying across his left knee.

"Hmph." Adam thought the young man's knuckles would crack open from the strain, but he said nothing else.

Ramona turned back to them as she tucked the phone into her jacket pocket.

"Kaminski." She gestured with her head.

"Stay here." Adam held a finger up to the young assistant. "Don't go anywhere, I'll be right back."

He followed Ramona to the other side of the room, where she leaned her head in close to his.

"That was one of Hennessy's men," she explained.

"Are they onto something?"

"They think so. They invited us to meet them back at FBI headquarters. They're planning an activity for this evening."

Adam nodded, then glanced back at the young man waiting impatiently near the double glass doors. "Look, you go meet up with them. I'll handle this interview on my own. We just need to find out if Towne really was there that morning. Maybe McFellan will confirm it if he thinks it will get him off the hook." Adam would take any lead that might get him home faster.

Ramona grinned. "Or if his lawyer thinks it will."

Adam nodded his agreement. "I'll give you a call when I'm done here?"

"Sure." Ramona patted his arm as she passed by him, heading back toward the elevators. "Have fun in there."

Adam walked back to the assistant, his hands in his pockets.

"Are you ready now?" The young man's voice was high and strained.

"Sure, lead the way."

Adam wiped the grin off his face as soon as he turned the corner through the glass doors. The lawyer they had met yesterday stood waiting for him, leaning against the door jamb of McFellan's office, one pointy heel pushing against the wall as if holding it up.

He was not looking forward to this interview.

CHAPTER TWENTY-FOUR

SAM TOOK THE CORNER at speed, this time not caring if his tires cried out. It was sixteen minutes since he'd first gotten the call from Jackie. Even with the siren going, DC traffic was tough to get through. He'd been lucky, managing to work his way across town avoiding the worst of the gridlock.

A squad car stood a block ahead, parked at an angle into the curb. He pulled up behind it and took a breath. Whatever was going on here, he needed to stay calm.

He stepped out of his vehicle, badge in hand.

A door opened on the car in front of him, front passenger side. The driver stayed in the car with the perp. Even with the glare from the afternoon sun, he could see a head in the back seat. Sitting at that familiar awkward angle of a man with his hands cuffed. Troy.

He turned his attention to the uniformed officer walking toward him, hand on his weapon. He held his badge out higher. "Diplomatic Security." His voice sounded loud to his ears in the otherwise quiet of the neighborhood. A dog barked as he spoke, then turned its attention to something else. He heard no other sirens. No sound of a chase. No friendly voices calling to each other over back fences, as he would around Howard's house. "Agent Sam Burke."

As the officer stepped closer, Sam smiled and breathed out. He hadn't realized he was still holding his breath. "Tonado. Good to see you."

"You, too, Burke. Whatcha doing here?" Gerry Tonado smiled in return. "Haven't seen much of you since you moved on to bigger and better things."

Tonado was old school. He'd been in uniform when Sam still worked with MPDC, and looked like he hadn't moved on. Sam knew he'd always enjoyed being a cop. A real cop, on the street, not behind a desk.

He'd grown up on a block not far from Sam's. Knew the dangers and strengths of the District's streets, the ongoing struggle to preserve the neighborhoods, the value of family. Their similar experiences growing up had sealed the friendship that started naturally between the two men.

Tonado's radio spit static into the air, the cop pausing to listen. Sam couldn't make it out from this distance.

"I hear you got someone there who's of interest to me," Sam explained. "Troy Davis."

"Yeah, we got him." He nodded his head in the direction of his squad car. "I recognized the name, too. Though it wasn't you I was expecting to see."

Sam smiled. "Davis would be here in an instant if he knew his boy was in this kind of trouble."

Tonado grinned, leaning back against Sam's car as his radio blared again. This time Sam heard the call, officers returning to the scene. Sam joined him against the car. The sun had already heated the fiberglass and Sam felt it burning through his trouser legs, but he didn't mind the warmth.

"I gotta help Troy. You understand that, right?"

Tonado jerked his head to one side. Half an acknowledgement. "We already called it in."

Sam nodded, looking around. "Where are the others? I heard there were two other perps."

Tonado pointed up the street the way Sam had come. "They ran off, Lewis and Murphy after them." He gestured to his radio with his chin. "Sounds like they got away. They're gonna want to keep Troy, he's the only one left."

Sam looked at his friend, his voice low. "He's Davis' boy. You know Davis. You know this would kill him."

Tonado frowned and turned to see the second squad car crawling toward them. "I don't know, Sam. Chief's never gonna accept this."

Sam grinned and stood, hearing the acceptance in the other man's voice. "You'll think of something, buddy, I know you will. You're doing the right thing."

Tonado pushed up off the car as the other two got close enough to call to him through an open window. Sam recognized one but not the other.

Tonado spoke to the others as he walked beside their car. Sam could just make out a few words... diplomatic security, federal agency. The unknown officer rolled his eyes and glanced back at Sam. Within a minute, he was pulling Troy out from the back of the squad car. Leading him over to Sam.

Sam stood and opened his back door. "You can take the cuffs off, I don't need those."

Troy glanced at him, recognition in his eyes, but he kept his mouth shut. The officer did as requested, leaving Troy in Sam's custody. He shook his head as he walked back to his partner. Sam didn't wait around for them to change their minds.

He glanced at Troy in the rearview mirror as he turned his vehicle around, heading back toward Howard's house.

"Tell me what happened, Troy. The truth."

Troy shrugged, his eyes staring out the window. He didn't speak.

Sam cursed and jerked the wheel to the right, his right tires bumping up over the curb as he pulled the car over. He turned around in his seat.

"I'm here to help you, Troy. I stopped them from

booking you, but I can only do so much. You gotta help me here. What's going on?"

Troy looked at Sam and smiled. He shrugged again. "It's dope, man, what else?"

Sam kept his lips tight. "Who were the other guys?"

"Like I know." Troy's anger seeped through his words, though his voice was quiet. "You think we exchange Christmas cards or something?"

"How did you find them? How did they find you?"

Troy shrugged again. "I dunno. A friend told me to meet them. Told me they could get me a score. And they woulda, too"— he turned his eyes on Sam — "if your asshole friends hadn't shown up."

"Who were they, Troy?" Sam repeated his question.

He wanted to reach back across the seat and smack Troy when he shrugged again. "I dunno, I told you."

"What do you know?" Sam did his best to control his voice, sound patient. He would wait Troy out if he had to.

"Look, I don't know who they were. French, I think. I don't know their names, okay?" He glanced out the window again, though the scenery hadn't changed. A chain link fence surrounded a ragged yard, a few weeds that couldn't cover the dirt that used to be a lawn. "There was a place."

"Tell me, Troy."

"They called it like… I dunno, I didn't understand. It reminded me of that hotel, the Embassy Suites. Maybe they would meet up at that hotel."

Sam kept his face clear, his voice calm. Only his fingers gripping the back of the seat next to him gave away his excitement, but Troy seemed not to notice.

"When'd they talk about that place?"

"I dunno." Troy looked up at the ceiling of the car, as if hoping to float up and out of the way of Sam's questions.

"Try again, Troy."

"They got a call," the boy was whining now, "that's all

I know. Some dude was making them mad. They were joking about him and sayin' they were going to their place to take care of him."

Sam thought about what Troy was telling him. It didn't make sense. He looked at Troy. "How do you know what they said? How good's your French?"

Troy grinned. "It sucks. I took it in high school, like Ramona. This wasn't normal French, either. They talked weird." He screwed his face up at the recollection of it.

"French Africa, maybe," Sam thought out loud. "A former colony."

"Whatever." Troy shrugged again. "I dunno, could be. When this guy made them mad, their voices changed. They'd like… say it slowly. But with a sneer. Like I said, weird."

Sam nodded, turning his attention away from Troy to the street outside his car. His mind was elsewhere, not seeing the peeling paint of the house next door, the rusted-out shell of a car parked ahead. He turned back to Troy. "Tell me more about the guy who made them mad. Did they work for him? Or were they afraid of him?"

"Yep." Troy smiled.

"What does that mean?"

"Yes, to both, I think. What the hell do I know?" Troy's anger flared again and he smacked the wall of the car. "Here I am, standing on a corner, knowing the cops are out there and trying to get clear before they show up. And these two assholes" — Troy screwed up his forehead and looked at Sam — "they're standing around having phone conversations. What a bunch of idiots."

"They are idiots, Troy. What the hell you thinking getting involved with them?"

"Here we go."

Sam turned again in his seat, putting his hands back on the steering wheel. "I'm taking you home. Your parents will have something to say about this."

Troy sneered, "That's not my home anymore. I moved out a year ago."

Sam glanced back at Troy in the mirror. "I'm going to have to tell Ramona, too. She'll find out soon enough, anyway. Do you want me to tell her, or will you?"

"You tell her, I don't care. Nothing she can do anyway."

SAM HEARD the anguish in Tish's voice as she called to Troy, her voice carrying from inside the house. Angry, but hopeful. Desperate even. The young man had thrown himself down on the couch in the basement, TV on, as soon as he'd walked in the house, and was now completely ignoring her. Sam shook his head.

"I'm so sorry, Howard."

The older man shook his head slowly. "I started asking questions, you know? And I talked to people who had heard some things." His lips turned up into a tight grin. "I thought I'd be bringing you news, Sam, not the other way around. Not this." He looked down the street to where the corner of the national park could be seen. "Not about Troy."

Sam looked down at his hands. "I'm so sorry," he repeated.

Howard nodded, slapping his hands against his legs. "We'll deal with him. At least we can now, thanks to you." He turned to face Sam. "I can't tell you how much it means to us, you watching out for our boy like that."

"You know I'm always here for you and your family."

Howard nodded again. "I know... and I'm here for you, too, old friend. Like I said, I made some calls since yesterday, found some people willing to talk about that ambassador and his staff."

Sam stood from his chair and walked to the end of the narrow porch. It was one of a line, stretching down the block, house after house filled with people with such promise, and at risk of such despair. He turned back to Howard. "What did you learn?"

"The guy's kind of an asshole."

Sam laughed. "Saint-Amand? I didn't expect that. He's always in such control."

"Well— " Howard shrugged. "He may be a great diplomat, but people can see through him. He's all about control, you know?"

"In his household? Or in his job?"

"Both." Howard nodded as Sam took the folding chair next to him again. Howard continued, "He's vocal on his position when it comes to France — tighter immigration restrictions. Tighter restrictions for immigrants once they're in France. Keep France French, that kind of thing."

Sam nodded, thinking. "Which is hard for some people to agree with."

"Oh, yeah. The man doesn't even want girls to be allowed to wear a cross or a burka to school. He's a fanatic."

Sam frowned. "So he gets in the way of the drug trade, which relies on immigrants, is that it?"

"Well…" Howard shrugged and put his head to the right side. "May not be that clear-cut, I'm afraid."

"Tell me."

"It's only rumors, you understand? I got nothing substantiated. Just cops who heard things on the street, but no one who's a witness, no one who could testify."

"I understand." Sam nodded. "And I'll treat it like a rumor. Every little bit helps, you know that."

"I do indeed." Howard smiled. "Hell, I taught you that." He blinked, looking down at his hands clasped tightly on his lap. Sam thought again how much time had changed Howard, his large, strong hands now bony and wrinkled, the skin turning gray around the knuckles and nails.

"Rumor has it," Howard said, "that the Ambassador

puts up a strong front, but turns around and benefits from the drug trade in secret. Behind closed doors."

Sam studied his friend's face for a moment, considering his next words. "That's not so uncommon, really, is it? The most fanatical can also be the first to fall."

"I guess." Howard shrugged. "Like I said, nothing substantiated. Nothing you could act on."

"Even if he didn't have diplomatic immunity." Sam stood again as he spoke. "Which he does."

The breeze had picked up again, always a welcome guest in DC's hot summer months. Sam watched as the flag across the street kicked up its patriotic dance. He loved this town and the people who lived here. The alleys like this one that made up the heart of District neighborhoods. Even when posted overseas, he had longed for the nights hanging out in his own back garden, messing with his greens, sharing fishing tips with neighbors. He closed his eyes and took a deep breath, and could hear again the blues sounds of Charlie Patton, the pungent smell of pork on the grill. The friends and the trust.

He knew that boys like Troy also faced challenges. For some, insurmountable challenges. Troy had all the advantages — a good home, good parents who cared about him. A sister.

"Do you think Ramona knows what Troy's gotten involved in?" Harold's question jolted Sam, following so directly from his own thoughts.

"I don't know." He raised his shoulders as he turned back to his friend. "If she knew, she'd be trying to help him. Same way I did today. Maybe she wouldn't tell you, I don't know."

"She's a good girl, our Mona. Don't know why her brother doesn't take after her more."

Sam smiled, remembering the two of them playing on this very front yard. Ramona had always been the one in charge. The one calling the shots. Sam had also noticed that Troy only played along when it suited him. He'd never really believed Ramona was in control of Troy.

Not then, and not now.

"I'll talk to her, Howard. See what she knows. See what she can do to help him."

Howard nodded and frowned. "Thank you, Sam. Thank you."

CHAPTER TWENTY-FIVE

"PETE, ANY NEWS?" Adam answered the call without preamble, glad his partner was calling so soon.

"Just wanted to let you know I'm on it. I'm here with Julia now."

"Thanks, buddy. I really appreciate this." Adam stepped toward the gray stone wall of the building next to him, out of the path of the busy flow of pedestrians moving up and down K Street. A river of gray and black suits, each tailored to its wearer, flowed seamlessly along the wide sidewalk. A choreographed dance of lobbyists, staffers, and political players.

"I checked in with Joe Smiley on my way over."

Adam nodded, watching an old black man leaning over into a trashcan across the sidewalk. He bent almost double, his head down into the can as he rummaged about through it, looking for something he could use. Perhaps something he could eat. The suits flowed around him, as if not even aware he was there.

"Good thinking," he said to Pete, knowing that Smiley, a small-time criminal who often worked in Julia's part of town, would be more than happy to turn on a competitor. "Did he have anything to say?"

"A few ideas, yeah." Peter's voice became muffled for a moment, as if he had turned his head to talk to someone else in the room. "Julia wants me to tell you she's fine. She says she doesn't need babysitting." His voice returned to normal as he conveyed the message.

Adam laughed. "No kidding. She needs a police guard, is what she needs."

"I guess that's what she's got then, partner." Adam heard the smile in Peter's voice. "I'm going to look into a couple of the names Smiley gave me."

"What about Julia? I don't want her staying there alone."

"No worries, bud. She's got a gig today, taking some shots downtown. She'll be surrounded by people."

"Any names I'd recognize on Smiley's list?" Adam asked, familiar with a number of the small-timers who worked Old City.

"Yeah, the usual. You know this was probably opportunistic. We think one of the other tenants may have left the front door unlocked. Someone passing took a chance, got in. The lock to Julia's apartment was jimmied. Nothing that required any special skills."

"That damn Danny, I bet." Adam pictured Julia's unkempt neighbor. "What kind of idiot doesn't lock a door in Philly at night?"

"It happens, you know that as well as I do. None of the residents have owned up to it, but they wouldn't, would they?"

"Any of the other apartments robbed?"

"Yeah, the floor below Julia's. I don't know which they hit first. That was it. I guess they took all they could carry and got out. Like I said, it smacks of opportunism."

"Thanks, Pete." Adam closed his eyes as he spoke, grateful once again, as always, for his partner. "The captain giving you any trouble for working someone else's case?"

"No… but then, he'd have to know I was doing it to do that, wouldn't he?"

Adam grinned despite himself. "Don't get yourself in trouble on my behalf, buddy."

"You should be more worried about yourself, partner.

The captain was asking about you this morning, before you called. He wants to know why you're still in DC, what's taking so long."

"What the hell?" Adam kept his voice low even as his anger mounted. "He knows the deputy commissioner sent me here, right? I'm not even back reporting to him yet, I'm still on my detail for a couple more weeks."

"I know, I know." Pete's voice was calm, rational. "He's eager to get you back, that's all. We all are. How much longer do you think you'll be down there?"

"I don't know, buddy, I really don't." Adam's voice was resigned. "Every time I think I have an idea where this is heading, I get thrown off target. I've got a couple of good leads now. Hopefully not too much longer." He thought of Julia alone in Philly. He thought of Sylvia, alone with her work parties. "Listen, no one wants me home faster than I do, believe me. I wish there was more I could do to help you out on this one, catch the bastard who attacked my sister."

"Don't worry about that, Adam. And look, she's fine. She really is. I was here when the locksmith came, and she's got a good lock on that door now. Nothing that anyone'll be jimmying again any time soon. And I'll follow up on the names Smiley gave me. I'll have this guy behind bars before you're back from DC, I promise."

"Thanks, buddy, I owe you one. Again." Adam paused, "I still need more from you. Take care of her. Until I'm back."

Pete laughed. "Julia's a big girl, partner, she can take care of herself." Adam heard the sound of hitting through the phone, and Peter laughed again. "I'm telling you, she's tough. You don't need to worry."

Julia was tough, Adam reminded himself as he tucked his phone back into his pocket. He knew that. He grinned as he thought of Julia in contrast to the lawyer he'd just had the displeasure of spending time with. Two strong women. Two very different women.

JASON MCFELLAN had taken a seat on the couch this time, part of a graceful seating area across the room from his desk.

The lawyer guided Adam to a chair across the narrow coffee table from McFellan, then took the other chair for herself. She perched on the edge of the seat, her knees together, her spiked heels once again digging into the carpet.

Adam smiled at them both. "Thanks for seeing me again. I'd like to run through your statement one more time."

"Of course, of course." McFellan spread his hands. "And I hope you don't mind that Ms. Monspear is going to join us this time." He glanced at his lawyer. "To make sure I don't say anything untoward." He grinned at Adam.

"Then can you please run through the chain of events that morning for me again." When neither spoke, Adam added, "From the time you finished breakfast."

"I see." McFellan raised his eyebrows. "Well, not much happened after that. Let's see…" He turned to stare at his lawyer, as if seeking answers from her tightly bound hair or pencil-thin eyebrows. She gave one nod.

"Well," McFellan repeated. "Let's see, breakfast was served in the morning room. More of a buffet type thing, you understand." He waved his hand as he spoke, fully expecting Adam to be well versed in the usual layout of a breakfast buffet in an ambassadorial residence. "The ambassador and senator left the house first—"

"They were the first out of the house?" Adam interrupted him. "Is that right?"

McFellan looked surprised. "Yes, I think so. I mean, other than their aides, that is."

"I see. So who left the house first?"

"Oh, I see what you mean." McFellan made a small

grimace toward his lawyer. "Look at that, I'm already messing up. I'm sorry, Detective, I didn't mean to misspeak. Yes. There were two aides there, Jay Kapoor and a young man associated with the ambassador. They had both been in the room during breakfast, and they both left — together, I might add — before the rest of us. They went out to make sure the cars were ready, I suppose."

"And were the cars ready?"

McFellan opened his eyes wide and shrugged as he took a deep breath. "Of course."

"Ahem."

McFellan glanced at his attorney as she cleared her throat, then turned back to Adam. "That is to say, I have no idea. I wasn't out there, so how could I know?"

Adam raised an eyebrow. "Please, go on. What happened after Senator Marshall and Ambassador Saint-Amand left the house?"

McFellan frowned. "Nothing. Nothing happened. John Marshall stood where he was for a few minutes, finishing his coffee..." He glanced at Monspear, who nodded silently. McFellan continued, "He finished his coffee, asked me if I was coming. I told him no, I was just there for breakfast, I wasn't joining them in Philadelphia. He left the room."

"He wasn't outside when the shot was fired," Adam pointed out.

"Then that must have been right at that moment. He left the room." McFellan stated with finality.

Adam pictured the layout of the residence. The bright morning room standing off the hallway, only a few steps from the open door. A few more steps from the ground floor office space, main staircase, and hallway to the back kitchen. How far had John Marshall made it before the shot was fired? If someone else had been in the house, would Marshall have seen them? Or heard them?

McFellan leaned forward, his eyes meeting Adam's. "Detective, what am I missing? Is there anything else I can say that would help?" He leaned back again, his hands open on his lap. "I want to help. I want you to find the guy who did this. And if anything I saw that morning can help you…" He shrugged as his voice trailed off.

Adam glanced at the lawyer, who was nodding silently, her lips pursed.

"I appreciate that, Mr. McFellan. I'm really looking for anything you didn't mention before. Anything that's occurred to you, now you've had some time to reflect on what happened that morning." Adam recognized a snow job when he heard one, but he was willing to play along if there was a chance he could learn something new. Something helpful. "Tell me again what happened after the ambassador and senator left the room."

McFellan sat back in his seat, his eyes screwed up tight. After a second, he opened his eyes and looked at Adam. "I heard them in the hall. Talking. Couldn't make out the words, then… yep, then I heard the door close behind them."

Adam cut him off again. "You heard the door? Are you sure?" Adam thought about the gentle sigh the heavy door had made on closing. No way that was audible in the morning room.

McFellan pursed his lips and glanced at his lawyer. "Well… I think so. I mean, I can't be one hundred percent sure. I'm trying to remember."

Ms. Monspear smiled at Adam. "Please understand that the events you're asking my client to describe are now a few days old. And they were traumatic events. If there is any discrepancy between my client's statement now and his statement at the time, I assure you his statement at the time was accurate."

Adam looked down at his hands. "If you heard a door, Mr. McFellan, that could be very helpful to us."

McFellan shook his head rapidly back and forth, his hands as well. "I think I heard a door. Maybe. I couldn't swear to it. Or maybe that was after John Marshall left the room. Yes…" He held up a hand. "It might have been after John left the room." He shrugged again. "I'm not sure." He glanced at his lawyer.

Monspear smiled sweetly at McFellan, then turned her face to Adam, her friendly look turning to ice. "Is there anything else, Detective Kaminski? I think your questions are getting my client flustered. Are you trying to trick him into saying something?"

Adam furrowed his brow and shook his head. "No, ma'am, nothing like that." He glanced at the lawyer and could have sworn he saw a twinkle in her eye. Was she playing with him? He couldn't help but grin. One corner of her mouth turned up in response as she looked away, crossing one leg over the other, her dangling foot tapping up and down in the air.

Adam looked at McFellan. "When does Senator Marshall start here?"

McFellan raised his eyebrows. "In the fall. Late fall. End of the year."

"And what will she be doing here, exactly?"

"Well" — McFellan blew his cheeks out — "the same as the rest of us, really."

"And what is that, sir?"

"Working on behalf of our clients to persuade certain people in power to make certain decisions. Good decisions, I assure you."

Adam nodded, trying not to look at Ms. Monspear's pale leg swinging to his right at the edge of his view. "Are there any particular clients she's expected to work with? Or topics she'll be working on?"

McFellan's eyes widened, and Adam noticed the movement of Monspear's leg stop. "I really couldn't tell you that, Detective." He held up his hands as Adam started to speak. "Not that I don't want to, nothing like that. I simply don't have an answer yet." He shook his head. "We haven't finalized her portfolio yet."

"You believe she'll be a useful employee for your company?"

"Oh, yes. Definitely." McFellan nodded vigorously. "With her background… local politics, the Senate, her husband a small business owner… well, a large business owner." He smiled as Adam raised his eyebrows. "Yes, she'll be a great asset."

"She's certainly familiar with this city. The people who live here, the culture."

"Culture?" McFellan almost giggled. "There's no such thing as DC culture, Detective. Scratch the surface and you'll see there's nothing there. It's an empty shell, waiting for the right person to come along and shape it. DC is whatever you want to make of it."

Adam tried not to let thoughts of Ramona and how she would have reacted to that statement distract him. He considered McFellan's position. His relationship to the senator. His belief that he was going to benefit from having her on his team. "And if she doesn't work out?" he asked.

"I don't see how that can be. It's pretty much the same skill set, you know, senator and advocacy consultant."

Adam grinned at the title, but said nothing. He still avoided looking at the lawyer.

McFellan continued, "Of course, nothing is permanent." He shrugged. "Her contract is only for one year. Renewable, obviously."

Adam wasn't surprised to hear that. McFellan certainly wasn't the type of guy to make a long-term commitment to anyone. For anything.

"Look, I can't tell you much else. Have you spoken to everyone else who was there? The staff? The drivers? They might have seen something, they were moving around the house and grounds." McFellan tapped his fingers on the arm of the sofa. "Or that little man, what's his name… Towne. Have you spoken to him?"

Adam glanced the lawyer, but her face was impassive. "Why would I talk to Greg Towne?" he asked, keeping his voice slow.

"He might have seen something." McFellan lowered his eyebrows. "That's all. I'm not accusing him of anything." He spoke as if the suggestion were absurd.

"Was he there that morning, Mr. McFellan?"

"Well, he was at the residence, anyway. I passed him on my way in, his car was pulling out as my car turned into the drive." McFellan shrugged. "Surely you knew that, Detective?"

McFellan and Monspear shared a glance. "Perhaps you should be focusing your efforts in a different direction, Detective." Monspear's smile was narrow, her eyes even narrower.

Adam had ended the interview with that. He had no doubt this man could sell cow dung to a dairy farm, but he seriously doubted McFellan was passionate enough about anything to kill for it. Greg Towne, on the other hand, was a whole different story.

CHAPTER TWENTY-SIX

"SORRY." The boy glanced over his shoulder as he kept running. His friend was already on the other side of the food court, dodging behind a cart stacked with hats, T-shirts, and baseball pendants.

"No problem." Adam spoke to the boy's retreating back, unconsciously wiping his hand along the side of the pants where the boy had slammed into him. The boy's parents or teachers were nowhere to be seen, but it was clear he was part of a larger group of preteens gathering in the food court of the Old Post Office Tower.

Adam paused to watch the group. Clumps of girls gathered around the stalls, picking through scarves and necklaces. Boys gathered in separate groups, occasionally breaking out into a gallop around the open seating area. Alive and full of life.

Turning away from the children and the dark memories they conjured for him, he glimpsed Towne heading toward the elevators that would take him up to the Bells of Congress. So his colleagues at the university were right when they suggested Towne might be here once again.

Towne carried a plastic bag from one of the stalls in the food court. It stuck out like a sore thumb against his Armani suit, his Italian leather shoes. It wasn't right. Even from this distance across the food court, Adam could see the shake in his hands, the fidgeting in his steps. Towne was even more nervous than usual. That couldn't be good.

Weaving his way around the late lunch crowd that surged in the food court, Adam worked his way toward the elevators. The line to go up to see the Bells couldn't be long; the end of the line didn't stretch out to the corridor where Adam could see it. By the time Adam had cleared the lunchroom floor, he could see Towne's white face staring down at him from the glass elevator rising up into the tower.

Their eyes met, and Towne's hand tightened its grip on the plastic bag, his other hand flattening itself against the glass of the elevator.

"Shit." Adam jogged toward the entrance. A uniformed park ranger stood behind the desk, occasionally glancing up as visitors lined up for the elevators. His eyes ran right over Adam, probably more interested in seeking out gum chewers than crazy architects.

As the elevator doors crawled open, the ranger spoke up. "Stay to your right, ladies and gentlemen. Let the others off the elevator first, please, then you can step in."

Adam baby-stepped his way onto the elevator behind a large man holding a child's hand. As the elevator rose, the child stared in awe at the scene unfolding below them, and Adam followed his gaze to the open seating area packed with noisy school groups, the grand arcades of the turn-of-the-century architecture, the glass ceiling glowing above them and slowly coming closer.

At the back of the elevator, Adam waited impatiently for the rest of the group to step off. The narrow hallway that led to the tower viewing platform didn't leave any room for running, but he managed to sidestep his way past the rest of the group, pushing open the door into the open bell tower.

Another uniformed park ranger stood here, engaging

a young couple in a discussion of the Bells of Congress and their significance. Large open windows on each side of the tower exposed miles of DC, a stunning view. Wind whipped through the open platform, and the ranger stood with his hand planted firmly on his flat hat.

The square tower was no more than twenty feet on each side, and it took only a second for Adam to see that Towne wasn't there. He turned to the park ranger.

"Excuse me, have you seen a gentleman, mid-thirties, curly brown hair? He looked nervous and carried a plastic shopping bag."

"I'm sorry, sir, we get so many visitors up here." The ranger shrugged and looked apologetic. He pointed Adam in the direction of the stairs leading down. "Perhaps your friend went to the next level down, to see the bells?"

"Thanks." Adam was already jogging toward the door. He took the stairs down two at a time, skidding out into the next level. Fewer visitors gathered here. Lower inside the tower, this room offered no views of the city. Instead, it offered a view of the resource Towne was fighting so hard to preserve — the Bells of Congress.

Towne stood on the far side of the display, Adam's view of him warped by the thick plastic case that enclosed the bells. Adam had taken a few steps in Towne's direction when he looked up.

"Stay where you are, Detective." Towne's hand was deep inside the plastic bag and his fingers shifted around whatever he held.

The few visitors in the room turned to look, first at Towne, then at Adam, who stopped walking and held his hands open in front of him.

"What's going on, Towne? What are you doing?"

The bag slipped away. Towne held a gun, its barrel pushed against the side of his leg. Perhaps in the future the contractors managing security for this building wouldn't be so eager to let VIPs skip the security line.

"What are you thinking, Towne? Talk to me." Adam kept his voice low, but Towne raised the gun.

A woman standing near him gasped and pulled her daughter close to her.

"You all should probably leave this area." Adam kept his eyes fixed on Towne. The other visitors in the space moved away as he directed. Hopefully one of them was going up to let the park ranger know what was going on.

Towne raised the gun even higher, turning to face the bell closest to him. "No one will listen to me. No one takes me seriously."

"And you think this will help with that?" Adam shook his head and frowned. "I don't buy that."

"This was supposed to be my legacy," Towne was whispering now, leaning in to the plastic case that covered the bells on display. "The one thing I thought I could do right." Towne's voice was calm. Too calm.

"What are you trying to do, Towne?" Adam asked, his tone of voice matching Towne's. As if they were simply having a friendly conversation. "You don't want to damage the bells that you're trying to protect."

"Why not?" Towne shrugged, and for the first time moved his eyes from the bells to look at Adam.

While his voice was calm, his eyes told a different story. Red rims encircled eyes worn out from crying. Eyes that showed defeat. Acceptance. Utter despair. Adam had looked into eyes like that before. When there was no hope left. Nowhere else to turn for solace. No more anger, no more fear. Just acceptance of the very, very worst.

"Give me the gun, Towne. Dr. Towne," Adam added as an afterthought.

Towne grinned and dipped his head in recognition. "Thank you for that. It doesn't matter anymore. I have no career left. No respect." He waved the gun vaguely in the direction of the bells. "I've tried and I've tried… I wrote papers. But… nothing. Even my own daughter won't return my phone calls."

"People will listen to you, Dr. Towne. Your daughter will talk to you. You have a position of respect, remember?"

"Yes." Towne nodded, smiling, his eyes miles away. "I did. Not anymore." He turned to Adam, his voice businesslike. "I haven't published anything new, you see. In years. My last three submissions were rejected. Too subjective, they said, not evidence based. Hah!" In the first sign of emotion, spittle shot out with his laugh, hitting the plastic case around the bells, lingering for a minute before starting its descent down the front of the case.

"You don't want to damage the bells, Dr. Towne. They're too important to you." Adam took a step toward Towne, who tensed.

"They are important. You're right." He tapped the plastic with his gun. "I couldn't get through this casing anyway, could I?" He laughed, the laughter growing louder, faster, as he turned his eyes to Adam. "I can't do anything right, can I?"

With a cry, he threw the gun. Adam jumped, watching the weapon as it hit the ground then grabbing and securing it. While Adam's focus was on the gun, Towne turned and lunged the other way, back to the stairs that led up to the open tower.

Adam chased after him, two steps at a time. How the hell did that little pudgy man move so fast?

Adam pushed through the door out onto the landing just as Towne launched himself onto the ledge of the open tower, reaching for the open air. The District of Columbia spread out below him, and he paused for a second, as if admiring the view before throwing himself out into it.

Before Towne had even taken a deep breath, the park ranger wrapped his arms firmly around him. He locked his hands around Towne's waist, dragging him back down to the safety of the platform, spinning as he pulled.

Towne struggled like a madman, twisting and pulling.

As the ranger stumbled, trying to regain his balance, Adam grabbed at Towne. The man twisted again, reaching for the ledge once more.

"Damn it," Adam swore as he let his right arm swing, knowing he was going to regret this. His fist landed firmly on Towne's jaw, and the other man went down.

"Cops on the way?" Adam asked the ranger without looking up.

"Be here any second." The ranger nodded, standing and wiping down his uniform.

"I got you, Towne. You're safe." Adam leaned forward and pulled Towne up into a sitting position. He slumped against the middle platform of the tower, his head lolling against his chest, blood trickling from the cut on his jaw.

"I have nothing," he mumbled into his tie. "Nothing left."

CHAPTER TWENTY-SEVEN

"SO IS THIS a Philly technique? Punch out the witness?" Sam smiled as he spoke, but Adam knew it wasn't a joke.

"I was saving his life, man. He would've jumped." The thin plastic chair creaked under his weight as he turned toward Sam, then looked back down at the floor, trying to ignore the looks he got from others in the hospital waiting area as his voice rose. Why shouldn't he be upset? It seemed pretty likely to him he had punched an innocent man. A potential witness. Not a good thing.

"Uh-huh." Sam sat in a plastic chair next to Adam's. Adam kept his eyes on his hands and didn't look up. "Get anything good from him? Before you punched him, I mean."

Adam shrugged. He stood and walked a few feet before turning back to Sam. "I don't know." He shook his head. "Nothing real. The man's angry, I can tell you that. Pissed as hell."

"Mad enough to kill?"

Adam nodded. "Definitely." A movement at the front desk to his right caught his eye, and he turned in time to see John Marshall being escorted back to the treatment rooms. Back to where Towne was currently getting stitches. "What is he doing here?"

"Who?" Sam turned, but Marshall was already out of sight.

"John Marshall. The nurse took him back." Adam frowned at Sam. "Is he here to see Towne?"

"I don't know." Sam stood and let his eyes roam over the waiting room. The reception area. No one else looked familiar. Just a room full of tired, frustrated people, some waiting for friends or family, others waiting for medical attention. "He could be checking up on Towne, I guess."

"No way." Adam shook his head. "That doesn't make sense."

"Maybe the senator is concerned?" Sam shrugged. "He came to check up on her colleague. After he was beaten by the police." Sam was clearly trying to bring the conversation back to what Adam had done, but Adam ignored him.

"Right, because she really comes across as the type to be concerned about a colleague. No. Unless she has an ulterior motive…"

"Kaminski." Sam waited, then added, "Adam. You need to talk to me. You just punched a witness."

"What do you want me to say?" Adam looked at him. "The man was going to jump. I hit him to save his life."

"If he presses charges…" Sam looked away.

"I know, Sam." Adam shook his head. "I don't know what I was thinking. I was angry, I was in a hurry. I need to get home, take care of my sister. I felt like I didn't have time for that crap, and I reacted. You don't need to tell me, I screwed up."

"I know he's an annoying little man, but he does have connections." Sam nodded in the direction Marshall had gone. "Senator Marshall, for example."

"Yeah, I know. I know." Adam touched his right hand with his left and winced. "So you think she sent Marshall to check up on Towne? Because she's concerned about him? And God knows she couldn't afford to be associated with this situation." Adam laughed under his breath.

"You really have it in for Senator Marshall, don't you?"

"It's not that, I swear. She's keeping something secret. I don't know what. I've got a feeling." He shook his head. "You know, it seems to me that of everyone involved in this, she's got the most to lose."

Sam shrugged and patted Adam on the shoulder. "Come on, I'll give you a lift. And don't let your gut lead you too far astray. I know the senator's a cool character, but she's had her own grief to deal with. And she deals with it in her own way. Right?"

Adam took a deep breath. "Maybe. Thanks for the offer, but I'm staying here. I need to talk to Towne again. Preferably when he's not pointing a gun."

Sam opened his mouth to respond. The ring of Adam's phone cut off whatever he was about say.

"Kaminski."

Adam recognized the voice of Deputy Commissioner White. "What the hell's going on down there?"

"You mean about Towne, sir?"

"Who the hell is Towne? No, I mean about Jay. The young man whose interests you're supposed to be watching out for?"

"I don't understand." Adam sank back into the plastic chair. "What happened?" He looked up at Sam, hovering over him.

"I just got a call from the Kapoors, Kaminski. They're not happy. Very not happy."

CHAPTER TWENTY-EIGHT

"A BLOG? Why're the Kapoors even reading political blogs?"

Adam understood Ramona's confusion. That had been his first question, too. "They weren't. A friend of the family saw it, let them know." He glanced up as Sam's car pulled away from the hospital entrance, then he headed toward the nearest Metro stop.

"So it's pretty bad, huh? I'm pulling it up now." The sound of Ramona's typing carried over the phone.

"Where are you?"

"I'm at the Bureau," Ramona explained. "I told you, they're gearing up for an activity this evening and invited us to join them. I'm using an open workstation to file my report, let my captain know the plan."

Adam nodded to himself. "D'you find the blog yet?"

"Oh, yes. Political Dish it is." Ramona paused, presumably reading the page in front of her. "Dark secrets... no surprise he's dead... did he get what he deserved? This stuff is toxic, Kaminski, no wonder the Kapoors are pissed. And your deputy commissioner. Why would someone write this stuff about Jay?"

"That's what I need to find out. And that means finding the person behind the blog. Can you help?"

"Um... let's see." Ramona's voice pulled away from the phone, and he could make her out calling someone's name. He heard a few scuffles, then Ramona's voice came back on the line. "Okay, Kaminski, I want to introduce you to Don Morris. He's a tech guy here at the Bureau."

"What can I do to help?" Morris' voice was loud and clear. He must have picked the call up on another line.

"I'm trying to find the author of an anonymous blog. Is that something you can do?"

There was a pause — Adam wondered if Ramona and Morris were conferring off line — then Morris' voice came back on. "Sure, no problem, but it might take some time. I can find the site and geolocate the IP address. Assuming this guy is trying to stay anonymous, we'd need to contact the ISP to get his name. That's the part that could take awhile, including however long it takes you to get the warrant."

"Okay, get started." Ramona had picked up Adam's urgency.

Adam stopped at the head of the deep escalator that would take him down to the Metro, far below ground. "Listen, Ramona. I'm going down, I'll be out of touch. How long does Morris think this is going to take? 'Cause I can head over your way if you think we can get the Bureau started on the warrant request."

"I'm right here, Detective Kaminski, you don't need to talk about me in the third person."

"Right, sorry, Morris. So how long will this take?"

"Weelll…" Morris stretched out the word and Adam heard his fingers flying across a keyboard. "Like I said, I can trace the IP address, no problem. In fact, there it is. Yeah, he's covered up his identity, no surprise. Thing is, we all leave breadcrumbs, don't we?"

"I have no idea, do we?"

"Sure do. You should pay more attention when you're online. I just need to follow his trail…" Morris' words faded into the sound of typing. "Who needs IP-based user identification, anyway?"

Adam took a deep breath. "I need the short version, Morris. I'm in a bit of a hurry."

When Morris didn't reply, Adam added, "Ramona, you still there?"

"Sure — wait, what?" Ramona cut herself off with her own questions.

"Ramona?" Adam squinted and turned his back to a crowd of people exiting the escalator, his hand over his free ear. "What's going on?" All he could make out was some muttering from the other end of the phone.

"He says he's online now. Morris. I mean, Morris says the blogger is online now. On a cell phone."

"So? What does that mean?"

"It means…" Morris' calm voice cut into their conversation. "It means I can get you a specific location… better than trying to trace an IP address and no warrant necessary…"

Adam took another breath, squared his shoulders. "Meaning?"

"Give me a sec… I'm just getting it…"

"When you say a specific location, do you mean his actual location?" Adam tried rephrasing his question.

Morris answered, but his mind was clearly following wherever his fingers were going. His voice was soft, singsong. "Wherever he is right now."

"Just like that? I can meet him face to face?"

"Yep, that's it," Morris answered. "It's that simple. For me, at least, thanks to the FCC and the Supreme Court. Let's see…"

"He's nodding, Kaminski." Ramona's voice was high and tight. "I think that's good thing, right, Morris?"

"Yep." Morris' voice was low. Calm. "Got him."

ADAM JOGGED up the steps, beads of sweat forming along his back as he searched the flow of visitors streaming away from the Capitol building. Another beautiful June day in DC. If you weren't chasing down an anonymous blogger who might or might not know something about a murder.

Morris had pinpointed the blogger's location to the north end of the Capitol building, a location he could identify down to the second. Now Adam had to find it. He glanced at his cell phone as he jogged, watching his GPS location as he moved.

"Detective Kaminski?"

Adam looked up, surprised to see Jason McFellan coming down the stairs toward him.

"Mr. McFellan, what are you doing here?"

McFellan smiled and waved his hand towards the monumental white building looming at the top of the marble steps. "This is where I work, Detective. That shouldn't surprise you."

Adam stopped. Examined the man smiling in front of him. "Jason McFellan. It's you, isn't it?"

"What's me?" The man's smile was disarming, but not enough to put Adam off.

"You're the man behind Political Dish."

"What?" McFellan's voice held laughter as he walked toward Adam, his arm outstretched. "Don't be ridiculous, have you read some of that nonsense?"

As he drew closer to Adam, he placed his arm over Adam's shoulder, leaning his head in to whisper in Adam's ear. "Keep your voice down, do you want everyone to hear? Do you know what a rumor like that would do to my career?" He lifted his head to glance around. No one seemed to have overheard. "Come, Detective, walk with me."

Adam shrugged away from McFellan's arm, but followed him down the steps. Together, they walked toward the reflecting pool.

"I don't understand. Why would you run something like that blog?" Adam looked over at the man next to him. "You said yourself, if anyone finds out, it would ruin you."

McFellan smiled, his face relaxed, his arms swinging naturally by his side as he walked. "I don't know, Detective. Maybe you can tell me. It's just something I do." His smile turned into a grin, and Adam felt he was playing against the Cheshire Cat. "Maybe it's fun."

Adam shook his head. Looked away. "What do you know about Jay? That was some pretty vile stuff you posted about him."

"Kapoor?" McFellan shrugged. Frowned. His hands found their way to his pockets. "To tell the truth, I don't really know much at all. Only the rumors I've heard. Lots and lots of rumors."

"Like what?"

They had reached the reflecting pool, and McFellan turned left, working his way along the edge of the water. "No one wants to speak ill of the dead, Detective. You know that. Sometimes people have things they need to share. Need to get off their chest, you know?"

"And they talk to you? Why, so you can post it on your blog?"

"Hah, hardly." McFellan's laugh was soft. Civilized. "They talk to me because I listen. I'm a very good listener, Detective."

"Then tell me what you've heard." Adam stopped walking, turning to McFellan. "What do you know about Jay's murder?"

"You're not listening to me, Kaminski." McFellan's voice grew hard. "I'm telling you, I don't know any more. Everything I heard — everything — I posted on that blog. Just rumors and innuendos. Rumors that matched my own assessment of the guy. That Jay enjoyed keeping secrets. Other people's secrets." McFellan turned to continue along the path around the pool.

"Why do you run that blog, McFellan?" Adam asked. "Really?"

McFellan shrugged, his comfortable smile back on his face. Relaxed once again. "Maybe because I'm bored?" He said it like a question, shrugging his shoulder as he spoke. "Maybe I like to live life close to the edge. Things come all too easily sometimes, don't they, Detective?"

He stared out over the pool as he spoke, his face a picture of introspection. "Things were getting boring and I needed a bit of a challenge. Something to spice things up. Make life dangerous again."

Adam nodded, listening. "Right." He pursed his lips. Let his eyes range over the same view McFellan was seeing. "Thing is, I don't believe a word of that."

McFellan started and turned, the two men standing face to face, alone among the crowds of tourists that roamed around the Capitol grounds, enjoying the plush grass, the coolness seeping off the reflecting pool.

"And what do you believe, Detective?"

Adam frowned, turning back to face the pool. "It's just a thought, Mr. McFellan, but I think that maybe, after all these years, you stopped believing the lies you've been telling yourself."

"Hmm." McFellan's voice was soft, his smile gone. "And what lies are those?"

One side of Adam's mouth turned up a fraction. "That you're only playing by the rules. That you're not doing anything wrong." He turned back to McFellan. "In your job, I mean. That's what you said, right? That you know how to work the system?"

"That's what I said, yes. I don't see—"

"Your blog is followed by thousands of people looking for an end to the big-money politics of Washington," Adam cut him off. "It exposes the payments made by corporations, wealthy individuals, and foreign countries. Payments that determine the course of politics in DC."

"Yes, Detective." McFellan voice was dry. "I see you've read it."

Adam shook his head. "I don't have to. I think I understand you. You're looking for power. You thrive on power. But you can't shake the guilt over what you're doing. Because no matter what you say, you know it's wrong."

McFellan laughed under his breath. Turned and kept

walking. "Maybe you're right, Detective. Who knows? Is it for the thrill? Or to appease my guilt? Or both, perhaps?" He ducked his head to one side. "It doesn't matter why, though, does it? You want to know what I know. And I don't know anything more than I've already told you. Honestly."

Adam watched him as he spoke. A professional liar. A man who would say anything for money. For power.

"Now I know your secret, what will you do?" Adam asked.

The question jolted McFellan out of his complacency, as Adam knew it would. "You know nothing, got it? This has nothing to do with your investigation. And you have no proof." He ran a hand over his hair as he regained his composure. "You can't beat me in this game, Detective, I've been playing it far too long."

"If anyone found out that you're behind that blog, you'd lose all your connections. No one would talk to you then. All that power you've accumulated."

They had reached the halfway point around the pool. Third Street was a few steps straight ahead, Independence Avenue to the south.

"What do you think is going to happen next, Detective?" McFellan smiled at him. "Do you think I'm going to join you back at police headquarters?" He laughed out loud as he spoke. "Make a statement? Share everything I know?" He shook his head.

"Yeah, something like that." Adam didn't smile back.

McFellan put his hands up to straighten his tie, adjust the handkerchief peeking out of his pocket. "No, Detective, I don't think so. You have no jurisdiction here. Not really." He raised an eyebrow at Adam as he spoke, grinning again. "In fact, I'm going to walk away."

McFellan smiled and waved his hand to indicate the street to their south.

"Damn," Adam swore under his breath as he realized his own impotence. He had no real authority here. He couldn't arrest McFellan. And no way he was going to bring McFellan in by force, or punch out another witness. Or suspect.

McFellan saw Adam's indecision. He turned toward Independence Avenue.

CHAPTER TWENTY-NINE

CROWDS SURGED on the dimly lit streets of Adams Morgan. They crawled along the sidewalk, moving in and out of doors that lined the street. Doors that led to small bars that could hold only a hundred or so people. Stores selling beads, bandanas, and incense. Restaurants that were nothing more than a counter at the front window, selling kebabs, fried chicken, pizza. Each venue drawing people in, then pushing them back out into the street.

People laughed, talked, called to each other. Waves of music blaring from within the buildings merged with each other, creating a raucous blend of rhythm, voice, and instrument.

A fistfight broke out, someone got pushed up against a pockmarked wall. The crowd closed in. A few minutes later, a winner emerged triumphant. The crowd moved on to replay the scene on the next block.

No one seemed to care about the black SUV parked along the curb, tucked behind an old blue van and in front of a silver Mercedes.

Farther up the street, Adam could see another similar SUV, which he knew held two more agents. A third team stood in a dark doorway that led to apartments above one of the bars, smoking.

"Business is good, looks like." Liu used his chin to gesture toward the tall African leaning against a graffiti covered wall.

As they watched, a young man approached the dealer, hands in the pockets of his leather jacket. They stood close together, the African looming over the shorter man, but even through the lines of people passing them by, it was clear that something passed between their hands. With a quick glance up and down the street, the younger man sauntered away, hands back in his pockets.

Fitzpatrick sat behind the wheel, his eyes peeled on the street around them. Liu glanced at Adam and Ramona in the back seat, then turned back to the road in front of him.

Adam made eye contact with Ramona, but kept his mouth shut. Did she share the FBI's focus on the drug dealer, or was she as worried as he was about McFellan? About Towne? About what was really behind Jay's murder and the time they might be wasting sitting here?

She nodded without speaking. Both of them knew perfectly well that though they had been invited by Hennessy to join this operation, they weren't wanted by the agents on the ground. Fitzpatrick had yet to even acknowledge their presence in the back of his car.

Adam knew the FBI was certain the cocaine trade with Cote D'Ivoire was behind the ambassador's attempted murder. It made sense. Fit with what Sam had learned from his contacts. It just didn't sit right with him. He was sure there was more to this murder, something they were missing.

This operation wasn't the time for second-guessing. Or for sharing notes.

"Heads up." Fitzpatrick's voice was tight.

Fitzpatrick and Liu turned their attention to the dealer. Ramona's attention, however, was caught by something down the street. Adam saw her face turn, a sharp intake of breath as her eyes flickered in surprise. She put a hand out to touch the door handle.

"What's up?" Adam leaned over and whispered in her ear. Liu's black eyes flickered toward them, then refocused on the dealer.

Ramona gave her head a quick shake and said nothing.

Adam scanned the street around them, trying to figure out what had startled Ramona. MPDC were patrolling the area on foot. A couple of uniforms in bright yellow jackets walked along the yellow line in the middle of the street. They chatted with the drivers of the cars that crawled along the congested roadway, trying to avoid the pedestrians who wandered in and out of the street. They kept an eye on the crowds on the sidewalks, but stayed out of the small scuffles.

Another man had approached the dealer, wearing the same uniform as the rest of the youth in the neighborhood. Dark leather jacket over baggy jeans that hung low, exposing swaths of gray boxer shorts. Unlike the African's previous clients, this one was an undercover agent. Part of the sting operation set up for this evening. As soon as he gave the signal, the rest of the team would close in.

They just needed to wait for the signal.

Ramona's hand moved. Adam saw her reach for the door. He put out a hand. To stop her, he supposed. It was too late.

She pushed the door open. Stepped out of the car.

The movement caught the African's attention.

"Shit." Liu pushed his door open, Adam right after him.

The agent with the dealer said something and the dealer's head jerked toward him, then his hand lashed out. The agent fell back against the wall.

"Shit! Shit!" Liu was running across the street, weapon drawn.

Two more agents from the car ahead of them came running from the opposite direction.

Adam started to chase Liu, then noticed Ramona. She stood still, her hand on the roof of the SUV. Her eyes were turned away from the chase, scanning the crowd along the sidewalk.

Adam's gaze followed hers. People were moving away, fast. Some were shouting, but the calls were lost in the noise of the music, the engines of idling cars and hundreds of voices. Some weren't even fazed by the sight of the agents closing in.

One man caught Adam's eye. A young man, hands in his pockets, walking away from the activity. Walking slowly and steadily, head down. Not looking back.

Adam glanced at Ramona. Saw her eyes following the young man. She nodded to herself, then turned to Adam.

"Let's get in on this." Her face was grim but excitement shone in her eyes.

SAM CLICKED another link on his computer. Scrolled through another old article. Then another. He sat up straight, pushing his hands into the small of his back, then leaned forward again, clicking another link.

Thirty minutes later, he reached his hand out to adjust the desk lamp, shifting the yellow beam of light away from his eyes. He sat back in his chair, rubbing his hands over his eyes. This was getting him nowhere. He could hear his wife downstairs in the kitchen, clearing up the dishes from their dinner. He should be down there helping her, he knew. God knows she worked hard enough during the day, she didn't need to be stuck with all the housework at night.

There had to be something here. Something more.

All the information he could find on the Marshalls was superficial. At best. Stories about their perfect house back in Pennsylvania. Their perfect community at their church that helped them through the loss of their only child. His success at his business. Her success at her campaigns. Even the dirt spilled about her on blogs like Political Dish was weak in comparison to some of the corruption exposed there. No one could be this innocent. There had to be something else.

He was stuck working on this from home, without access to his classified system. After the business with Troy and Harold, he had returned to his office earlier that day. Once again reading through cable after cable, looking for something that would connect Lisa or John Marshall to Ambassador Saint-Amand. Something that would reveal a motive. And the true victim.

He was only halfway through the cables he had pulled up with his search when a shadow fell across his screen.

"What you working on, Burke?"

Sam glanced up at Deputy Assistant Secretary John Waters. "Looking for background information on the Saint-Amand incident, sir."

Waters leaned forward over Sam's desk. "You're not going to find anything helpful there. I thought the Bureau had narrowed it down to a drug deal. Something to do with Saint-Amand's staff?"

Sam frowned and shook his head. "That's what they're thinking, yeah. They're following that lead now, in fact."

"You're not with them?"

Sam grinned as he leaned back in his chair, turning to face his DAS. "I'm a little too old for that kind of action, sir. Searching cables is more my speed."

Waters laughed. "I guess so. Don't waste your time on this. If there was anything in our records that gave a clue about this, it would have been flagged by now. Our people in Paris or Abidjan would have let us know."

"I know, but—"

Waters cut him off. "I said drop it, Burke. If you can't help with the final stages of the investigation, there's plenty else you could be working on."

Sam bit his lip, looking up at the man who didn't run his department, but wanted to. A man with lofty goals that weren't matched by his skills. "I'm trying to get more on the Marshalls, sir, not just Saint-Amand."

Waters frowned. "Why the Marshalls?"

Sam considered his answer carefully. He had no facts,

only Adam's hunch. "I met with him the other day, sir. He was pumping me for information about the investigation."

Waters shrugged. "Makes sense. Though his wife probably knows more than you do." Waters grinned at Sam.

"Yes, sir. There was just something about his attitude. I don't know." Sam thought about the phone call Marshall was unwilling to answer, the look that had crossed his face when he saw who was calling. "He's got a secret, I'm sure of it." He looked up at his DAS. "I'm trying to find out what it is. Part of any investigation, right, digging up secrets?"

"Everyone's got secrets." Waters pushed himself off Sam's desk. "Doesn't make him a killer. Or a target. Leave the senator and her husband alone, they've been through enough."

Sam was surprised that Waters cared about their privacy. That wasn't like him. "But, sir—"

Waters cut him off yet again. "I don't want to have to write the letter to the senator explaining why we're digging through her private life, you got that?"

Sam nodded. That sounded like the DAS he knew.

Sam rubbed his eyes again, bringing his focus back to the sites open on the screen of his personal computer at home. If the Marshalls had a secret, he wasn't going to find it here. Anything worth killing over — anything worth getting killed over — wasn't going to be posted online for anyone to see. He couldn't justify going back to the office. He thought about the files Adam had found on Jay's desk. Newspaper clippings, hard copies cut out and saved. Where they couldn't be rewritten, updated, or faked.

What had Adam said? He closed his eyes to think about their conversation that morning. Noise complaints. Exorbitant hospital charges. A break-in. A hit-and-run. Had Jay found something important? A secret worth keeping?

Sam leaned forward in his seat and pulled up one more website. Pivoting in his chair, he reached for his phone, glancing at his watch as he did so. It was late. Not likely anyone would answer.

Someone picked up after the third ring.

"Sheriff's Office." The voice was gruff, tired. As it would be after a long day.

FITZPATRICK TURNED the corner into the alley, Liu right behind him. The two agents who had been positioned on the street were far ahead, closing in on the dealer as he made a run for it. The two agents from the other SUV squatted next to their injured colleague, sitting him up against the brick wall, bandaging his head, waiting for the ambulance that was on its way.

Adam glanced at Ramona and shook his head. She slowed her pace, falling into step next to him. They both holstered their weapons.

"Look." Adam jerked his head to the right, and Ramona's eyes turned in that direction.

A tall, thin black man moved quickly along the sidewalk. Not running, but not walking either. As he moved toward the alley, his hand reached into his jacket.

Adam and Ramona saw the heft of the gun at the same time, the shape of something solid beneath the leather of his jacket. They both tensed, put their hands on their own weapons.

The man turned the corner.

"Damn!" Adam picked up his pace, Ramona right behind him.

Adam was the first to turn the corner after the suspect. He took the turn at a jog, keeping his right arm close against the wall. Thank God for the wall. And thank God he was first, and not Ramona.

The bullet hit his left arm, tearing through the fabric of his jacket and shirtsleeve and through the muscle of his arm. He threw himself back against the wall with a grunt, the weight of his Kevlar vest comforting against his chest. Keeping his back pressed against the wall, he stepped to his right, taking shelter in an old window well, the bricks of the ground-level sill loose beneath his feet.

With the sound of the shot, all hell broke loose. Adam kept his eyes on the shooter, ignoring the sound of screams, running feet, revving engines coming from the main street to his left. He focused on the sound of Ramona's footsteps, stopping just around the corner.

"Kaminski, talk to me."

"I'm good, stay where you are."

"The shooter?"

"I got eyes on him, about twenty feet up, behind a Dumpster."

"You hit?"

"Just a graze." Adam grunted as he shifted his weight, tentatively moving his left arm. "I'm fine." The trickle of blood from his wound was growing. Adam felt dampness running down his arm, saw the drips of blood pooling on the ground below him. He let his arm dangle, keeping his grip on his weapon with his right hand.

"So it's a standoff." Adam heard the grin in Ramona's voice, sensed the absurdity of his situation.

"'Til he moves, I move, or reinforcements arrive."

"And I'm here now, aren't I?"

Adam shook his head, but kept his arm firm, his sights clear on the suspect as he heard Ramona move with a quiet "on your left" under her breath.

She slipped into the alley in only three steps, throwing herself behind another Dumpster across the alley from Adam. The shooter caught the movement, took a shot. The bullet went wide, whistling through the air between them. Adam heard the shatter of glass as it hit a storefront across the street.

"Shit." He risked glancing at Ramona to make sure she was okay, then kept his eyes trained on the gray

Dumpster twenty feet up the alley. "We can't have a shoot-out on a DC street."

"You think it'd be the first time?" Ramona spoke without moving her jaw, her face tense. Adam heard her take a raspy breath, then she yelled out, "MPDC. Drop your weapon, put your hands in the air."

The only response came from the street, where the wail of sirens grew louder, then stopped. Footsteps approached from the street.

Ramona tilted her head toward her radio, keeping her eyes and her weapon firmly trained.

"One shooter, about halfway up the alley. I need someone up at the other end."

Adam couldn't make out the response, but Ramona straightened up, both hands clasped around her weapon. She repeated her call. "MPDC. Drop your weapon and stand up."

They both saw the movement at the same time. The man pushed the Dumpster as he stood, turning to run farther up the alley. Ramona took aim and fired at the suspect. Her bullet dented the Dumpster. Adam lifted his left arm, using it to balance his weapon, and aimed ahead. The ring of the bullet hitting the large, square drainpipe that ran up the side of the building stopped the suspect in his tracks.

"*Merde.*" The man turned back toward the Dumpster, ducking down again.

"We got him cornered. We'll have officers coming in from the other direction any second." Ramona turned to Adam. He half stood, half slumped against the broken glass in the window well, his left arm hanging by his side. "You okay, Kaminski? Hold on there."

"Just part of the job, right?" He grinned, but didn't take his eyes off that Dumpster.

Ramona stood taller, her feet apart, eyes on the Dumpster. She glanced in his direction for a second, keeping her weapon pointed. "Why are you here, Kaminski, really?"

"Gotta keep the world safe, right?" He blinked to keep the sweat out of his eyes. The pool of blood at his feet seemed to have grown larger and darker.

"Stay with me, Kaminski. Who are you keeping safe?"

"Julia." Adam spoke softly, not sure if Ramona could hear him.

"Tell me about Julia." Ramona's voice sounded distant. Adam blinked again. Caught the scent of lilies at his students' funeral, the sound of dirt hitting three plain wooden coffins.

Adam tightened his grip on his gun, pushed himself into the brick wall next to him, willing the rough feel of the brick to bring him back to the present. "She's my sister. I take care of her. She needs me."

"I get that, about siblings, I mean. I have a brother."

"Is that who you saw? On the street earlier?"

"You noticed that, did you?"

"Yeah, not just me. You'll be getting hell about that false start." Adam grinned, then his grin faltered. "It's all about what you need to protect, isn't it?"

"Of course it is, Kaminski."

Adam heard the shuffle of feet and uniforms carrying from the other end of the alley.

"MPDC," a man's voice called out, "you're surrounded. Drop your weapon."

"What you would die for. What you would kill for." Adam was speaking to himself, but Ramona stepped across the alley, taking her eyes off the shooter for the two steps it took her to throw herself into Adam's window well.

"You're not dying for anyone today, Kaminski." She put her hand against his right shoulder.

He dropped his gun back into his holster, let his left arm hang loose by his side, and slid down the brick wall until he was sitting on the ground. "No, partner, not today." He grinned at her and the white of her teeth caught the dim light of the alley as she smiled back.

CHAPTER THIRTY

"I'M GLAD we were on this together, Kaminski." Ramona adjusted the blanket that lay across Adam's shoulders, covering up the sling the EMTs had applied as a temporary measure. "Thanks for having my back."

Adam chuckled. "I'm pretty sure I should be the one thanking you. If I hadn't been so careless, running around the corner like that…"

Ramona laughed, a deep, joyful sound that released all the tension she had been holding in for the past hour. She patted him on the shoulder as she did so, and he flinched. "Oh, sorry. Really, we make a good team, don't we?"

Ramona's eyes glowed as she smiled, the adrenaline still pumping through her veins. Her hand, as she adjusted Adam's blanket again, felt like silk against his face, and he closed his eyes for a moment, letting his cheek rub against the back of her hand, breathing in her familiar scent of vanilla, now mingling with the odor of her sweat.

He opened his eyes. She was looking at him. He coughed, and turned on the ambulance cot, adjusting the line that ran to his arm. "Look, Ramona…"

"I know." She spoke quietly. "Other obligations, right?"

He looked up at her. "I'm involved. And I want to make it work. At least" — he adjusted himself again —

"I need to try to make it work. And, hey, after this case, maybe she'll be happier with my career choice."

"I get it." Ramona's lips turned up at the edges, but her eyes gave her away. "You're a good guy, Kaminski. A one-woman kind of guy. That's what I like about you. Don't lose yourself in your relationship."

"You okay in there?" They both turned to look at Fitzpatrick, leaning in the back of the ambulance. "You going with him to the hospital, Davis?"

"I could, why?"

"We were thinking, since you helped catch the perp, you might want to be there for the interrogation."

Ramona raised her eyebrows, then glanced at Adam.

"Go," he said. "See what you can learn."

Ramona looked back at Fitzpatrick. "I'm surprised you're asking, after what happened earlier."

Fitzpatrick shrugged and tapped the door of the ambulance. "Look, whatever. You reacted too early, it's true." He looked at Ramona and Adam. "But if it weren't for you two, we wouldn't have this guy now, so if you want in, you're in." He turned and walked back to his SUV.

"Will you be okay?"

Adam smiled at her. "I'm fine. It's a small wound, I probably won't even spend the night in the hospital. Go."

"Sorry you can't be part of this."

"Don't worry about it." Adam frowned. "To be honest, I'm still not convinced."

"Not convinced?" Ramona's voice rose a level. "The man shot you, and you're not convinced he's the guy we want?"

Adam shrugged, then flinched as pain shot through his shoulder. "It's like I said back there, I can't stop thinking. What would you be willing to die for — or kill for?" He looked at Ramona. "There's more to this. It wasn't some drug dealer knocking off the competition. That wouldn't happen at the residence. With the senator there. No." He shook his head again. "Someone took that shot — at that time, at that place — for a reason. Something worth killing for."

Ramona was about to respond when her cell phone rang. She hung up after only a few words. "Sam's going to meet you at the hospital. Make sure you're okay. He says he's got some news of his own to share."

"Good luck with the questioning, then. We'll catch up in the morning."

Ramona jumped down from the ambulance. Adam smiled as he watched her move between the vehicles parked on the street, then step up into Fitzpatrick's SUV.

CHAPTER THIRTY-ONE

"DARLING, HOW ARE YOU?" Sylvia answered on the second ring.

Adam let out his breath. And realized he'd been holding it. "I'm glad I caught you at home… I wasn't sure if I should try your cell." He swung his feet up onto his hotel bed, leaning back against the headrest.

"Of course I'm here, where else would I be?"

Adam tried not to think of an answer to that. "I tried to reach you last night, but you weren't answering. Were you working?"

"What's wrong, Adam? You sound tired." Sylvia's voice rose a notch as she spoke. "Did something happen?"

"I'm fine. I am… well, I got shot last night."

"What—"

Adam cut her off. "I'm fine. I didn't even spend the night in the hospital. The bullet grazed my arm. It bled a lot, but no permanent damage. I tried to reach you…" He shifted against his pillows, then inhaled sharply as pain shot through his arm and up into his shoulder. He grimaced as he glanced at his sling, tossed on a chair in the far corner.

"Don't worry about me," Sylvia scolded him, "tell me about you. You sound like you're in pain. What happened? Are you sure you're okay?"

"We brought one of the suspects in last night. He's

involved in the drug trade. We think there might be a connection between him and someone on the ambassador's staff." Adam heard Sylvia's gasp. At the connection with the ambassador, no doubt, not that they caught a drug dealer. "We're not sure."

"How did you get shot?"

Adam started to shrug, then caught himself in time. "He didn't want to come in for questioning. We did it the hard way."

"My love, I can't believe you were shot…" Sylvia's voice trailed away, and he could picture her, standing in their apartment. Tears running down her face. Well, he was imagining the tears part. He'd never actually seen her cry.

"It's okay. I'm okay."

"And you caught the killer?"

"The drug dealer. The guy who shot me. Yeah. Not sure yet if he killed Jay."

Sylvia took a deep breath. "This is good news then."

"I guess…" Adam shivered as he accidentally moved his arm. "If you can call this good."

"It means you were successful in your assignment. You can come home. And you're a hero." Sylvia spoke with finality.

A sharp rap on the door prevented him from asking if he'd've been welcome back home if they hadn't caught the guy.

"Room service," a voice called out from the hallway.

"Go, eat, take care of yourself." Sylvia's voice held nothing but concern. Adam wished he could see her face. "Get better and come home, darling."

"I will, I just… I was going to tell you… something happened to Julia."

"Is she all right?"

"She is now, yes."

"Call me later then, after you've rested more. Go now. Please."

Adam hung up, telling himself that her concern was

for his health, nothing more. As he opened the door for the food delivery, he realized she never told him where she was the night before.

Settling back on his bed with the tray of food balanced next to him, Adam turned back to his phone. Julia took a little longer to answer.

Expecting her voicemail, he was surprised to hear her answer. She sounded out of breath. "Adam? Hi, how are you?"

"I'm fine. I wanted to check in with you, see how things are going. Are you okay?"

"Yeah, yeah. I'm fine. I spent the night with a friend, so I wasn't home alone. Look, I'm in the middle of something. Can I call you back?" Julia's voice was rushed, low.

"Of course, sure. You'll let me know if you hear anything more from Pete about the break-in, right?"

"Right... um... look, I really gotta go. I'll text you later." Julia disconnected.

Adam lay back on his bed and stared at the now familiar piece of non-art hanging on the wall across from his bed. He wondered which friend Julia had spent the night with. Hopefully not that Danny. Adam didn't trust him as far as he could throw him. At least if this case was over, it meant he could get back to Philly. To take care of Julia like he should be doing. And to pay Sylvia the attention she deserved.

He picked up a piece of cold toast, sniffed it, and dropped it back onto his plate. He tried a sip of orange juice. A gulp of coffee.

He picked up the toast again.

Finally he picked up his phone again.

"Pete, partner, good to hear a friendly voice." Adam took a bite of the toast.

"Hey, buddy. How's it going?"

"Not great, man. I got shot last night."

"What? What are you saying? Are you okay?"

"I'm fine." Adam laughed. "I'm bored. I'm sitting in

my hotel room while the feds question the perp we brought in."

He could hear water running in the background before Pete responded, "Is he looking good for the shooting? Of the aide, I mean… not you."

"Ha ha, very funny." Adam grunted as he moved his arm to grab more coffee. "I don't know. The FBI seem to think so. A connection between the ambassador's staff and the cocaine trade with Cote D'Ivoire."

"International narcotics ring, eh? You sure did hit the big time on this one."

"Yeah, whatever. I want to get off my butt and back into the investigation so I can wrap this up and come home. Listen, man, tell me what's up with Julia's case. Where are you on that?"

"Good, good."

The water on Pete's end stopped running, and Adam thought he heard a woman's voice. "Am I catching you in the middle of something, partner? Do you want to talk later?"

"No, it's fine. It's good. And the case is moving, too. That lead Smiley gave us?"

"Sure, I remember, you said he tagged someone else for the break-in?"

"He sure did. And it panned out. We got him in lock-up now, holding him for twenty-four."

Adam nodded, grateful that Pete had acted so quickly on the case. "Does it look good?"

"I think so." Adam could hear the shrug in Pete's voice. "He had means, motive, and opportunity. He's known to work in that neighborhood. He's got a record of petty theft and selling stolen goods." Pete paused, then added. "He's a real bastard, Adam. Julia was lucky."

Adam closed his eyes, refusing to let the anger and guilt back in. "So you got him?"

"Yeah, he even left prints at the scene. Like he didn't care if he got caught. He'll talk, I'm sure of it. And if he's smart, he'll name his fence and Julia can get her stuff back."

"That's great, man, really. Thank you."

"Don't mention it. So now that you've got your perp and you're the big hero, getting shot in the line of duty, when're you coming home? Today?" Adam thought he heard a woman's voice again, but Pete said nothing more.

"I don't know, partner. I might try to hang around here a little longer." He moved again, this time not surprised by the pain. "I'm not sure."

"Not sure when you're coming home?"

"Not sure we caught the right guy."

MARSHALL SLAMMED the newspaper down so hard, other visitors turned to look.

"Mr. Marshall," Sam greeted him as he pushed the folded paper away from him on the concrete bench. "Thank you for agreeing to meet me."

"Agreeing? Hah." Marshall spun around and planted himself on the edge of the bench, the newspaper between him and Sam. "Believe me, I wanted to talk to you too, Agent Burke. Have you seen today's papers?" He glared at Sam and leaned toward him, his hand resting on the very paper in question. "Looked at some of the blogs?"

"I'm sorry sir, I haven't." Sam let his eyes stray to the folded paper for a fraction of a second, otherwise keeping his eyes on Marshall.

"Hmm," Marshall grunted. "Of course not. That's what you all do, isn't it? You screw things up royally, then pretend you don't notice."

Sam looked around at the hall in which they sat. The entrance gallery of the Library of Congress. It had seemed a reasonable enough place to ask Marshall to meet him, but now Sam was regretting how public it was.

After his initial outburst, Marshall kept his voice low. More of a growl than a whisper. Perhaps the curious visitors who had turned their way earlier would move along. As long as Marshall didn't do anything else to attract attention.

"What's going on, Mr. Marshall? What's wrong?"

"The damn rags are already reporting a connection between Lisa and Towne. Look at this nonsense." Marshall gestured again to the newspaper that still lay between them. "Senator's colleague implicated in murder. Friend of Senator Marshall attacked and arrested." His voice mimicked the headlines, mocking them. He stared at Sam. "She's all over the news, in print and online. That's why she wanted me to talk to you now. Can't you see why we're concerned? After what she went through after Debbie's death…" Marshall shook his head and his voice trailed away.

"I heard about your daughter, sir. I'm truly sorry."

"Yeah, yeah." Marshall waved Sam's concern away with his left hand. "It doesn't matter. It's over. Lisa got through that just fine. But this—" He jabbed his finger into the newsprint, his voice rising once more. "This is now. We can't let it happen again. If I could get my hands on the assholes who hide behind their pansy anonymity on those blogs…"

"The best way for us to stop it is to find the truth. You know that as well as I do, sir."

"Hmm," Marshall grunted again. A regular part of his vocabulary, apparently. "Someone needs to find the truth." He raised an eyebrow at Sam. "I have my doubts that it'll be you."

Sam bowed his head to acknowledge the truth. "I'm not working on this alone—"

"Right," Marshall cut him off. "Kaminski. The detective from Philly."

"And the FBI, sir, and Diplomatic Security." Sam furrowed his brow. "We're all working together. Anything you can tell me, anything at all you haven't thought of, could really help. You never know what's going to tip the scales."

Marshall frowned as he nodded, looking around at the grand marble staircase that opened up below them, the tall stained glass windows that cut the light into this national library. "What are you looking for?"

"Well…" Sam considered his words carefully. "For starters, I wanted to talk with you about Jason McFellan. How much do you know about him?"

"McFellan? That jackass?" Marshall laughed. "He's greedy as all hell, no doubt. I don't think he has any secrets. He's completely aboveboard in his willingness to break the law for a buck." Marshall laughed again, sliding back on the bench.

"Was McFellan really alone in the morning room after you headed out?" Marshall frowned and nodded, so Sam continued, "Any chance he could have stepped out of the room? Maybe run upstairs? After you were outside, I mean?"

"McFellan?" Marshall raised his eyebrows and squinted at Sam. "Are you out of your mind? You think McFellan fired that shot? Why?"

Sam shrugged. "You never know what's going to drive someone to murder, sir. I know your wife has agreed to work for him. Maybe he decided he didn't want her on his team after all, but there was no legal way to get out of it."

Marshall scowled and slid forward on the seat. "And why the hell wouldn't he want Lisa on his staff? Hmm?"

"I don't know." Sam put up his hands. "I'm just speculating."

"Well, speculate less, Agent Burke. Could McFellan have run upstairs? Yeah, I suppose so. I left the room, then…" Marshall seemed to be concentrating. Counting. He frowned, then said. "Yeah, maybe five seconds later, the shot was fired." He looked at Sam. "McFellan didn't do this."

"How can you be so sure?"

"I'm sure."

Sam looked at the man sitting next to him. His elegant suit. The tip of a silk handkerchief sticking out just so from his front pocket. Everything about him shouted money. And power. He was the husband of a sitting U.S. senator, after all. What else was he?

"How's your wife holding up under all of this?"

"How do you think?" Marshall shook his head as he spoke, his hands clenched by his side. "She's upset. Another family losing a child. She's getting raked across the coals in the press." Marshall grabbed the newspaper and looked as if he were about to throw it across the room.

Sam put his hand out to take the paper and Marshall jumped as if Sam's touch burned him.

"Keep your distance, Agent Burke. From me. From my wife."

"I'd like to know about her."

"Yeah? Then Google her. There's lots of juicy stuff."

Sam let a lopsided grin crease his face.

"Oh, so you've already done that," Marshall acknowledged, then looked away. "Well, don't trust everything you read on the Internet, Agent. Believe me."

"I have no doubt, sir. So what should I believe?"

Marshall looked at him. "Believe that when Debbie died, it nearly killed Lisa. Debbie had been sick—" Marshall turned away again, and Sam figured it was to hide the tears that were forming in his eyes. "Debbie had been sick for a while. Damn doctors didn't have a clue what was going on." He turned to smile at Sam. "No better than your lot."

"How did she die?"

"How? Who knows?" Marshall looked down at his hands, now folded neatly in his lap. "It was an accident, they said. She was accident prone. That didn't explain why she got hurt so much. Other kids, they fall…" Marshall paused for a moment. Swallowed. "Other kids fall off the swing set, they get right back up.

Debbie would have a broken leg."

"She had some kind of disease?"

Marshall nodded, still looking down. "That's what the doctors said. They didn't know what. They couldn't figure it out. She kept getting hurt. And it got worse." He breathed in hard through his nose and held his breath, then let it out in a long exhale through his mouth. "And then it killed her."

Sam looked at the grieving father before him. No way he was faking that kind of grief. That deep, abiding sorrow that only a parent who had lost a child could know. He looked away.

Marshall took a few minutes to compose himself. When he looked back at Sam, all the anger had faded from his face. He was pale. Exhausted.

"What can I do to help, Agent? I want this case closed. I want this nightmare to end."

Sam watched him as he asked his next question. "Why were you at the hospital yesterday? To see Towne?"

Sam saw the surprise register on Marshall's face. "How did you know? Never mind." He shook his head and held a hand up to stop Sam from answering. "It doesn't matter. I was there because of this." He poked at the newspaper. "Because Lisa knew this was coming. She asked me to go."

"What did you hope to accomplish? Didn't your presence there lend more fuel to this fire, make it even more likely her name would be linked to this?"

"Hmm." Sam was getting familiar with Marshall's grunts, and this one seemed less definitive. More questioning. "I don't know." Marshall sounded defeated. "Lisa wanted me to talk to Towne. Find out what had really happened." He looked up at Sam. "If that Philly friend of yours really had beat him up for no good reason."

"There was a reason, Mr. Marshall. Towne tried to kill himself. Do you know why he would do that?"

"Do I?" Marshall stood. "He didn't say anything

about that to me, that bastard. Just said he was concerned about Lisa, warned me to stay away from the Philly cop. Said he was out of control." Marshall started pacing in front of Sam. "Tried to kill himself? That bastard. It all fits."

"What fits, sir?" Sam stood eye to eye with Marshall. "What do you know?"

"I know he's pissed, Agent Burke. I know he's pissed at Lisa. And isn't guilt one hell of a good reason for suicide?"

CHAPTER THIRTY-TWO

SAM'S DARK BLUE SEDAN pulled into the curved drive in front of the hotel. Adam watched as Sam rolled to a gentle stop in front of him. The medications were keeping the pain in his arm to a low burn, but he felt a jolt with every move. He did his best to let his arm hang loose in the sling as he slid into the car. His best wasn't quite good enough. He grimaced as the door slammed shut beside him.

"Getting a late start today? What, you think one bullet wound is enough to get you off a regular schedule?" Sam didn't smile as he spoke, but his raised eyebrow gave him away.

Adam grinned. "Thanks for picking me up, I appreciate it." He shifted as he pulled the seatbelt across his chest and grimaced again. "I am really not in the mood for dealing with Metro today."

"No, I guess not." Sam waited until Adam was settled, then pulled out into the road. "You shouldn't be working today at all." He glanced at Adam as he spoke. "You're not carrying your weapon, are you?"

"No, but thanks for checking, Mom." Adam frowned. "What were you doing last night while Ramona and I were chasing actual criminals?"

Sam laughed. "I was chasing my own ideas, I guess." He paused as he pulled into the flow of traffic heading over the Theodore Roosevelt Memorial Bridge into the

District, then continued, "I called the Sheriff's Office of Clarion County, Pennsylvania."

"The Marshalls' home town?"

"Been doing your homework, too, huh?" Sam smiled at Adam. "Yeah, I'm still looking into the Marshalls."

"You really have a bug up your butt about John Marshall, don't you?"

"Nice. Is that a Philly expression? Remind me never to use that one. I was going to fill you in last night, but the way you looked at the hospital, man, I figured I'd be wasting my breath trying to tell you anything. Plus I got a little more from Marshall this morning."

Adam laughed, then coughed to cover up the gasp of pain that shot through his arm as he moved. "You talked to Marshall again? So what'd you find out?"

"Hmm." Sam shrugged. "Not sure. Sheriff was friendly enough. Happy to talk about his town's most famous couple. Most beneficent couple, too, apparently. Senator Marshall's made sure to use her position to bring home the pork."

"A lot of well-funded projects in town?"

"You got it. Going on about how much the senator's done for their town. As soon as I started asking about some of the stories Jay was looking into, he warned me off. Told me I was heading in the wrong direction."

Adam let his mind wander back over everything they knew about the Marshalls. And about Jay. "Jay found something, didn't he? Something in those news clippings, I bet. Any story in particular get his goat up?"

"Hard to say. He turned cool as soon as I said I was looking for something in her past that would be a motive for someone to take a shot at her. Said she had been great to that town, and if I was looking for someone who wanted her dead, I'd have to look elsewhere."

"Makes sense. You can't blame the guy."

"Yeah. I pushed a bit. I can't be sure, but..." Sam's voice trailed off as he edged his way through three lanes of traffic to get to the left turn lane. "I think it was questions about her home life that finally shut him up. Told me we were done talking."

Adam frowned, considering. "Look, I'm sure he's a good man, trying to do what's best for his town. If she brings in the bucks, he's not going to spill the dirt on her. Just because he didn't want to talk about it doesn't mean he's keeping a secret. Maybe he didn't want to gossip."

"I agree. And I'll tell you what else." He looked at Adam. "It's just a feeling, mind you."

"A feeling based on years of hard-earned experience," Adam pointed out.

Sam nodded and smiled. "True. I'm pretty sure as soon as he hung up with me he was making another call. To let someone else know I'd been asking."

"OKAY, TELL ME again why your commander wanted to see us?"

"We're not waiting for the commander, Kaminski." Ramona glared at Adam. "We're waiting for the assistant chief."

"I thought you said your commander—"

Ramona cut Adam off. "I said my commander called. He called to tell me the assistant chief wanted to see us. That's all I know." She held up a hand as Adam started to speak again. "You know as much as I do. I got the call. I called you. Sam dropped you off here."

Adam looked around the station. From the outside, the red brick building of the MPDC Patrol Services looked more like an old school. In fact, that's probably what it was. This building and the one across the street. Though at least that one had added the stained glass windows to give people passing by a clue that it was now the home of the Seventh Day Adventist Church.

From the inside, this was all police station, from the uniforms stationed behind the main counter, to the lines of benches inside the front door, to the rough looking customers who occupied those benches. Along with Adam and Ramona.

"Can't we wait in your office?"

"What the hell world do you live in? You think I have an office?" Ramona's glare could have cut through steel. "Besides, this isn't my district." She shook her head. "I was hoping for a chance to see the assistant chief, to talk about getting transferred to the Investigative Services Bureau, but somehow I don't think that's what we're here to talk about."

"Great, fine. I'm all for talking about where we're directing our focus next, too. But how long is he going to keep us waiting?" Adam checked his watch for the third time, then sighed and looked around again. Finally turning back to Ramona, he asked, "How did the interrogation go last night? You haven't said anything about it."

"Yeah…" Ramona shrugged and looked at her hands. "We got nothing. They're trying again this morning." She grinned. "I sure wish I was there instead of wasting time here with you."

"Thanks. I take a bullet for you, and this is what I get?"

She leaned to her left, gently nudging Adam's good shoulder. He bit his lip, refusing to let her see that even that caused him pain.

This was taking too long. Waiting. And for what? He had no idea why they were being called in, hanging out in the lobby with the thieves, dealers, and lowlifes he spent his days chasing.

A woman passed by him heading toward the restrooms, her gray hair pinned in tight curls against her head, her body bent forward as she leaned heavily on her cane. Adam coughed and chided himself for jumping to conclusions.

Someone up the hall started shouting. Another angry voice shouted him down. Adam shook his head and glanced at the clock on the wall.

"Oh." Ramona jerked her head up. "I did find something else out yesterday, I never got a chance to tell you." She moved her foot back as a young man stumbled close to her, emanating a stench that made Adam think of dead fish and burnt rubber, then continued, "I talked to Elise yesterday. She backed up McFellan's story that Towne was at the ambassador's residence that morning."

"Elise specifically ID'd Towne? Does she even know him?"

Ramona shook her head. "I brought along a few pictures from the Kendall reception." She wiggled her phone in her lap and grinned. "To show her what a nice party it was, how nice of the ambassador to invite us. Happened to have a few shots of Towne, and she recognized him."

"Smart." He laughed as he thought about what this information might mean. "If Towne was there that morning, why wouldn't the senator mention it? What would she have to hide?"

Ramona shrugged. "I think he came and went before the rest of the group arrived. At least, that's the way Elise tells it. He wanted to see the senator. Elise shooed him away."

Adam nodded. "I guess McFellan saw Towne leaving as he was coming in. The senator was there when McFellan arrived, so she must have known Towne was there. Why the hell didn't she tell us? She's got no reason to protect Towne."

"Hmm… keeping secrets and not sharing information with local officials. That doesn't sound like a US senator." Ramona raised an eyebrow as she spoke, her tone making her sarcasm clear.

"Maybe so, but still."

"I don't get it either." Ramona shook her head. She was about to say more when the clerk at the desk caught her eye and waved her over.

Adam waited, watching her leaning against the

counter, her face calm, smiling at something the clerk said.

Ramona's expression was grim as she returned to the bench. "The assistant chief's almost ready to see us. Seems he had a long call this morning with your deputy commissioner."

"White? That doesn't sound good."

Ramona shrugged. "We'll find out soon enough. So" — she tapped her fingers against her knee as she spoke — "if you're still not happy with the drug dealer as the killer, tell me, could Towne have been the shooter? We know he was there that morning. After his performance yesterday, it's possible he does have it in him."

"Yeah, but what's his motive? Opportunity, fine, but I still don't get his motive."

"Anger, pure and simple. Revenge." Ramona shrugged again. "The senator sold his pet building and he wants her dead."

Adam checked his watch one more time. His right knee started bouncing up and down. Ramona glanced at his knee and shook her head. "He told you himself while you were saving his life. His career's shot. Maybe he's lost all hope."

"I don't know." Adam's knee stopped moving as he spoke. "Threatening to damage a historic bell — and just threatening, mind you. I don't believe for a second he would've actually done it. That's hardly the same as killing someone."

"He tried to kill himself," Ramona pointed out.

"Maybe. Only when he knew I was there. Knew I'd stop him."

The clerk's voice carried across the room, breaking into their conversation. "Davis, Kaminski, you're up. Assistant Chief Luess is waiting in his office."

"Here goes." Adam stood. "Let's see what the day holds for us."

CHAPTER THIRTY-THREE

ADAM'S OVERNIGHT BAG landed with a thump on his bed, bouncing a little before settling down into a depression on the covers. Adam sighed and dropped down next to it. Reaching around with his right hand, he pulled up the pillows, then lay back carefully, lifting his legs onto the bed, pushing his bag out of the way.

Damn it, how could he get pulled off the case like this?

He closed his eyes, enjoying for a moment the familiar smells and sounds of home. Sylvia's lavender scent from the pillow mixing with those from a hotdog vendor on the corner. A horse and carriage clopping by on the street. The hydraulics of a bus following along behind the carriage. The paradoxes and joys of historic Philadelphia.

He hadn't been kicked off the case, not really, he told himself. It was closed. Criminal caught. And at least partly thanks to him. Him and Ramona.

It didn't matter, he'd screwed up. His supervisors might not realize it, but he did. Hitting Towne. Letting McFellan sneak away. Either of them could know the truth of what was going on, and he'd let them slip through his fingers.

He opened his eyes. A photograph Julia had given him years ago hung on the wall across the room, an image of him much younger. When he was teaching. Smiling, not thinking about death, or murder. Not yet, anyway. It was a welcome change from the paint blob in his hotel room, and he smiled and closed his eyes again.

Orange light filtered through the blinds, the sun low in the sky, when he heard the front door open. Heard the jangle of Sylvia's keys as she dropped them in the bowl by the door. The sound of her feet moving toward the bedroom.

"Adam, are you here?" Her voice pulled him finally out of the haze of sleep. "I heard you're a hero." She perched on the edge of the bed next to him, leaning forward to run her hand across his face, through his hair. She touched a finger gently to his sling and pouted. "You poor thing, does it hurt?"

"Only a little. I'm fine. And I'm not a hero." He shook his head as he reached his own hand up to touch her face. "I ran into a blind alley. I'm an idiot. I'm lucky this is all I got for it."

She pouted again. "That's all you got because you did everything right, I'm sure of it." She touched the sling one more time, then leaned forward to kiss him lightly on the lips. As he leaned forward to return the kiss, she stood, opened his bag and started pulling out the dirty clothes. "And now the case is solved, correct?"

"I don't know, maybe." Adam toyed with the bedcover under his arm. "I wanted to talk to you about that."

Sylvia paused, a pair of boxer briefs dangling from her hands. "You arrested someone, didn't you?"

"For drug dealing, sure."

"And that was connected to the case." Sylvia tossed the briefs into the hamper across the room, as if putting a closing remark on the conversation.

Adam smiled. "Connected, yes. That doesn't mean he pulled the trigger. He wasn't even in the house."

Sylvia had turned to carry the now empty bag to the

hall closet and stopped in the doorway, looking back at Adam. She frowned. "You caught him. The police are satisfied. So there must be a reason. Perhaps he was working with someone in the house?"

"Yeah, that's possible. We know there was an unknown visitor that morning. Maybe the maid Beth is part of it...." He pictured Beth, thinking about her unnamed visitor. It's true, she could be part of it. But he didn't like it. It didn't seem right to him.

Sylvia nodded and turned back to the hall closet. "So there is, as you say, motive, and the opportunity. And if he is a drug dealer, then I'm sure he has many guns, yes?"

Adam laughed. "Yes."

"Well, that's an end of it anyway. And tomorrow you go back to your detail at Dignitary Protection?"

Adam inhaled deeply before answering. "Nope, I'm done with that. Captain wants me back at the Sixth District."

"Oh." Sylvia frowned. "That's too bad. Well" — she brightened up — "but you are a hero. Injured on the job, catching the bad guy. Everyone is happy, I am sure."

"I guess."

Sylvia turned to look at him. "Adam. I know you. Do not pursue this. Go chasing some imaginary bad guy. The case is closed." She sat down on the bed next to him. "Isn't the deputy commissioner happy with your work?"

He shrugged and looked away from her. "It's not enough. Something's not right."

"No!" She pushed hard on his shoulder as she stood, and he flinched. "No. What's not right is you not accepting that it's over." She threw both arms in the air as she paced their room. "You can never be happy. Take the credit, Adam. Take the credit for solving this case, and be done with it. If you push, who knows where this will lead?"

"I know, I know." Adam watched her, shaking his head. God knew, she was probably right. He should just let it go.

"WHERE'S OUR HERO?" Sam smiled as he slid into their regular booth carrying two slices and a paper cup. If nothing else, this case had brought him closer to Ramona. And back in touch with her dad. He l ooked up from his pizza and frowned at Ramona's expression.

"Gone." She took a bite of her slice and chewed.

Sam watched her jaws moving up and down for a moment before prompting, "And what does that mean?"

She shrugged. "Case is closed. Our Philly cop has gone back to Philly."

"Huh." Sam ran his tongue along his teeth before taking a sip of his soda. "Closed."

"Yup." Ramona kept eating.

He watched her again, then took a bite of his own slice. Thinking.

He had finished his first slice before either of them spoke again.

"Okay, we both know the case isn't closed, right?"

Ramona grinned at him. "I guess you're right about that. FBI says it is. And it's their case."

"I guess." Sam wiped his fingers off on a thin paper napkin, then tossed it back on the table and picked up his second slice.

Now it was Ramona's turn to watch him. She didn't wait long. "What are you saying, Sam? You think you can reopen this?"

"Probably not." Sam spoke with his mouth full, then swallowed. "That doesn't mean I have to stop looking into it, does it?"

Ramona shook her head. "They've got a motive, you know. Saint-Amand was a thorn in the side of some dangerous people. And they tried to take him out. Jay Kapoor got in the way."

"And they had the opportunity, assuming someone on Saint-Amand's staff let them in to the residence that morning." Sam nodded as he spoke, fully aware that the FBI's case was strong. "They just need to find some physical evidence that placed the shooter in the house, and they're good."

"They haven't found any." Ramona put her head on the side. "Short of a confession, I don't think our guy is going down for this."

"And that's not likely. Look, my options are let this go, knowing that the shooter — if it was our friendly neighborhood drug dealer — will get away. Or..."

"Or?"

"Or start with the assumption that those maids are telling the truth, trusting my gut on this one, and finding out who really pulled that trigger." He raised an eyebrow at Ramona.

She took a long sip from her cup, watching Sam. "Okay, I'm in." She smiled.

"Good." Sam leaned forward. "What do we know? We know the shot came from inside the house. I think Beth and Elise are out of this, I don't like them for it at all. Not even for letting the shooter in. If Beth knew something like that, I'd have seen it in her eyes."

"Agreed."

"Oh, yeah?" Sam smiled.

"Yeah, don't sound so surprised." Ramona laughed. "I've learned a lot from my dad, and one of those things is to trust your judgment, Sam Burke."

"All right, then who's left?" He counted off on the fingers of his right hand. "McFellan and Marshall were both alone in the house."

"And Towne was there," Ramona added.

"Towne? Are we looking at him seriously?"

Ramona shrugged. "Could be, I don't know. He went crazy yesterday in the Old Post Office tower."

"True. All right, we add Towne to the list. How do any of them fit with all the other clues about motive?"

"That's the thing, isn't it?" Ramona asked. "Motive."

"We figure that out, we got our killer."

"And without it, we've got nothing."

CHAPTER THIRTY-FOUR

SAM BLEW ON HIS COFFEE before taking a sip, pulling his lips back in a toothy grin as he inhaled in appreciation. One thing he knew he could always count on was Tish's coffee.

To his right, Howard sat back in his chair, cradling his own steaming mug, watching the evening light settling down over the quiet street.

"Why's Troy still hanging around?" Sam asked. "I thought he'd've hightailed it back to his friends by now."

"Friends?" Howard grunted. "Some friends, getting him tied up in this mess."

Sam dipped his head. "He's gotta take some responsibility for his actions, Howard. You can't blame his friends."

"No kidding." Howard leaned forward and rested his mug on the porch railing in front of him. "Tish seems to be getting through to him with some help from next door." He shrugged as he nodded his head toward the house to their right, home to a woman who had been like a grandmother to both his children. "The boy's still angry, but... I don't know."

Sam smiled, taking another sip. "There's hope for him yet. I know, that's why I wanted to take care of him."

"And thank you for that—" Howard cut himself off as Tish stepped out onto the porch, followed by Troy. She carried a tray of cinnamon bread, its sweet scent so strong it carried over the smell of the damp yard and the pungent odor of the coffee.

Sam grinned and reached out for the plate Tish offered.

"Still getting visitors, I see. That's good." Sam gestured with his chin to indicate a group of three young people, two men and a woman, walking toward the entrance of the Frederick Douglass home up the street.

"He sure is. A man to remember." Howard glanced at his son. "Right, Troy?"

Tish nudged Howard with her shoulder as she took the chair next to him, but Troy didn't respond, simply sat on the porch step in front of Sam.

"We fought to be free. To be free, you hear that son? Not to be jailed."

"I know, Dad, I hear you."

Sam heard the weariness in Troy's voice. Saw the deep shadows gathering under his eyes. He knew how hard it was for Troy, growing up in this neighborhood, trying to do the right thing. As much as he was surrounded by people willing to watch out for him, he was also surrounded by poverty. By the continual, futile struggle to get ahead. It was too easy to get sucked in to the lure of easy money. To the lie that it didn't matter what he did, he'd end up on the wrong side of the law anyway.

As if reading his thoughts, Tish spoke, echoing her husband's sentiments. "It's a tough neighborhood, but it's a good one. It was good enough for Douglass, it's good enough for us. We've got some good friends on the alley and we'll watch out for each other."

They sat in silence for a few minutes more, enjoying the coffee and cinnamon bread, the last light of the sun calming and soothing them, a strain of Muddy Waters barely audible from within the house.

"It's not the neighborhood that makes the man," Sam finally said. "Look at this case I'm working on."

"I thought that was closed?" Howard's voice was sharp.

"Maybe so, maybe so." Sam moved his head from side to side. "Like I said, look at this young man, Jay. He grew up in the right neighborhood. He got a good education, got a good job. And what happened to him?"

"You can hardly blame him for getting shot, can you?" Tish asked, surprised.

"That's the thing, isn't it." Sam turned to look at his friends. "If someone shot him—"

"I thought he wasn't the intended target?" Howard jumped right to the point again.

"I know" — Sam held up a hand — "but let's say he was. Then there was a reason. We've been looking into his background, to see if we could find a motive. A reason someone might want him dead."

A sound escaped Troy's lips. A cross between a laugh, a cough, and a snicker. He wiped his hand over his mouth, as if to wipe the sound away, and took a bite of his bread.

"You got something to say, son?"

Troy shrugged and smiled, glancing back at his parents, then turning back to stare at the house across the street. "Nope."

Sam watched Troy's back, strong and firm. Steady. Able to handle whatever came his way. "Did you know Jay Kapoor, Troy?" he finally asked.

Troy shrugged again.

"He was involved with the dealers we picked up yesterday, we know that." Sam thought a little more. "The same guys you were caught with the other day, right? Maybe you two crossed paths."

"Maybe." Troy played with his bread. "It's a big world, lots of people dealing. No reason I should know him."

"No." Sam took a last sip of his coffee, then placed the mug on the worn wood below his chair. "But you did, didn't you?"

"What if I did?" Troy shifted, turning to face Sam and his parents.

"What do you—" Tish started to ask, but Sam interrupted her, lifting his hand to stop her question.

"Talk to me, Troy, tell me what you know. It could really help me out, you know."

Troy lifted one side of his mouth in a lopsided smile. "I owe you one, don't I?"

"Yes, you do."

He shrugged again. "Yeah, I knew him. A bit. We dealt together a couple of times. Nothing more, Mom," he added as Tish made a high-pitched sound. "Look, it was no big deal. I'm getting out of it, Mom, I told you."

As Tish sat back in her chair, Sam pushed Troy harder. "So what do you know about Jay? What was he into?"

Troy frowned as he thought. "He seemed like the kind of guy who always had the next thing lined up. He planned ahead, you know?"

Sam nodded as Troy continued, "He wasn't going to get stuck with the drugs, it was a means to an end for him."

"For the money?" Sam asked.

"Nah, that's the thing." Troy smiled. "He didn't do it for the money. He had other income sources, he made that clear."

"Then what?" Howard asked.

"Information." Troy shrugged. "He wanted to know who was buying. Who was using."

"Why would he care? He doesn't care about us." Howard let his anger seep through his words.

"Not us, Dad, them." Troy jerked his head. "Up on the Hill, in the northwest. The rich and powerful. He wanted to get dirt on them."

"Ah." Sam nodded. That made sense. That was who Jay Kapoor had been.

Sam was still digesting this information when Troy spoke again. "He was getting out, he had a better thing lined up."

"Do you know what it was?"

"Not really. He mentioned it in passing one time. That this would be his last deal. He had something big, something to do with someone getting killed. An accident, I think." Troy shrugged. "Didn't matter, it was something Jay knew was going to pay off for him. Big time. He was one happy customer last time I saw him."

CHAPTER THIRTY-FIVE

"SERIOUSLY, HE CONFESSED?" Adam tossed back the last of his whiskey and gave Pete a look of disbelief.

"Yep, it was that easy." Pete shrugged and raised a hand to get the bartender's attention. "You have time for another?"

Adam glanced at his watch. He'd left Sylvia in the apartment an hour ago, telling her he needed to catch up with Pete about work. He knew he'd find him at Blackie's, their usual haunt. "Sure, why not. So tell me about this confession."

"Smiley fingered him. I don't know what he'd done to Smiley, but he even agreed to sign a witness statement."

"Huh, go figure." Adam wrapped his hand around his glass. "Getting rid of the competition, I suppose. Good ole capitalism at work."

Pete smiled. "I guess so. When Jake confessed, he gave us everything. Even his fence."

"What?" Adam laughed out loud. "So it's a twofer?"

"A good day all around, buddy. At this point, we've actually got back almost everything that was taken." Pete shook his head as he sipped his beer. "A couple of art pieces gone. The fence didn't have them, says he never got them."

Adam patted Pete on the back, then winced as the vibration hit his bad arm. "Not bad, considering."

"Considering how many cases go unsolved in this city?"

Adam raised an eyebrow and nodded his agreement.

Pete shrugged. "Well, that's just a fact of life, you know how it goes. We need to take our victories where we can get them, you know?"

"I do, partner, I do. So what else is going on now? Captain told me to take a few days off, heal myself, then I'll be back on the streets with you."

Pete eyed Adam's sling suspiciously. "Is that what you think? I'm guessing you'll have a bit more light duty in store first, buddy. Sorry."

"Nah, that's fine. I probably need it." Adam reached over the bar to grab a bowl of peanuts and tossed a few into his mouth. "Hey, thanks again for helping out with Julia — not only catching the guy, but taking care of her, you know?"

Pete shook his head and glanced down. In the bar's dim light, it almost looked like his face turned a little red. Adam laughed to himself. Not a chance. Pete could handle a little praise, that much he knew.

"Just helping out a friend. And it was a lucky break, really." Pete's words were swallowed by his pint cup coming up to his mouth.

"Hmm." Adam shrugged. "There really isn't any honor between thieves, is there?"

"Hah, as if. They'll turn on each other faster than a pack of jackals. 'A plague upon it when thieves cannot be true one to another!'"

"Umm…" Adam brought his eyebrows together and stared at his partner in a parody of concentration. "Benjamin Franklin?"

"Close. Shakespeare." Pete grinned and took a sip of his beer.

Adam grinned and laughed softly under his breath. "I guess the rule to live by is, if anyone gets anything on you, make sure you've got something on them, too. Kept running into that in DC, too." Adam's thoughts ran to Jason McFellan, the challenges he'd face once word got out about his blog. As it was bound to do, eventually.

Pete laughed gently. "That's right, they'll either make you pay or they'll turn you in."

Adam put his whiskey back on the bar, his head on the side. "They'll make you pay…. That's it. That must be it." He pushed his stool back as he stood, almost knocking it over.

"What is, partner? What did you figure out?"

"I'm catching the first train back to DC in the morning."

"Sylvia won't be happy with that. She wants you to toe the line. Get in the commissioner's good graces. Not ignore his instructions."

Adam shrugged. "He told me to take a few days off, get myself healed before coming back to work."

"I don't think going back to DC is what he had in mind. I'm telling you, Sylvia'll be pissed."

"I'll deal with Sylvia. I gotta get back there. I know what's going on."

"OF COURSE, SIR. Yes" — Adam shook his head no as he spoke into the phone — "I understand." He frowned as he listened, one hand in the air like a supplicant. "No, I don't agree. No."

Adam ran his free hand through his hair, grabbing a handful and almost pulling it out of his head.

His voice rose. "I really think you're making a mistake—"

He stopped talking, his mouth in a thin line.

"Yes. Sir." The sarcasm punctuating his last word followed the phone as he threw it onto the sofa.

At this time of night, he hadn't been able to get through to Deputy Commissioner White. Only the lieutenant in charge of Dignitary Protection. Who had no interest whatsoever in listening to Adam's suggestion that the FBI had it all wrong. Or that a U.S. senator was involved.

He let out a small laugh as he realized he couldn't entirely blame him for that.

He was still standing there, in the middle of their living room, when Sylvia came in through the front door.

"Hey, I'm glad you're here." He put his arms around her, inhaled her familiar scent. "Where've you been?"

"Meeting a colleague for a drink. Just like you were." Sylvia stepped out of his embrace and moved across the room.

"You didn't mention you were going out."

She didn't look at him as she responded. "You didn't ask." She stood at the low counter that separated the room from the kitchen, her back to him as she dug through a pile of letters that lay unopened.

Adam shut his eyes for a moment, took a breath. "Okay. I need to talk to you. I'm going back to DC in the morning."

Sylvia stopped her search and turned to him. "They asked you to go back? I thought the case was closed."

"Not exactly." He let out his breath. He had a feeling where this was going to go. "The case is closed. I'm just not so sure."

"Does anyone else agree with you?"

Adam shook his head. "Nope. In fact, the lieutenant ordered me to stay out of it. Not to go back to DC."

"You're going to go anyway. Because you think you know better than anyone else."

Adam shrugged. "I have to go back."

With a sudden turn, Sylvia grabbed the letter opener from the counter and threw it at him. It bounced harmlessly off the sofa, but she exploded with violence. "The hell you do. You'll piss people off. That's the opposite of good for your career."

"I don't care about my career. Don't you get it?"

"And I do. Don't you get that?"

They both stopped, Sylvia with her hands on her hips, her eyes glaring, Adam with pleading in his.

"I have to go back. I think I know what's going on," he tried to explain.

"If you leave… if you screw things up…"

"What? What will you do?"

"I don't know, Adam. I just don't know."

CHAPTER THIRTY-SIX

"THANKS for the lift, buddy."

Sam looked sideways at Adam and raised an eyebrow. "Glad to see you back in town, Kaminski. Why the return?"

Adam stowed his bag in the trunk before getting into Sam's car, pulling the door closed behind him. "We're not done on this case, are we?"

Sam grinned and shook his head as he pulled around Union Station. "Not by a long shot. So where to?"

"The Hill. It's gotta start there."

Sam pulled into the right lane, his eyes on the morning traffic around him. "I can't imagine it was easy for you to get permission to come back here."

"Easier than you might think. I had some leave coming."

Sam took his eyes off the road. "You crazy? Your lieutenant doesn't know you're here?"

"And he's not going to find out, unless this pays off."

"Yeah, or unless you get yourself snagged by the Bureau for harassing a sitting U.S. senator."

Adam kept his head turned, staring fixedly out the window. He knew Sam was right. And it wasn't just his job at stake, it was his whole life. He took a breath and focused. Running over and over again through the few facts they had. Trying to put them into order — into an order that would support what he now knew to be true.

"All right, one." He spoke aloud. "We know Jay was a blackmailer."

"Check." Sam nodded, still looking askance at Adam.

"Can we prove it, though? That's the question."

"Blackmail's always tough to prove, you know that as well as I do." Sam glanced over his shoulder as he changed lanes. "I did a little research last night."

"Research?"

"Yeah, spent the evening at the library, digging through archived newspapers."

Adam laughed. "You? That's hard to imagine."

"You know they still use microfilm at those places?" He shook his head and laughed. "But it paid off."

"What'd you find?"

"Those news clippings you found on Jay's desk? You were right about them."

"How'd you mean?"

"All the stories online are either gone or revised. I compared the stories I could find online with the stories that were actually printed — and still in the library's archives. They're different."

"Anything that relates to the Marshalls?"

"Yeah, but not what I was expecting. It was about their daughter. Debbie."

"What was?" Adam asked, confused.

"The article about hospitals. The journalist used the Marshalls — just prominent citizens at the time — as an example. Their daughter had been in the hospital six times over the previous year, and they used the costs associated with her various injuries to show how crazy hospital fees can be."

"Was it only about her?"

"No." Sam shook his head, his eyes still on the road. "She was one example. She was hospitalized a lot."

Adam frowned. "Marshall said she had some kind of disease. Was that what they were treating her for?"

"Didn't mention it. Just the accidents."

"So why was Jay so interested in Debbie?"

They sat in silence for a few minutes, each considering the options.

As the car turned onto Constitution Avenue, Adam voiced his thoughts. "We know Jay was a blackmailer. I know he was targeting the senator. It must have had something to do with Debbie. We need to find out what."

"If he had the goods on them..." Sam shook his head. "Even if there was something questionable about the way Debbie was treated that they wanted to keep secret, maybe they would pay to keep that quiet. But to kill? I don't know about that."

Adam shrugged. "That's what we need to find out."

CHAPTER THIRTY-SEVEN

"I COULD LOSE my job for this, you know." Denise looked up from her computer screen to glare at the two men sitting opposite her in the cramped office allocated to her by the Department of Health and Human Services.

"I know, Denise. I can't tell you how much I appreciate this."

"And how important it is," Adam added to Sam's thanks.

"Mm-hmm." Denise pulled her lips into a tight frown and looked back at her monitor. "Debbie Marshall, you said? Spelling?"

"Exactly like in Senator Marshall."

Denise looked up again at Sam's tone. "Wait a minute, you didn't say this had anything to do with a senator. You just said it was about a girl who was killed."

"And it is, Denise. The senator's daughter."

"I don't think so." Denise sat back from her keyboard and folded her arms under her ample breasts. "If the senator's daughter had been killed, that's something I would have heard about."

"Look, Denise, I understand what kind of position I'm putting you in, I really do." Sam leaned forward toward his friend, his face earnest. He had brought Adam here, the headquarters of Health and Human Services, because of his long history with Denise.

Growing up together on the alley, playing hookie together, learning to trust and rely on each other when so many people couldn't be trusted. "I know I'm asking a lot, but you have to trust me on this one."

Denise tipped her head to the side and smiled at Sam, her eyes softening. "Of course I trust you, Sammy, you know that. What you're asking me to find... I can't."

"Please."

Denise cut him off. "No, you don't understand. I can't. There's nothing here." She waved vaguely in the direction of her computer.

"I thought Marshall said—"

"He did." Sam cut off Adam's question. "Debbie was in and out of the hospital all the time. Her medical records must be pages and pages long. How could you not be finding them?"

"There's no way," Denise said. "If they were here, I'd see them." She pointed again to her computer. "Between HIPAA, Obamacare, and all the recent work that's gone into computerizing medical records, I have access to records from all over the country. And with my HHS access, there's not a lot I can't see. What I can't see right now are any medical records for Debbie — or Deborah — Marshall."

"Is it because they're too old?" Adam asked. "Maybe records get deleted after a while. Or not digitized?"

"Sure." Denise nodded at him. "If all that you're talking about happened more than fifty years ago."

Sam shook his head. "Uh-uh. This would have been in the last twenty years or so. The records should be there."

"Who has the ability to change these — or erase them?" Adam asked.

"Ability?" Denise shrugged. "I don't know. Any good hacker, I suppose. The authority to change them? That's a very short list: nobody. These records are not supposed to be changed. That's a federal crime. Huh..." She turned back to her computer, tapping furiously on the keys.

"Now what?" Sam asked.

"I was just thinking that it should be possible to find out who deleted them. Every time we log into the system we leave a record of our presence. We should be able to trace this back. Agh!" She slammed her finger down on a key and spun her chair away from the desk, her earrings jangling as she turned. "That's beyond my pay grade. Someone has done a pretty good job of covering their tracks."

"But it can be traced? If we can convince the FBI to put one of their specialists on it?"

"Sure. Like I said, anytime we log on it leaves a record. Sets off little alarms. The system is set up intentionally to prevent the type of fraud you're describing."

"Not fraud. Murder." Sam shook his head again. "What do you think, Kaminski? Is this enough to convince the Bureau?"

Adam wasn't listening to Sam's question. He was still focused on something Denise had said earlier.

He took a breath, tried to still his thoughts. "You're saying that someone can tell that you were just in there looking for Debbie's records?"

"Sure. Like I said, the system is designed to set off an alarm whenever someone tries to mess with it. "

"And who gets that alarm?"

Denise's lips turned down into a frown. "That depends. It could be the doctor who's currently working the case, or a hospital administrator who's responsible for the records... or anyone who's responsible, really."

"Like the parents of the patient?"

"No." Denise's earrings jangled again. "No, not the parents. Or the patient."

Sam gave Adam a look, but he ignored it, continuing to direct his questions to Denise. "How about law enforcement? If the patient's death was suspicious, would local law enforcement be alerted if someone tried to change the medical records?"

Denise nodded, but Sam spoke before she could. "You're thinking about the Sheriff up in Clarion County, aren't you?"

Adam's lips pulled tight. "I'm thinking that we just set off those alarms. And someone's going to let the Marshalls know."

"Shit." Sam stood. "How long do we have?"

Denise's head moved only a fraction, her eyebrows raised. "It could be days."

"Or less?"

She raised her shoulders. "If someone's watching that account, paying attention, sure. Hell, it could be hours."

"We gotta go, Sam." Adam put a hand on Sam's arm. "Now."

"Thanks a bunch, Denise. I owe you one. Big time."

"Yes, you do, honey, but then again, you already did."

Sam stepped around the desk to plant a kiss on her cheek, then followed Adam out the door.

"My guess is, by the end of the day they'll know we tried to access those records."

"So now what?"

Adam pushed past a crowd near the entrance, picking up his pace as he headed for Sam's car. "We need to move forward, we have no choice. And I don't care how tough she is, I need to talk to Lisa Marshall."

CHAPTER THIRTY-EIGHT

MIRANDA SAT BEHIND the desk in Senator Marshall's outer office. Adam was struck again by how thin and pale she was. She needed to get outside. Get some exercise.

Right now, she looked bored. For her, this was just another day at the office, waiting for the Senate to run out the clock on its summer session so she could leave DC along with the rest of the Hill politicians.

"Good morning, Miranda. Is Senator Marshall in?" Adam asked.

Miranda smiled up at them, but her brow lowered at the same time. "Is she expecting you?"

"I doubt it. It is important," Sam answered.

"We found something that could definitely affect her chances of reelection," Adam added.

Miranda frowned and started to speak. Sam cut her off, glancing at Adam. "He means her future job prospects."

"Oh, is it about Barton McFellan?" Miranda asked.

"Yes, it is," Adam said, "something she really needs to know about Jason McFellan. Now."

"She's in the main Senate chamber now. She'll only be in there for twenty minutes or so. Do you want to wait here for her?"

Adam leaned forward over Miranda's desk, shifting a pile of papers that floated gently down to the floor. Miranda watched their progress before turning her attention back to Adam, who was already speaking. "This can't wait, Miranda. She'll really want to know this now. Not in twenty minutes."

"Oh." Miranda stood, turning at her desk, then turning the other direction to a file cabinet behind her. She turned back to the men. "Now? Are you sure?"

"Now." Adam's voice betrayed not a hint of the doubt he felt about this course of action. He had to be right. He had to be.

Miranda pulled two laminated cards out of a file and handed them to Adam and Sam, who clipped the IDs onto their lapels.

They followed her through a warren of hallways until she stopped and swiped her ID over a lock. Elevator doors slid open.

They emerged into a subway, one Adam hadn't seen before. Only a few people lingered here. Some who Adam recognized from the news. A lot more he didn't recognize. Those nameless aides who operated behind the scenes, writing all the bills that became the law of the land. Making all the deals. Running the country. Not at all the image most Americans had of the way their Congress worked.

As they stood there, a short subway car pulled up, its doors sliding silently open. A handful of men and women in gray and black suits got off, each talking intently with the person with them or focusing on paperwork in their hands. One or two cast sideways glances at Adam and Sam as they approached the car, as if trying to place a semi-familiar face.

"You'll be okay from here." Miranda waved them onto the train. "Get off at the first stop, follow the others. It will take you right into the Capitol. The senator's in the main Senate chamber."

"Thanks for your help, Miranda."

"You won't be able to talk to her until she leaves the chamber…" Miranda's warning was cut off as the doors slid shut.

The ride took only a few minutes. Adam had just sat down on a bench next to Sam when the car pulled to a gentle stop. Sam and Adam followed the other passengers off the train.

Small, discreet signs were sufficient to clearly mark the path before them. Only one main hallway ran between the subway and the Capitol, sloping gently up to the Crypt. The low-ceilinged room seemed to be supported by the marble columns that filled the space, though surely the number of columns was overkill. Unless they were supporting the weight of the work being done above, not just the ceiling.

Sam led the way up the stairs to the main hallway as Adam tried not to think about the implications of their actions. The disaster he was courting by ignoring a direct order. Worse, by ignoring Sylvia.

Crowds of tour groups pushed past them, their eyes moving from one painting to another as they followed the guide through their headphones, oblivious to the people moving to and fro around them on congressional business.

On the second floor, they passed through the small Senate rotunda to approach the main door of the Senate chamber. A guard stopped their progress there.

"Sorry, you need to go to the public balcony." The guard pointed to their IDs. "You can't go in here."

Sam pulled out his DS ID card. "We gotta talk to Senator Marshall. It's important."

The guard shook his head, his face like stone. "Is there a threat I need to know about?"

Sam paused for a second, but knew better than to create a panic. "No, sir, no imminent threat."

"Then you need to wait here or go to the public balcony." The guard folded his arms in front of his chest and planted his feet.

Sam nodded and took a step back. "We wait," he said, turning to Adam and glancing at his watch.

"How long could this be?"

"It's June, so not long." Sam looked around at the smaller groups of tourists gathered in the small Rotunda. "Senate's killing time at this point, keeping themselves in session so the President can't make any recess appointments."

Adam fiddled with the ID card Miranda had given him, making sure it was clearly visible on his jacket, then leaned over the waist-high marble railing to look down through the circular hole in the floor in the middle of the Rotunda. Tourists below stared back up at him. He smiled and stepped back.

Despite its name, the small Senate rotunda where they waited was a striking reception room, though admittedly more intimate than the Grand Rotunda below the Capitol Dome.

Images of historical scenes and the beautiful city shone before them. Images of hopes. Dreams. Fears. A city that was proud. And a city that was vulnerable.

A guide stopped on the level below, and Adam could hear her voice carrying up through the rotunda. The words were a blur, more white noise than anything else, until a phrase jumped out. 9/11. Adam stopped to listen.

The guide had been working here that day. She spoke softly. Slowly. Doing her best to share an experience that could never really be shared.

Adam stood, transfixed, listening to her story. Her experience of knowing what was happening but not truly understanding. Hearing of death. Destruction.

Running out of the building and seeing the plume of smoke in the distance. Being very afraid.

She finished talking and the group moved on. Adam stood where he was. Remembering. Thinking.

He thought about what people would do to protect their way of life. Even if that meant protecting their secrets.

The footsteps approaching from behind startled him.

Senator Marshall had walked quickly from the front of the room, her heels tapping along the marble floor. A trio of aides deeply engaged in a whispered discussion trailed along in her wake.

"Yes." Her voice was curt. Abrupt. Impatient. "What can I do for you?"

"We need to talk with you, ma'am." Adam glanced at the aides before adding, "In private."

The senator looked at the young man to her right, who checked his watch and shook his head.

"I'm sorry, gentlemen, this morning is not a good time for me. I have a lot going on." The senator nodded at them both, then turned as if to walk away.

"We know why Jay was killed." Adam paused. "Senator."

She frowned. "I would certainly like to hear about that. I'll contact the commissioner, I'm sure he can fill me in. I understand it was something to do with drugs. That Ambassador Saint-Amand's staff was involved."

Sam was letting Adam do all the talking, and he wasn't sure if he appreciated it or not. "That's not it, Senator." Adam added nothing more, waiting to see her reaction.

She didn't even blink. "I have meetings all day, then late lunch plans. I cannot talk with you." She glanced down at her phone, vibrating in her hand, then back up at Adam and Sam.

She didn't pause. Just turned and tapped away, lifting her phone to her ear.

CHAPTER THIRTY-NINE

"DAMN." ADAM TURNED on his bar stool to keep his arm from touching the oak bar. Every unexpected nudge still sent shivers of pain up his arm into his shoulder.

"You okay, Kaminski?"

He nodded at Sam and ran his eyes around the room before glancing back at the door of the steakhouse. Looking at the other clientele in the restaurant and bar, he wasn't surprised the senator had scheduled her late lunch meeting here.

Distracting Miranda long enough for Sam to look through the senator's appointment book had been easy. Talking to her surrounded by groups of lawmakers, lobbyists, and influence peddlers wasn't going to be, but he had to give it another try. He wasn't ready to give up yet.

He took another sip of his Tullamore Dew as he waited. Sam was drinking beer, though drinking wasn't really the right word. He moved the pint glass around on the bar, sometimes tapping it in his impatience.

They'd been waiting for over an hour. Apparently a "late lunch" really meant cocktails, and the senator didn't care if she kept her dining companions waiting.

Senator Marshall swept in from 14th Street like a shark who sensed blood in the water. Adam sniffed and realized he could smell blood buried within the aroma of rare steaks and peaty whiskey.

A swarm of men in suits surrounded her, gray and black pilot fish circling, feeding off her leftovers. As long as she was strong and successful. Once she lost her edge, they would find another host to swim with.

The hostess saw the group coming. She grabbed a handful of menus and greeted Senator Marshall. She then followed the group to a round booth tucked into the corner, where she distributed the menus as most of the group slid into their seats. Their usual table, apparently.

Adam downed the last of his whiskey. He shared a look with Sam, who nodded and stayed where he was, then he stood, straightened his pant legs, and walked over to the senator's table.

He picked up the stream of her conversation as he approached. Something not particularly witty, but everyone at the table laughed anyway. She saw him coming, he knew that. They made eye contact as she glanced his way out of the corner of her eye without turning her head. She didn't change her position or stop her flow of chatter.

He stood by the table and didn't wait for her to acknowledge him. "Senator. I had hoped to talk to you privately."

She didn't turn her face toward him. "Please leave, Detective, this is not appropriate." She spoke as if addressing a man across the round booth from her.

"I know why Jay was killed."

By now all other conversation at the table had stopped and Adam felt every eye on him. Every eye except the senator's. "Leave now, Detective," she said, again not to him.

"I know about the deleted hospital records." He didn't want to bring up blackmail in front of this group, but he would if he had to.

He didn't have to.

She sighed and slid off the end of the bench. "Excuse me, gentlemen. I'll be right back." She walked across the room to the end of the bar, apparently expecting Adam to follow her.

She spoke as soon as she reached the bar. She was used to people following one step behind her. "Listen to me, Detective. I don't know what you think you know, but you've gone too far."

Adam nodded, as if considering her words. He frowned as he answered. "I think Jay died because of what he knew — and what he was willing to do with that information."

She shook her head. "I don't know what you're talking about."

"Jay Kapoor was a blackmailer, among other things. I think he was blackmailing you."

"Me? That's absurd. I've done nothing wrong. My record is spotless."

Adam frowned and raised his eyebrows. "Well" — he grinned and shrugged his shoulders — "except for those accidents Debbie kept having that you worked so hard to cover up."

Her eyes flashed. Adam had never really understood that expression before. It had seemed impossible to him. How could someone's eyes flash? Now he understood. He felt the rage surge out of her as if he had been struck by lightning, though her body language didn't change. She still stood by the bar, one hand resting on it lightly, a smile just visible on her lips.

Her words came out like the hiss of a snake. Or perhaps the way a shark would talk, if it could. "If you breathe one word of that to anyone, ever, I'll ruin you, Detective. I'll see you living in rags in the gutter before I'm done with you."

"It's no use threatening me, Senator." Adam didn't miss a beat. Didn't take a breath. "I'm not the only one who knows."

She glanced at Sam, who raised his beer in a toast. She bit her lip. Her posture still hadn't changed. The smile hadn't left her face. Any paparazzi looking for a shot would see her having a friendly conversation with a constituent. Adam knew she was thinking. Furiously.

Finally, she looked up at him and her smile widened. Her voice was normal when she spoke. "I couldn't have done it. I was on the drive when the shot was fired. How could I have shot Jay?"

"Maybe. It was someone inside the house, that much we know. Mr. Marshall was inside the house at the time. Alone."

Lisa Marshall shrugged as she laughed, her voice now light and airy. "I seriously doubt my husband would have the balls to kill anyone. But" — she changed tack without batting an eye — "if he did, I don't know anything about it."

Adam loved the way she was willing to throw her husband under the bus in the same breath as castrating him. He laughed along with her. Just two friends having a pleasant conversation. "We'll see," was all he said.

She stopped laughing as she turned from the bar. She took only one step, then paused. She stepped back toward Adam. So close he felt swamped by the sickly sweet scent of her perfume. He took a step back, then wished he hadn't as he saw the satisfaction in her face. "You'll see all right, Detective." She smiled. "I'll be contacting your commissioner about this baseless accusation."

The tip of her tongue touched her blood-red lips as she looked him up and down. He felt like a steak she was sizing up for lunch. "And once you're unemployed and unarmed, Detective? I'd watch your back if I were you." She smiled as she returned to her table.

CHAPTER FORTY

"JOHN MARSHALL PULLED the trigger. He must have."

Adam acknowledged the truth of Sam's statement with a nod. "We can't prove it."

"Not yet." Ramona's optimism was still appealing. Adam smiled at her, but looked away when they made eye contact.

They had gathered in the earthy maze of the Franklin Delano Roosevelt Memorial, surrounded by dripping fountains, fresh green plants, and galvanized steel. Hidden in plain sight as they toured the monument with other tourists. Ramona hiding from her captain as she used a sick day to help expose the killer. Sam hiding from his DAS as he pursued a case that had already been closed. Adam not sure what he was hiding from. Or who.

"We know who." He shook his head as he spoke, as if correcting his own thoughts. "We know why. We even know how. So what are we missing?"

"Proof." Sam's answer was simple. And impossible.

"There's something else." Adam looked out over the Tidal Basin. Thomas Jefferson's monument glowed back at him across the water. Joggers passed by in single file and in groups as they took advantage of the evening light to get in a run at the end of a long day. "What's her role in this? If he pulled the trigger?"

"She's the one behind the killing. He wasn't working alone." Ramona's lips pursed as she frowned. "I've been telling you that. Just 'cause he's the man…" She shook her head as she cut herself off.

"Which leaves us where we started," Sam said. "Proof." He stood with his hands in his pockets, his eyes running along the text carved into the stone. He stopped and read the words out loud. "'We must remember that any oppression, any injustice, any hatred, is a wedge designed to attack our civilization.'"

"So's that why we're here?" Ramona turned and smiled at him. "To protect civilization itself?"

Sam laughed quietly and turned away, his hands still in his pockets. "Maybe so," he said as he turned.

Ramona looked at Adam. "How're you going to explain this to your people back home?"

"Work, you mean?"

"Sure, that too." She grinned.

Adam put his head on the side, considering the words Sam had just read. "Once we wrap this up, I won't need to explain anything." He looked at her, and this time didn't turn away when their eyes met. "So let's figure this out."

They walked into the next segment of the maze. Sam nodded as they approached him. "So what do we know?"

"Marshall pulled the trigger," Adam answered, ticking the points off on his fingers as he said them. "He was aiming for Jay all along. Jay was blackmailing them over what they did to their daughter."

"What they did?" Ramona frowned. "Or what she did?"

"He's the one who pulled the trigger."

"So we're back to him. I thought we'd moved beyond that." Ramona shook her head.

"Uh-uh. I believe it." Sam shook his head. "I know there's something off about him. I didn't peg him for a killer… I should have seen that."

"No way," Ramona said. "I don't buy it. So what, the senator's an innocent bystander in all this?"

"No. She's the mother. She knew what was going on, but she kept quite about it. Let him get away with it. Used her influence to keep it out of the news."

They had stopped in the section of the memorial dedicated to FDR's second term, coming in from the wrong end as they worked their way through the maze backward, in reverse chronological order. Surrounded by stone and brass symbolizing the president's determination to create work for the unemployed, provide opportunities for those who had none. After a moment, Sam moved ahead and the other two followed.

"That doesn't make sense." Ramona spoke to Adam under her breath as they walked. "She's not afraid. Not the type of woman to let a man bully her."

"Hah." Adam couldn't stop the laugh from coming out as he pictured the woman he had confronted that afternoon. "More likely she was the bully herself."

Sam stopped. Turned toward them. "Think about it. That fits the profile. I've been looking at him all wrong."

"What do you mean?" Adam turned to face Sam, turning his back to a statue of FDR in his wheelchair, his dog sitting faithfully by his side. Dog and master green with age and weather.

"He's a victim." Sam spread his hands wide. "That's what's been bugging me. He acts like a victim. Seeking out help without being able to ask for it. Avoiding her calls when he can, running at her beck and call the rest of the time."

"Maybe he's just a man in love?"

Sam shook his head at Ramona's suggestion. "He's a man in fear."

Adam nodded. It fit. "Fear enough to kill for her?" he wondered out loud.

CHAPTER FORTY-ONE

THE FRONT DOOR swung open as Sam knocked on it. As if they were expected. Or someone was.

Sam stepped into the carpeted hallway, Ramona following behind. Adam glanced up and down the road. Acres of neatly trimmed lawn lined the wide street. Three other driveways were visible, curving off into the bushes. He could see only one other vehicle. A BMW, pulled up to the curb in front of a neighboring property.

A lone figure moved at the end of the block, a silhouette at this distance in the twilight. A smaller figure hunched on the ground near it. A man out walking his dog after dinner. Normal. Routine. What you'd expect in the suburbs.

Adam turned back to the stuccoed McMansion and stepped inside, passing through the imposing double-storied hallway into a living room that ran the length of the house.

Sam and Ramona had stopped inside the doorway. Marshall stood by a mahogany end table at the far end of the room, his hand still on the receiver of the phone that sat atop the table. He didn't seem surprised to see them.

Adam took a breath and looked around. Beige walls surrounded a beige carpet and gold and beige furniture. An expensively furnished room, no doubt. It looked like something right out of a catalog. It told him nothing about the people who lived here. About the man who stood facing them.

Adam stepped around Sam and moved toward John Marshall. John took a step back, behind the table, his back up against the pale gold curtains.

"We talked to your wife, John. She says you did it."

John shook his head and mumbled something.

"What was that?" Adam took one more step forward then stopped, his head to the side. "Did you say something?"

Marshall shook his head, his eyes jerking from Adam to Sam to Ramona, who blocked his exit.

"I have nothing to say. She'll protect me." His voice was calm, quiet. As bland as the room he stood in.

"She threw you under the bus, John. You can tell us what really happened. Before she takes her story to the cops."

"I don't know what you're talking about." Marshall's face hadn't changed. His voice remained monotone. "I don't know what her story is."

"She says you shot Jay, from inside the house." Adam was glad Ramona had spoken from where she was, without stepping farther into the room. Marshall was scaring him with his calmness, his monotone.

Marshall was shaking his head even as Ramona spoke. "She'll protect me," he repeated like a mantra. "She'll know what to do. I trust her."

Sam moved slowly, carefully. Flanking Marshall. He stood surrounded now, the three of them encircling him.

His cool broke. Adam saw the tremor in his hands first, before Marshall shoved them into the pockets of his gray silk trousers. But it was too late, he'd lost his control. His legs buckled and he took a quick step forward to the sofa, almost falling down onto it. He kept his hands in his pockets, looking up at Adam and Sam as if he had already been arrested, his hands no longer free.

Adam stayed where he was, casting a warning glance

toward Sam. Marshall was trapped and scared. Unpredictable.

"We know your wife was behind the shooting." Adam kept his own voice calm. Rational. Reasonable. Just explaining the facts. "We know about your daughter. And the blackmail."

He paused, glanced over at Sam. He sensed Ramona shift behind him, but didn't turn his back on Marshall.

Marshall sat on the sofa, first looking up at Sam and Adam, then turning his eyes down to the floor. His head moved back and forth, shaking a silent no. Adam waited, watching as the tremors took over, as Marshall's whole body shook. With anger? With fear? He couldn't tell.

"Talk to me, John. Tell me." After a beat, he added, "I can help you. We can help you."

"We know it's not your fault." Ramona's voice was quiet, soothing. "We know you were only doing what you had to do."

Marshall looked up at her, his eyes suddenly clear and alert.

"She was our daughter. Our beautiful daughter." His eyes flickered back and forth between Adam and Sam. "I loved her."

"Okay." Sam spoke softly. "Tell us about it."

Marshall's head jerked to the right, one eye blinked. "I loved her. I loved them both. I didn't understand what was happening."

"What was happening?" Ramona's voice was a whisper, matching Marshall's.

He licked his lips. Looked around the room, but never at any of them. "It was small accidents at first. Nothing major. Nothing that would get anyone's attention. Kids get hurt, you know?" He finally turned his eyes to Adam. Pleading eyes. Begging to be understood.

Adam nodded but said nothing.

Marshall looked away and continued, "It started when she was only three. Just a toddler." He shook his head.

"Kids are supposed to be resilient at that age. Not easily hurt." He shrugged. "The doctors were surprised. Not surprised enough to ask too many questions."

"And you?" Adam kept his voice at a whisper as well. "Did you ask questions?"

The look Marshall gave him ran right through him, made him pity the man. Not just rueful. Desperate. Agonizing.

"Of course I did. I never thought... I mean, who would?" He shook his head, then sat up straighter on the sofa. "Lisa was on City Council by then, not a school nurse anymore. She kept having to leave early to take Debbie to see a doctor. The other council members, they felt bad for her. They were very supportive... Lisa appreciated that so much. Appreciated the support, the kind words... the attention."

"When did you guess the truth?"

"I didn't, don't you see?" The strength of Marshall's response surprised them all. The words echoed around the room. Sam and Adam both took a step back.

Marshall started shaking again. "There was one doctor. She asked questions. She said it didn't add up. She sent us copies of the hospital records, all of Debbie's injuries." Marshall frowned and shrugged. "Then she was involved in a scandal — something about fake prescriptions. She lost her license. Went away. No one else was looking into it. Watching out for Debbie."

"I remember it," he moaned then, his eyes still. "I remember it every day." He shook his head as he spoke, the tremors fading as he let loose the memories. The fear. "I saw it the day she killed her. The day Debbie died. Do you know how hard that was?" He looked up at Adam seeking understanding, so Adam nodded.

Marshall continued, "It was in the back yard. Debbie on the swing set, Lisa playing with her, rough-housing." He shook his head as he spoke and finally pulled his hands out of his pockets. They lay on his lap, the tremors only an occasional shake now. "I remember thinking she was being too rough. It was dangerous."

"She — what? Pushed her?"

"From the top of the slide. She went over the side. Hit her head on the cement that was supposed to stabilize it. Supposed to make it safe. There was nothing I could do. I watched her fall. I ran to her. There was blood, so much blood."

Adam shuddered, he couldn't help himself.

Marshall glanced and him and smiled. Nodded. "Yeah. We called 911. They took her to the hospital, but it was too late." He shook his head, and his lips turned up into a smile. "I saw Lisa do it. I couldn't tell anyone. I'd just lost my daughter. I couldn't lose Lisa as well, could I?"

Adam felt Ramona move then, stepping farther into the room. He put his left hand out, signaling her to stop without turning around.

Marshall saw the gesture but didn't look at Ramona. "I don't care anymore. It doesn't matter what I say."

He looked up at Adam. "She was already considering running for mayor at that point. When Debbie died." He smiled a thin smile. "It helped her, the papers said. The sympathy vote. It helped her win."

"Why didn't you say anything? Go to the police?"

Marshall grinned again, then jerked forward on his seat, leaning toward Adam. Adam held his ground but tensed, not sure what to expect from this man.

"We're not monsters." He said it like a cry. A plea. "Lisa's not really a killer, I thought. She would never do it again. And we had no more children." He shrugged, his eyes seeking out the corners in the room as if he could pull an explanation, a justification, from the pale furniture. He shrugged. "Once she won the election, she never had to look back. To think about what had happened."

"What she had done," Ramona pointed out.

Marshall dipped his head. "I tried asking her about it once. To see if it had been an accident." He laughed softly to himself. "Of course she was furious. Denied even having pushed her. Accused me of making things up, of trying to blame her for Debbie's death." His voice trailed off as he added, "She told me to never bring it up again. If I did, she would leave me."

Ramona's voice startled Adam. "And you did what she told you?"

Marshall shrugged. "I always do. Then it came back, and I saw that she would…" He shuddered. "She would do it again. She needed it to be public, she enjoyed the attention, the condolences. And soon she'll be even more powerful."

He stopped talking. He had said everything he had to say.

He slid back on the sofa as if exhausted. Adam felt his own tension ebb, then Marshall jumped up. Adam tensed again, stepped toward him. Marshall was pacing, back and forth in front of the colorless sofa. Talking with excitement now.

"I kept the reports. From the doctor. Lisa never knew."

"You kept the reports?" Adam tried not to let his surprise carry through in his voice.

Marshall smiled. He looked at Adam, then laughed. "I always kept them. They were nothing at first, something I shoved into a drawer and forgot about." He turned and strode across the room, grabbing at a small drawer tucked into one of the low shelves that bookended the marble mantlepiece. "Then they were a connection. To Debbie, don't you see?"

He pulled out an envelope, turned to Adam, grinning. "I kept the reports. She never knew." He stood grinning like a child. Happy. Hopeful.

Adam had no problem crushing his spirit. "So why did you kill Jay?"

His words had the anticipated effect. Marshall frowned, dropped his hands, the envelope hanging loosely by his side. "Jay knew. I don't know how. He figured it out."

"Jay knew the senator well enough," Sam suggested. "Knew she was the type who would enjoy the attention she got when her child was injured. When her child died."

Marshall looked at Sam out of the corner of his eye and grinned. "Knew her? Not well enough, I guess. He really thought he could blackmail her and get away with it." He turned to Adam, pleading. "I had no choice, you see that, don't you? I had to do what she asked. I love her. With these, can it end? Can it stop now?"

Marshall might have wanted to say more, but he shut his mouth and turned his eyes to the living room door when the banging started. Someone was going to break down the front door if it didn't open.

Adam glanced at Ramona and she turned and left the room. She was back within seconds, trailing behind a team of men in dark suits. The lead man took one look into the room and held up a hand. He crossed to stand in front of Marshall.

"I don't know what's going on here, but I don't like it." He turned to Marshall. "Don't say anything else."

Marshall looked down at the envelope in his hands, holding it up as if at a loss as to what to do with it. A second, younger man stepped sideways across the room, coming up to Marshall crablike. Marshall handed him the envelope, and the young lawyer slid it into his briefcase.

The older man turned to glare at Adam, Sam, and Ramona in turn. "Nothing he said here can be used against him. You understand that, right?"

Adam shrugged. "I don't know who you work for or who's paying your bills, Marshall or his wife. You might decide to let him speak after you've heard what he's got to say."

The lawyer shook his head. "Leave. Now."

Ramona was the closest to the door and the first out of the room, Sam not far behind. Adam stepped into the hallway, then glanced back at the man who was John

Marshall. He sat again on the silk sofa, his hands loose on his lap, his eyes downcast. He said nothing, simply shook his head as the team of lawyers surrounded him, talking down to him.

A man who was a killer. A man who was a victim.

Adam blinked and followed Sam and Ramona back to their car.

CHAPTER FORTY-TWO

RAIN WOULD have been nice. For the senator, at least. An umbrella or two to block the view. Adam looked up at the blue sky and smiled. Not a cloud in sight.

He turned his gaze back to the front of the Marshalls' home, just visible from where he sat in Sam's car. He was happy staying where he was. The others could jostle over vantage points.

John Marshall's lawyers had taken him to FBI headquarters that morning. Apparently they did work for him. Not for her.

Faced with the evidence of Debbie's abuse and possible murder, the Bureau'd had no choice but to invite the senator to speak with them. At her convenience, of course.

He glanced at his watch. They would've made the call forty minutes ago. He did the math, calculating how long it would take for her to contact her lawyers. For them to advise her to deal with this right away. For them to get here.

As if on cue, a black SUV turned into her driveway.

The cameras went crazy. Nothing to see but a bunch of lawyers in dark suits, but it set the photographers off.

Adam chuckled to himself. Forty minutes to get a crack legal team on site. Only twenty minutes for the news about Marshall's accusations to leak and for the paparazzi to set up in front of their house.

The lawyers scuttled into the house, the door shutting the cameras out. The group clustered on the lawn fell silent. Even from where he sat, Adam could sense the anticipation. There was definitely blood in the water now.

It wasn't blood he could smell. It was the scent of freshly turned earth exploding into the air as it hit the top of a simple wooden coffin. Adam shut his eyes. Remembering. Accepting.

This was justice. If not for his students, then for another child who had been killed. This was what mattered to him.

Only a few minutes later, the door opened again. At first she was hidden, tucked behind a well-formed wall of gray and black suits. But they couldn't hold their formation as they moved toward the car. First one stepped out of line. Then another.

The cameras were on fire once again. Photographers jostled for the best angle, shoving their equipment as close to the shuffling group as they could before getting pushed aside by one of the legal defense team.

The senator seemed unfazed. She shuffled forward in the middle of the scrum, her eyes fixed on some distant point. A smile pasted on her face. A vacant, wild smile.

Adam shook his head. She was enjoying this. Enjoying the attention. He nudged Sam and nodded. Sam started up the car and pulled away.

SAM'S GRIP was firm. The two men nodded at each other as if sharing an inside joke.

"Hope we get a chance to work together again soon, Sam." Adam grinned as he released his grip. "This was fun."

"Hah, right. It was a pleasure, Detective Kaminski. Surprisingly." Sam laughed. "It was good to be back on the street, investigating again, you know?"

Adam understood. "I got a call from my deputy commissioner congratulating me. For showing off the skill of the PPD down here with the big boys."

"Lucky you. My involvement got me in the doghouse with my DAS. He is not happy with me… not that I care."

"Isn't that funny… I don't really care either. It's not about the title or pay grade, is it?"

Sam glanced to his left as Ramona jogged up to them. "Now here's someone whose career may actually have been helped with the case."

"Glad I caught you." She smiled at them both, though her eyes lingered on Adam.

Sam stretched his arm out to expose his wrist, tapping on his watch with his other hand as he spoke to Adam. "Don't forget you have a train to catch." He gave Ramona a look before turning and walking away.

Adam watched Sam go before focusing on Ramona.

She stood haloed in bright sunlight from the grand entryway behind her. Marble arches soared overhead while a broad staircase swept in a graceful curve to her right. She touched her tongue to her lips as she looked at him, and Adam thought, just for a second, of tearing up his ticket.

A passing traveler came too close, his rolling suitcase bumping up against Adam's leg. Adam stepped to the side, and the light changed. Ramona still stood in front him, but now looked merely mortal.

That morning had been as crazy as the previous evening. Lisa Marshall's image was splattered all over the front page of websites around the world. One in particular had already become a favorite of social media, a shot of the senator holding a hand up in front of her, her head held high, a madman's smile pasted to her face.

Adam cleared his throat and looked at the ground.

"Thanks for everything." Ramona spoke first.

"You got it." Adam looked up at the vaulted ceiling. "The Marshalls both being arrested for murder should make for some interesting reading in the news cycles for the next few days."

Ramona shrugged. "I guess." She shrugged again and moved her head. "She was arrested an hour ago... it's probably already old news on social media."

Adam laughed. "You're right about that. The trial will bring it back."

Ramona's smiled broadened. "Sam's right. I did get everything I wanted out of this case. You're looking at the new external liaison officer for the MPDC." She tilted her head to one side. "At least, almost everything. I know you've got your own life back in Philly..."

Adam didn't wait for her to finish her sentence. "I'm sorry, but I do."

"I get it." She smiled but it didn't carry to her eyes. "I guess... well... good luck with that."

"It's not just Sylvia."

Ramona shrugged. "I know... I think I get it."

"I do want to make it work with her." Adam looked around the station as he spoke. At the crowds passing by them heading toward the train tracks. At the business men lunching in the Tex-Mex restaurant that opened up into the station as if it were a street-side cafe. He looked everywhere except at Ramona.

"You've got nothing to be ashamed of, Adam." She looked confused. "You're a good man. And if things don't work out between you two, you know where I am."

Adam turned his eyes to her. Fixed his gaze on hers.

"I do. It's Julia, too. After what she went through this week, I want to be there for her. To take better care of her."

Ramona grinned. This time she looked away. "I have a feeling Pete might be taking care of that for you, buddy."

"What? Nah, he's a good guy," Adam waved away her comment. "He watches out for her when I'm not around, that's all."

"Uh-huh. Okay, if you say so."

"He did a great job on her case, even though he wasn't even officially on it."

Ramona turned her lips down. "No kidding. You said they caught the guy within 24 hours, right?"

"Yeah, and got most of her stuff back."

"That's great. The way it should always work."

Adam nodded, no longer watching the crowds, only watching Ramona. "I know that, and you know that, and Pete knows that. Julia… she's still bummed about the one statue we didn't retrieve."

Ramona laughed. "Not grateful enough for you, huh?"

Adam shrugged and smiled. "She goes on about how it's one-of-a-kind, made just for her, a stylistic rendering of some Norse god." Adam's voice took on a stilted tone as he described the statue, recalling Julia's description as best he could.

"Well, someone else will be praying to that god now, I suppose." Ramona grinned. "Good luck to you, Kaminski. With Julia. With Sylvia."

He took her hand. "Thank you. For being a great partner. And for understanding."

He leaned toward her, took a quick breath as he felt himself surrounded by the scent of her vanilla perfume. He let his lips linger a little too long on her cheek before pulling away.

"Thank you."

He turned and walked toward the train platform.

Author's Note

Thank you for reading *A Thin Veil*. I hope you enjoyed reading it as much as I enjoyed creating it. Of course, writing a book is never a solo effort. I am grateful for all the support I received from my early readers, mentors and friends who took the time to read, comment and critique, particularly Marty Peter for her review and comments and Nancy Weiss for putting up with me in DC. I also want to thank the Sisters in Crime and all the Guppies for sharing their wisdom, their experience and, when necessary, their commiserations. Most of all, I want to thank Chuck, for his unwavering belief in my writing.

Adam Kaminski lives on, in my mind and in the later books in this series. If you liked this book and want to read more, please visit my website to see the other books featuring Adam Kaminski as he steps up to the challenge of catching the killer, no matter where in the world he is.

www.janegorman.com